THE OLD DUCKS' CLUB

MADDIE PLEASE

Boldwood

First published in Great Britain in 2021 by Boldwood Books Ltd.

This paperback edition first published in 2022.

1

Paperback ISBN: 978-1-80415-289-8

Ebook ISBN: 978-1-80162-109-0

Kindle ISBN: 978-1-80162-110-6

Audio CD ISBN: 978-1-80162-117-5

Digital audio download ISBN: 978-1-80162-108-3

Large Print ISBN: 978-1-80162-112-0

Boldwood Books Ltd.

23 Bowerdean Street, London, SW6 3TN

www.boldwoodbooks.com

For Brian, who took me to Rhodes. With love. M xx

1

There's no reason for you to resign, he'd said.

We can work through this, he'd said.

Hear me out, he'd said.

Well there was and we couldn't, and I didn't. That was the truth of the matter.

Finally, *finally* I'd had enough.

* * *

Three weeks later

I rummaged in my bag for the plastic wallet of unfamiliar euros and paid my driver. He was pretty fluent in English and had talked all the way from the airport to prove it, almost without drawing breath it seemed. I was guessing his were the complaints of taxi drivers the world over. He told me his wife was difficult, his children greedy and ungrateful. The economy was dreadful, all politicians were corrupt and stupid.

Then, as we had neared the old town and the unchanging,

breath-taking view of the towers of the Palace of the Grand Master, his mood had lightened. He declared Rhodes was a marvellous place; there was nowhere better in Greece, in the world. And the Rhodians were the best; the men were the handsomest, the women delightful and caring. Added to this, the local food was unsurpassed, the pace of life calming and pleasant, and the people the most generous.

Tired after my early flight and the stress and disruption of the last few weeks, I didn't have much spare energy for the discussion. I agreed with everything. But suddenly, as I scanned the faces of the strangers on the streets, it really did feel as though I had escaped from England to somewhere I could regroup and recover. I needed time to myself, time to think, to plan what on earth I was going to do next.

The beauty of it was that no one knew me here. I would not feel the need to peer uncertainly around street corners, or dread the phone ringing, or, even worse, the late-night knock on my door that would unleash yet more embarrassing scenes. I felt safe here; I was on my own at last.

For the first time in ages I felt I might be able to relax and disentangle my tangled thoughts. Peace, solitude, quiet; things that had been in short supply for me recently could all be found in those ancient streets in front of me.

As we drove slowly towards the harbour, I craned round to watch a huge white cruise ship berthed in the distance. The famous Colossus of Rhodes had once looked out over that same wonderful blue water. I bet he would have been surprised to see *The Odyssey of the Seas* out there too.

On the other side of the car, I could already glimpse delightful little alleyways and a square seductively fringed with shady trees. The high season was over now but there were still quite a few couples sitting in the dappled shade with a glass of wine – the deep red of Mandilaria perhaps, or the crisp bright taste of Athiri – a dish of fat glossy olives, salty cubes of feta, *pitaroudia* fresh with mint... I'd done my research.

My mouth watered. That's what I had in mind once I was settled into my rented house. Yes, I was here for work – I had Lucian's editing to do and a limited time in which to complete it, but that didn't mean I couldn't enjoy myself. After all, I had to eat sometime.

That in itself was a nice feeling. I usually liked cooking, it was something I did well, but I hadn't wanted to eat much recently; I'd existed on hastily snatched snacks, half-finished ready meals and toast. There's always toast. None of it had been very satisfying or healthy for that matter. And I seemed to have incipient heartburn all the time. Perhaps the two were linked.

Nor had the late-night solitary drinking done me any favours. I certainly wasn't going to do that here. Perhaps I might think about turning over a new leaf and make this an alcohol-free trip.

Well, maybe not. I'd see how I felt.

Getting out of the aggressively perfumed, air-conditioned taxi into the heat of the afternoon was yet another shock to my already overwhelmed system. After one of the wettest Septembers on record back in Oxford, I'd forgotten what it felt like to stand in the clear Mediterranean sunshine.

My driver – Andros – took my case out of the boot of his taxi. I had no raincoat, no slightly damp shoes, no umbrella. Instead, just wonderful warmth, the fresh air scented with the sea and the hint of suntan oil. Why had I hesitated? What had kept me away from places like this for so long? These days people seemed to go off all over the world at the drop of a hat... to exotic islands and luxurious resorts, or maybe African safaris, temples in Thailand, road trips and – as I'd just seen – cruises. I felt a shiver of irritation at having allowed myself to become so closed off to the world.

* * *

Much cheered at the prospect of discovering my holiday home and finding my way around on my own without anyone behind me complaining about the language difficulties or the prices, I set off.

I passed under a stone archway, the alley leading deeper into the old town, pulling my case behind me, the wheels rattling on the cobbles. The air was warm and dense, trapped between the high fortifications. It smelled of history and secrets and new possibilities. It held promise.

I stopped for a moment and checked the map on my phone; it wasn't far. I'd done this a dozen times at home, looking at the app, wondering what my little alleyway would be like.

A dusty black cat scowled at me from the top of a wall, paws folded, golden eyes blinking. I liked cats; perhaps when all this was over, I would get one.

At last I stood in front of a simple wooden door set into an old stone archway. There was a blue and white painted porcelain plaque on the wall – *Iremía* – I now knew that meant *serenity*, which is exactly what I needed, and yes, the key was there, hidden under the flowerpot as I had been told it would be. Talk about trusting. You wouldn't do that in Oxford.

I felt suddenly exhilarated and clever. All my plans had worked out beautifully. No one had stolen my luggage or sneered at my passport. I'd bought a new plug adaptor at the airport and remembered all my cables.

I'd cancelled the milk, hadn't I? Perhaps I should email one of my lodgers, Nigel, and ask him to check. He was so vague, I wondered if he would even realise I'd gone.

As I reached to put the key into the lock my mobile rang. Foolishly, I answered it.

'Where are you?'

'Hello Lucian,' I said and sighed.

'Where on earth are you?' he repeated, this time slightly impatient.

'You know where I am.' I hitched my laptop bag up onto my shoulder.

I was tired, I'd had an early start that morning. I wanted to get inside and sit down; my back was aching.

'You said you were going to Rhodes. You didn't mean it did you? It's ridiculous. I know you. It was just something to say.'

'Was it?' I replied unhelpfully. 'Was it really?'

There was a moment's silence while Lucian thought about things.

'But Sophia. Sophia darling. There was no need for that. It was just a gesture wasn't it? A silly one from a silly billy.'

'God you are a condescending idiot, aren't you? Just leave me alone,' I shouted.

'You're overtired—'

'I'm not overtired, I'm ordinary tired.' I realised that didn't make much sense. 'I've been travelling all day, I've just arrived.'

'Oh well done. You actually made it there without any disasters.'

His tone was so familiar, but I could tell what it was now. Patronising and guaranteed to make me feel insecure. Well, I wasn't going to put up with it any more, I was thousands of miles away from him. He couldn't look at me with his mesmerising grey eyes and win me round with flowers or expensive wine. Always white wine though, never the red I preferred. And always blowsy lilies, which I don't like, dropping pollen over everything and making my house smell like a funeral parlour. How had I understood him so well, while he knew me so little?

I looked up at the sliver of deep blue sky which I could see between the high stone walls on either side of me and despite my resolution, I felt my good mood evaporating.

'Yes, actually I have. I'm quite capable—'

'No one's saying you're not,' he said in a sing-song voice that I assumed was supposed to calm me down. It had the opposite effect.

'Yes, you flaming well are! You're astonished, aren't you, that I could actually do this?' I shouted back.

I was suddenly aware that someone was watching me. Further up the narrow street a man was standing on his doorstep. It looked as though he had come out to water the rather glorious floral displays in the window boxes outside his house. We exchanged an uneasy glance and I turned slightly away from him.

'Lucian, we have said all we need to say. There's nothing else—'

'Of course we haven't! Not by a long chalk. We have to sort this out. We have to,' he said, his voice suddenly losing its heat. 'Come on, you know you want to. You're just being difficult. You're just trying to make a point. And it's a valid point, I accept that. I know you're hurt by what I said but – well, never mind all that now. Think about it. I need you Sophia, you love me, isn't that all that matters? Really?'

My mind shuffled through all the things I might say, the discussions we might still have, the arguments we might resume. I knew then that I didn't love him and I didn't actually like him much either. And, to be honest, in my new holiday frame of mind I couldn't be bothered. In addition, just a few steps away that man was still messing about with his task, probably eavesdropping on our conversation.

So I hung up.

I stood and looked at my phone for a moment, absolutely astonished at myself.

I was usually so polite and proper. I'd never, *ever* done that before. Not even with scam calls telling me my broadband was about to be cut off. Although I did leave one listening to *Woman's Hour* once while I went off and made coffee.

Not so long ago the sight of Lucian's name lighting up my phone had filled me with a thrill of excitement, a dizzy feeling of anticipation that he needed me, that he might slip away from his unsatisfactory life and dip into mine for a snatched hour or two of me making a fuss of him. Cooking his favourite meals for him. Now all that had changed. I just felt irritated and annoyed that he should try to impose himself on my escape. He had no place in my life any longer, we both knew that. Not after everything that had happened.

I tucked my phone into my pocket and hitched up my laptop bag again. Then I sneaked a look at the man who was now dead-heading some flowers. Men didn't do things like that, did they? It was obvious he was using it as an excuse to keep spying on me.

'*Kalispéra*. Good day to you, madame,' he said, catching my eye. His voice was as warm as velvet, his smile white and friendly.

'Good day,' I said rather brusquely.

'You are the English lady?' He took a step towards me.

I tried to look unapproachable and busy, and fussed about with the house key which had somehow got tangled up in the red tasselled cord attached to it.

'I am the English lady,' I said rather brusquely.

I could have said I was actually half English, half Scottish, but I doubted he was that interested. I wanted to get inside and see if the welcome box of groceries I had ordered would include some proper tea bags.

He smiled again. His face was open, kind, friendly. I was not used to men looking at me like that.

'I wish you a pleasant stay. Tell me if you have any – um, *provlímata* – issues; I'm sure I can help out.'

I had to admit he sounded lovely, and I've always had a weakness for a Greek accent. They make even tedious things sound interesting. And he didn't look half bad either. Tall, silver-haired with a slim build, he was barefoot on the warm stones, simply dressed in a white cotton shirt and faded jeans. I can't be doing with men of my generation who dress like teenagers or hippies with straggly beards or silly little hats. He was rather attractive actually.

Stop it. I certainly didn't need any of that sort of thing. I was here for peace and quiet and for work. I didn't want him lurking about being charming and asking about my *issues*. If he knew the half of it, he would have taken his watering can and his secateurs back indoors pretty sharpish.

'Thanks,' I said, finally untangling the key and managing to get the door unlocked.

I dragged my bag indoors behind me and sighed with relief; at last I had reached my destination.

It was lovely, far better than I'd dared to hope. There was just one very large white painted room, stone floor tiles and a wooden staircase to one side. On the opposite wall was a strange beehive-shaped fireplace filled with artistically arranged logs. There was a small but perfectly satisfactory kitchen and some simple white furniture in the dining area. Beyond that was a sitting area with a coffee table and some conservatory-type furniture softened by blue and white striped cushions. Most excitingly there were French doors opening onto a small, sunlit patio complete with a brick-built barbecue.

I dumped my laptop bag and my handbag onto the sofa and opened the doors to let in the warmth of the afternoon, with it came the scent of something floral and herby. Rosemary, perhaps, and basil. The patio was enclosed by a high stone wall on three sides; a vine rambled lustily over a pergola, some of the leaves tinged with red. On the other side, to my right, was a low fence and a gate into the neighbouring garden. Perhaps this was useful when friends or a large family were renting both houses. Next door I caught a glimpse of a large shady garden complete with a hot tub.

Lucky them. Still, I was entirely content with my choice. Everything was perfect.

I flexed my dodgy knee that hadn't been helped by hours sitting in a cramped airline seat. For a moment I seriously considered doing downward dog, a yoga pose I had been assured would help with the stress in my back. I had only been to yoga twice and both times I wasn't able to get up afterwards without a struggle. You don't realise how old you are until you sit on the floor and try and get back up again. My favourite so far had been the corpse pose which consisted of lying down at the end, not moving.

Instead, I stretched my arms above my head, relieving the ache, revelling in the peace and imagining myself sitting out there in the morning with some coffee and pastries from the bakery I had passed at the end of the alley. I would be clear-headed and rested from a sound night's sleep. I would not wake in a tangle of bedclothes, my new flamingo-printed pyjamas rucked around my knees like tourniquets.

Thinking about that, I took my bags upstairs to find the bedroom which was equally as charming as the rest of the house. More white walls, some blue-striped curtains, a wide bed with a white cotton bedspread and big glass doors opening onto a tiny balcony and a view of a garden. I was thrilled.

So often the photos of holiday rentals could be misleading; a pretty garden photographed three years ago which had now been concreted over to make a car parking space, a kitchen cleverly dressed with a fruit basket and a posh toaster to disguise the fact that it was small and badly planned. Or worse than that, a whole place grubby and reeking of other people's meals, with tumble-weeds of fluff under the furniture. It wasn't like that here. Everywhere was spotless and smelled of lavender and furniture polish.

In this place I would recover from the anxiety of the last few weeks, I would get all my notes in order, finish editing Lucian's book without him breathing over my shoulder, correcting and distracting me. In my spare time I would behave like a local, buying fruit and vegetables from the Laiki market; I would find golden bottles of olive oil and fat crusty loaves of bread.

Maybe I would even walk to the harbour and buy fresh fish straight off the boat. Although, to be honest, despite being quite a good cook, fish was not my specialty and what to do with said fish might prove challenging. Never mind, I would find out and later sit quietly in my little garden with an aesthetically pleasing meal and a small glass of wine, marvelling at my good fortune and being very happy. I would also buy a round, colourful tablecloth decorated with sunflowers and olives to get into the spirit of things.

Considering I had only spent half an hour on the internet on a rainy Sunday evening searching for somewhere to stay, I had obviously struck lucky. I couldn't have been happier, and that in itself was worth the journey. Lucian and his excuses and treachery, all those wasted years, were a world away.

* * *

I took my time unpacking because I liked to put my things away tidily. That way I can feel grounded and I can settle myself into any new place. There was a wardrobe with proper wooden hangers which was a definite bonus; I detested wire coat hangers. There was a chest of drawers lined with new paper that smelled faintly of sandalwood. I put my toiletries into the bathroom, which was also spotlessly clean and tiled in blue and provided with fluffy white towels which looked new and not like the much-washed, threadbare things I had been expecting. I placed my reckless airport purchases of overpriced cleanser and moisturiser on the glass shelf in front of the mirror. Not only would I return to Oxford with a tan, I would have smooth, unlined skin too.

There was a cubicle with a huge shower head that looked particularly impressive. I washed my hands with some expensive French soap I had also bought in the airport and felt a childish little jump of excitement. I was at the start of my adventure. I was ready.

* * *

By the time I'd settled myself in it was early evening and the sky above the garden was starting to fade to a delicious pale lavender with a single star – or it could have been a planet – winking through the pergola. I made myself a cup of tea (there was milk in the fridge and – hooray – some proper English tea bags in the cupboard) and took it out into the garden. I would have to go out and find something to eat soon, but for the moment I was just happy to relax and soak up the atmosphere and the reality of being here.

There was a single church bell tolling somewhere and the far distant sound of traffic, muffled by the thickness of the stone walls. It was bliss.

Perhaps I should make a start on some of Lucian's editing?

I closed my eyes and gave a heavy sigh. Perhaps not, I was owed a little breathing space surely?

2

I finished my tea, changed out of my travel clothes and into a new grey linen dress and cardigan and went out of the front door into the warm, quiet evening. There were a few people about, the numbers increasing as I reached the square. I found a lovely place with some tables set out under the trees which were illuminated with fairy lights.

There were couples studying menus, some with babies in pushchairs beside them. One couple had a toddler in a high chair between them, gnawing on a strip of bread. No one was arguing or bickering about what wine to have. None of the women looked as though they were about to push their chair back and storm off home. It was just a normal, pleasant evening. And no one here knew me. I could do what I wanted, eat what I wanted, and no one would raise an eyebrow or question my choices.

I was shown to a table and handed a menu. A green glass carafe of water and some pita breads swiftly followed, deposited on my table by a distracted waitress who was already rummaging about in her apron pocket for a notepad and pencil.

I did some similar mental rummaging for my Greek phrases.

'*Mia stigmí parakaló*,' I said proudly.

'No problem,' the waitress replied in a strong Australian accent, her attention already diverted to another table, 'I'll come back in five minutes.'

She went off and started clearing away plates and chatting with the customers.

I was used to that; I'd been finding now I was approaching sixty that there had been a gradual increase in my invisibility. I supposed it was to be expected that younger people were more able to see other young people rather than an ordinary, lone grey-haired woman on her own like me. But sometimes that was a good thing, to be able to merge into the background. It meant I'd probably make a good shoplifter. Not that I ever would of course.

I decided on *keftédes* which I remembered from my last visit many years ago, meatballs with a Greek salad and a small carafe of local red wine. It all arrived very quickly, the bill tucked in between the oil and vinegar bottles on the table. The food looked wonderful and I realised I was really hungry for the first time in ages.

Having hoovered it all up at top speed I finished up with some baklava, which was so sweet it set all my teeth jangling rather pleasantly.

On the table next to me I noticed the couple who had been sitting there before I had even arrived, were still eating their first course; it looked like moussaka. He was a tall, thin silent type with an unattractive beard, and she was small and vivacious with expressive hands. She was talking non-stop in French about someone called Carlo who had seriously annoyed her by the sounds of it, and her companion was nodding and chewing, his eyes on the far distance, occasionally grunting his agreement. There was a dog under their table, its head on its paws, looking similarly vacant.

I'd forgotten that here people took their time over eating, they took the opportunity to talk to each other and savour their food, not ram it down as fast as possible in silence as though they were still at school. I made a mental note to try and slow my eating speed next time.

Even so, I reasoned, I didn't have anyone to actually talk to. In a way that was a shame as well as a plus. It would have been nice to share this feeling of being somewhere new, of freedom. Someone to compare food with, to discuss our journey here, to think about what we might do tomorrow. Perhaps I should have brought my book with me to read. But then again I had been jolly hungry, so perhaps on this occasion...

'Ah, *kyría*, madame, I hope you have settled in?'

There was a man standing on the other side of the table. Talking to me. He looked familiar. Tall, silver-haired and definitely handsome.

I wiped the last flakes of my baklava from my mouth. Ah yes, he was the man who had spoken to me earlier on at the house.

God, hang on, was he *following* me?

Had I, as a woman travelling alone, already attracted a *stalker*?

'Fine thank you, *éxochos*. I mean, excellent,' I replied, my tone a bit frosty.

'Good, good. Remember to call me if you have any problems during your stay.' He pulled a white business card from his pocket and slid it across the table.

I picked it up. Why was he giving me this?

'Theo Demetrius,' I said, 'that's a very Greek name.'

What an unbelievably stupid thing to say. I fidgeted about, moving my wine glass and almost knocking the empty carafe over.

He flashed a wide smile and nodded.

'But of course, I am Greek after all.'

'Of course, you are. Thank you.'

I put his card into my handbag and clicked it shut. And then opened it again to find my purse.

'I hope you have enjoyed your meal? You should try the *dolmades;* they are fabulous here. If not, the owner is a friend of mine. I will complain on your behalf.' He raised one warning finger and put on a mock stern expression for a moment.

'No, absolutely not. The meal was fine.' I could feel myself getting rather hot. I was probably blushing. I thought I was past all that nonsense.

He smiled again. '*Éxochos*. Excellent.' He put one hand on the back of the empty chair opposite mine. 'Are you having coffee? And perhaps an *amygdalota* – an almond cookie? They are very good here.'

Was he planning to sit down? I hadn't bargained for this at all. I was immediately flustered at the thought of spending time with him, talking and perhaps giving away details about myself I would rather keep private.

At that point the Australian waitress came gliding over and they exchanged three cheek kisses that spoke of a great deal of familiarity.

'Cass, how are you?'

'Theo, you old devil. How are you more's the point?' she said, her smile as wide as his.

Perhaps they were in a relationship? He wasn't following me at all, he'd come along to see her, of course. She did seem a bit young for him, but then men do that don't they? Get away with having much younger partners whereas if women do that they are discounted as some sort of disgusting predator.

She was tall and slim and tanned, with an artlessly tousled blonde ponytail.

She could have been in one of those pretentious perfume commercials where everyone is glossy and golden and laughing and living a life the rest of us can only dream of. I found myself thinking about that sort of thing these days; what were they trying to sell us if we bought their overpriced scent? The promise of friends you could skip around a beach with, all of you wearing cleverly casual clothes and the same fragrance? Perhaps a night slinking in and out of dark nightclubs looking furious, in order to meet up with an equally bad-tempered man who had thoughtfully coordinated his aftershave with your eau-de-toilette?

I grabbed at my purse and started to scrabble about in it for some euros.

'Coffee Theo? The usual?' Cass said, collecting my cash without looking at me and handing back a few coins that I left on the table.

'*Naí*, that would be lovely,' he said.

Cass did some pouting and ponytail flicking and wriggled off between the tables.

Theo turned his dark eyes on me again.

'Are you sure you won't join me for coffee?'

'No. I must be going. It's been a long day. Travelling. You know.'

'Of course. *Lypámai poly*. So sorry,' he said. He was still smiling as though he knew I was panicking inside at this simple encounter. 'I wish you a pleasant evening.'

'Thank you.'

The belt of my new dress had somehow come loose and I took a few embarrassing moments disentangling it from the ironwork chair and nearly knocking it over while Theo stood patiently watching me, a half-smile on his face.

It was a good job Lucian wasn't here, he would have made an awful fuss. I thanked my lucky stars my husband Peter wasn't around to see what I'd been up to either. After the pickle I'd got myself into since he died, he would have thought I'd lost my mind, which occasionally I'd wondered too.

Then I set off confidently, walking back the way I had come. The sky was dark now and the lights from the cafes brighter. I hoped I wouldn't get lost in the maze of alleyways and felt a twinge of panic. It was a rather uncomfortable feeling for a moment, being on my own in unfamiliar territory. What if I was mugged? If I did get lost, I'd have to go back to the café and start again, and hope Theo Demetrius wasn't still there flirting with Cass and drinking coffee and probably laughing at the dithery woman who had darted off into the night like a startled rabbit.

No, I was fine; after a few false turns I found the right street and the right door and with a sigh of relief let myself in.

Something else I'd achieved. You see Lucian, you were wrong. I was more than capable of looking after myself.

There was a little bottle of some golden liqueur on the kitchen worktop. I hadn't noticed that before. It was even moulded into the shape of a map of the island and sealed with red wax. I wasn't sure if it was cute and worth keeping as a souvenir, or rather kitsch. Anyway, I opened it – I liked liqueurs – and took a cautious sniff. I read the back of the label, but it was indecipherable. Honey. Possibly rum. What was the worst that could happen?

I poured out a small tot and knocked it back. Yum! Delicious! I poured out another, slightly larger and took it outside onto the patio to enjoy more slowly as I had vowed I would. I had the feeling it was rather powerful stuff.

Obviously, on the current evidence, I wasn't going to make this an alcohol-free month after all.

I felt calm again now, my flutter of insecurity over. I was confident I could do this. Everything was going to be all right.

There was a slight chill in the air – well it was nearly October; I couldn't expect it to be boiling hot all year round. Tomorrow I would start some actual work. That was, after all, why I was here.

* * *

I got ready for bed and sat up with my laptop for a while so I could send off an email to Nigel about the milk. He'd probably still be up, mooching about, looking for biscuits. Then I lay in the dark watching the stars flickering outside my window before sinking into sleep with a happy sigh.

That night I slept wonderfully well. Not something I'd done for quite a while.

The bed was spacious and restful, the sheets smooth and cool. Even the pillows, which I usually had a big problem with, were comfortable and just right. For once I didn't wake up with a stiff neck. Or a numb shoulder which occasionally happened.

In the morning I showered, applied my expensive unguents, dressed and went out again feeling quite the local. A few minutes later I stood in the corner bakery inhaling the wonderful aromas of bread and pastries as men in white aprons shovelled loaves out of the brick ovens with wooden paddles. Eventually I decided on an almond pastry, managing the purchase in reasonable Greek which pleased me a great deal, and took it home to eat on my patio with a mug of tea and the company of two delightful Rhodian sparrows.

I would start work that morning. Definitely. But not until I had been out to reacquaint myself with the Palace of the Grand Master of the Knights of Rhodes. It was acceptable research after all, not just an excuse to put on another new linen dress – cream this time – rather impractical flat sandals and sunglasses and wander about the courtyards with a dazed expression admiring anew the crenelated towers, statues and crisp stone staircases. Of course, it wasn't.

The rest of the day then passed in similar fashion, which I hadn't really been expecting. One little road led to another; there always seemed to be another delightful vista to walk towards, or an elaborate fountain bubbling away in the sunshine to admire. I must have walked for miles; my feet and my knee were aching. I stopped occasionally, firstly to buy a pistachio ice cream which was beyond delicious and then later, to indulge in a toasted panini in a place with yellow-striped blinds and the most spectacular view of the harbour. I sat feeling emancipated and confident and even made a few notes in a little notebook I kept in my bag, so I felt as though I was achieving something work-related. People were wandering around, looking at the boats – which were lovely – and enjoying the sunshine. It was absolutely nothing like Oxford.

By the time I got home it was late afternoon. I kicked off my sandals, looked at my laptop which was still resting comfortably on the sofa, and hesitated for a moment. Then I opened the bottle of red wine I had bought and poured myself a large glass.

Out on the patio it was warm and quiet and I congratulated myself, perhaps incorrectly, on a day well spent. I hadn't actually done anything work-related if I was honest. But in my defence, I *had* been getting back into the zone, soaking up the atmosphere of Old Rhodes and getting my head around things I needed to do. This then deteriorated – as I could have predicted – into a snooze. I really shouldn't drink in the afternoon. Still, at my age, I thought it was acceptable to have forty winks occasionally and it was too good a chance to miss.

I then spent a messy but enjoyable evening behaving very recklessly, ripping chunks off a crusty sourdough loaf I'd bought and slapping on dollops of Manouri cheese while flicking though the television channels.

I was pleased to find I had satellite TV and could even catch up with the sport, doom and disaster in England. When I got fed up of that, which didn't take long, I investigated some Greek soaps which seemed just as confrontational and complicated as those in the UK.

There was a huge amount of arguing, door slamming and close-ups of angry faces and women with huge eyebrows and too much make-up and occasionally too few clothes. This was followed by the

Greek equivalent of *MasterChef* which required a lot of flammable ingredients and shouting, and then after that a current affairs programme where several fast-talking people yelled at each other, and in one case ripped off their microphone and stormed out. I quite enjoyed that one. I think they were talking about Italy.

By the time I turned the television off, most of the wine was gone and with it the majority of the cheese. I was feeling quite sleepy again, so – now being able to please myself – I put on my new pyjamas and went to bed. I'd had a marvellous day and was looking forward to getting down to some proper work in the morning. After I'd found breakfast of course. Perhaps I should have bought more than just wine, bread and cheese? My imaginary meals out on the patio with my colourful tablecloth, beautifully cooked food and some of the hand-painted crockery in the cupboard would not materialise unless I did.

* * *

That night, I was in the middle of a pleasant dream about cooking – which is something I did quite often – when I was rudely woken by an enormous crash. In my fuddled state it sounded as though a ceiling might have fallen in somewhere. Then there was the sound of crazy laughter.

I held my breath for a minute, wondering if I was properly awake or just in that strange half place between waking and sleeping.

I lay and frowned in the darkness for a few seconds, trying to decide if I had dreamed it all. Perhaps that hadn't been laughter but a hyena loose in my *MasterChef* kitchen?

I turned over to go back to sleep and then there was a piercing scream. I sat bolt upright in bed, making myself momentarily a bit dizzy. Now I definitely hadn't imagined that.

I looked at my watch; it was two-thirty in the morning.

Two-thirty in the morning accompanied by screaming couldn't be good.

I got out of bed and pulled on my dressing gown. Then – imagining there might be someone on my patio actually strangling a hyena – I tiptoed to the window and looked out.

The lights – which were reminiscent of Wembley Stadium on a match day – were on in next door's back garden and there were three elderly women out there – well, perhaps not actually elderly, they looked about my age – making one heck of a row.

One of them was already in the hot tub splashing about and laughing (the source of the hyena type laugh) and there were two others waving wine bottles and, bizarrely, a Union Jack. I think they were trying to do a Zorba the Greek-type dance in their garden until one of them fell over and landed in a bush like a beetle on its back, still clutching the wine bottle and laughing.

For heaven's sake!

I rapped on the window but of course they didn't hear me. Nor did they hear the choice epithets I sent them. The third woman – a brunette in an unwise leopard print tankini – had wrapped the flag around herself and was busily slugging back some wine straight from the bottle. I mean, that was a bit sordid as far as I was concerned.

Then the blonde one on the ground struggled to her feet and in one fluid motion stripped off her dress, revealing scarlet underwear, and clambered into the hot tub with her friend. She was clutching another wine bottle and busied herself unscrewing the top. Surely that wasn't allowed? Alcohol in a hot tub? If there were only three of them – and they looked as though they were plenty old enough to know better – how were they making such an incredible noise and, more importantly, how long was this going to continue?

I watched for a while, mentally composing a letter of complaint to someone. Perhaps I would push it under their door in the morning.

Unable to think of anything more helpful to do which didn't involve getting dressed and going downstairs, I went back to bed after finding the earplugs I had bought for the rare nights when Lucian stayed at my place. No one could sleep through that level of snoring without help.

For heaven's sake... I could still damn well hear them. I sat up and removed the earplugs.

They were noisily shushing each other now, but the hyena laughter continued. What the hell was so damn funny? And how much longer were they going to be out there? Didn't they realise there were people trying to sleep?

I lay fuming for a bit, listening to them *cavorting*, there was no other word for it. Occasionally I got up to open my bedroom window and glare at them. Naturally enough they didn't notice me.

I wondered who they were. They were obviously having a lot of fun. For a moment I wondered, a bit wistfully, what it would be like to be on holiday with friends like that who were game for a laugh. I hadn't seen much of my friends recently, they seemed to have just drifted off into their own lives. Of course, it was probably my fault. It's hard to have friends round for the evening when you are constantly on edge waiting for someone else to phone or turn up with white wine and lilies.

All three were now in the hot tub and glugging back wine from the bottle. Then the grey-haired one got out, stumbling slightly on the steps in a way that made me wonder if she was about to smack face down on the stone slabs, and lit up a cigarette. She coughed a bit and that made them all laugh some more.

'Bloody marvellous,' she shouted, sending a plume of smoke up into the still night air, 'I should never have given up! Sod you Stewart! This one's for you!'

I went back to being irritated. Couldn't anyone else hear them? They must be annoying more people than just me. The police would be round in a bit. I didn't like to think what the Greek police might do; I wasn't sure they would be as amenable as the police were in Oxford. The last time I'd seen the local constabulary called to the complaints about a student party in my road, they had ended up dancing in the street with some half-clad girls. Community policing at its finest.

By then it was nearly four o'clock and I was losing the will to live. I threw myself into bed yet again and this time, unexpectedly fell asleep.

3

I woke just after nine the following morning which annoyed me greatly as I was usually an early riser. I had been expecting to get down to some work this morning too. I waited for a moment, hoping my new neighbours had indeed gone to bed. There was no noise at all out there. Thank heavens.

I showered and got dressed. I was going to be late for the bakery too, which irritated me even more. I bet all the best things had gone by now. There had been a warning about that on Tripadvisor.

After resisting the temptation to bang loudly on my neighbours' door as I passed it, I walked down the street towards my breakfast treat and tried to be reasonable. They were excited, that was all. They were on holiday, three middle-aged women apparently on their own. Who knew what had brought them here? They were bound to be slightly over the top having arrived so late.

I decided I probably wouldn't complain. I wasn't very good at it anyway.

If we ran into each other, as seemed highly likely, I would try to be understanding and reasonable. I was sure – I hoped – it was a one off.

I had cheered up by the time I reached the bakery and realised there were still plenty of lovely-looking choices. I chose another delicious-looking pastry for breakfast plus a cheese pie thing – marked as *topiki eidikótita,* a local speciality – which I would heat up for my lunch.

When I got home the street was still quiet. I would start work after breakfast.

I went outside and peered over the gate into my neighbour's garden. The lid had been left off the hot tub so there were a few leaves floating on the surface, there were three empty wine bottles on the table and an ashtray piled high with fag ends. Lovely.

I hoped, rather unkindly, that they all had hangovers.

I settled myself outside on the patio for breakfast with my pastry on a lovely blue pottery plate, my tea in a matching mug. I fidgeted for a bit because something was missing. Then I remembered about the tablecloth I was going to buy. I could imagine it so clearly too, perhaps I had seen one on the stalls in the local square. The more I thought about it, the more I knew I wanted it to make the picture complete. What did people say? Instagrammable? If I was going to immerse myself into the local vibe, I probably *needed* it.

I ate slowly and thoughtfully this time, enjoying the delicious flavour of the apricot and sweet custard filling. The Greeks had it right, such delicious food deserved to be properly savoured and appreciated. I wondered what my cheese pie lunch would taste like. I could imagine myself appreciating that too, with a small glass of red wine. Which of course I didn't have.

Hmm.

Perhaps I needed to get the practicalities sorted out. Get some stock in and then I wouldn't have to keep popping out. After all, it was a waste of my time buying things for each meal.

Ten minutes later I was walking towards the market.

It was absolutely fantastic; I loved places like that. It was exactly as I had hoped and I could take my time. There were colourful wooden stalls set out with the most delicious-looking food, local wine and beautiful cheeses, huge, seductive piles of tumbling olives, wooden crates of bread and bottles of olive oil. Irresistible.

I bought a cute straw shopping basket embroidered with a map of Rhodes and made a few purchases, each of which was handed over with a smile and thanks. That was nice.

Then I wandered on to the small supermarket where I found some wine with a very attractive label – my only measure of whether it was okay or not. Unless it actually tasted like vinegar, I was very easy to please really – and bought three bottles. Well, why not? It would save me having to go out again.

Just as the weight of my shopping was starting to slow me down, I spotted the tablecloth lady. She was about five feet tall, brown as a berry, her hair hidden under a headscarf. We locked eyes and she sprang into action.

'Lovely things, lovely things,' she said engagingly.

I replied in my best Greek-lish. 'I'm looking – *thélo* a *mantilo*. A big one. *Megálo.*'

She looked blank for a moment, possibly because, I later realised, I had asked for a big handkerchief. She tried her best, pulling out tea towels and cushion covers, until eventually I pointed at some unattractive embroidered cloths and at last a round, cotton tablecloth printed with garish blue flowers and olive branches. It wasn't exactly what I had in mind, but by then we had attracted a small crowd who were all trying to help out and offer advice. I could feel myself sweating slightly.

'My brother has a stall, just a little way, lady. I will show you,' said one helpful chap who was plucking at my sleeve.

The first stallholder unleashed a torrent of abuse at him, some of which I understood – it mainly related to his parentage and appearance – and the helpful stranger retreated, muttering and throwing reproachful glances over his shoulder.

Then another nearby stallholder crept up with several table-cloths over her arm and tried to lure me away with many smiles and nods and a beckoning finger. It was as if she was selling drugs. Not that I'd ever bought any of course, but it's how I imagine it would be if I did. Well, that provoked another heated exchange of views and a great many gestures, and in the end I bought the original cloth just so I could get away. I didn't even haggle.

By then it was late morning and I returned to my little house well pleased with my purchases. My mobile phone rang.

'Darling! We were cut off I think,' Lucian said, his voice uncomfortably intimate in my ear.

'No, I hung up on you,' I said.

'Don't be daft,' he laughed, 'you'd never do that. I was wondering how you were getting on with The Book?'

I huffed with irritation.

I'd recently realised that Lucian always spoke like that. In capital letters. His lectures were always referred to as My Work. Students were always My Students. His dissatisfaction with life was the fault of Gina My Wife. I wondered why I had put up with him for five years. What on earth had I seen in him, apart from his dazzling good looks, his undeniable charm when it suited him and his all-pervading aura of glamour and intelligence? I now knew the truth, what an untrustworthy, lying weasel he was. Thinking about it, I didn't remember there being much talk recently about My Divorce although it had been an unspoken thing that had been hinted at and tacitly understood. Well at least by me.

But now, with the comfortable distance between us, I was beginning to realise the depth of my many mistakes with Lucian. Shelving my own research and helping him with his. Lending a sympathetic ear, tidying up his chaotic study, fetching his dry cleaning, even the evening shirt that was almost ruined when Gina My Wife threw a glass of red wine over him. Knowing what I knew now, I didn't blame her; over the last few weeks I would have liked to have done something similar.

'Are you still there?' Lucian said rather sharply.

'Yes, I'm still here.'

'Well please don't hang up again, I do need to talk to you about The Book.'

'To be honest, I haven't looked at it yet.'

'Haven't you? Well I do have a Strict Timetable; it really does need to be done. Come on Sophia, I know you won't let me down.'

'I told you; I've just been getting over the travelling and settling in,' I said.

'Of course, I do understand, what time is it over there?'

'Twelve fifteen,' I said, thinking about lunch and the delicious cheese pie waiting for me in the fridge.

'And what's the weather like?'

'Lovely. Warm and sunny,' I said, 'I've bought a tablecloth.'

There was a pause when neither of us spoke and I could hear him breathing down the phone.

'I miss you Sophia,' he sighed at last, 'I miss your spaghetti alla puttanesca. I miss you being here.'

There was a heart-rending little catch in his voice that almost fooled me for a second.

'Where are you?' I asked, curiosity getting the better of me.

'In my study, just moping about and trying to mark some papers. I can't find my blue stapler. Have you put it somewhere? At least it's stopped raining for five minutes. I'm waiting for my new Tutor Group to arrive.'

I could imagine it so clearly, him sitting in his leather armchair, leaning back so that it touched the windowsill. The view over the grassy quadrangle below, students milling about being busy and important, the new intake on their mobiles to their anxious mothers.

I can't talk for long; I have Professor Hunt in twenty minutes and I haven't had him before. I'm terrified. He's supposed to be really tough unless you're one of his favourites...

New intake, new students, a few of them new targets for Lucian's successful blend of urbane charm and flattery. Someone else to catch his eye and think herself blessed because the very handsome Professor Lucian Hunt had noticed her, taken the time to ask how she was getting on.

'I have no idea where your stapler is and no interest either,' I said crisply. 'Have a good afternoon.'

'But—'

I turned off my phone, went to the fridge and took out my lunch. Ten minutes in the oven should do it. I was going to eat it in peace, in the garden, with that glass of wine I'd promised myself.

4

Why couldn't life always be like this? I wondered.

I was sitting outside in the dappled shade of the pergola with my new tablecloth – which looked marvellous under the blue pottery – on the table, and I was thoroughly enjoying my lunch. The *topiki eidikótita* with a small green salad. Eating slowly, savouring every mouthful. It was quite hard to do, after the last few months of eating as fast as I could. Snacking, picking at leftovers, rushing off to do something else, usually with indigestion.

The friendly sparrows were back, pecking at crumbs on the ground near my feet. I felt a bit uncomfortable for a moment. I'd gone from the bustle of Oxford, the students, the traffic wardens looking for cars abandoned on double yellow lines, the tourists clogging up the pavements, to somewhere where I was absolutely alone with only sparrows for company.

More of the leaves on the vine were turning red, a few had already fallen. Autumn was definitely here. I turned up my face to the sun and closed my eyes. This was what I had been seeking wasn't it?

What was it that people were always saying? Listen to your

body, enjoy life, be *mindful*? I'd often wondered what that meant. It always reminded me of the police saying *mind how you go*. It was something I'd read about but not really understood. Was I too old to be mindful? Or was being mindful what people like me learned to do? Perhaps I should find out. I wouldn't want to miss out.

Suddenly there was the sound of a door squeaking open in the next-door garden.

Aha!

Now I would see who it was who had kept me awake half the night and maybe, unless there were full and frank apologies, I would make some waspish but *mindful* comments to them. My decision to be reasonable seemed to have evaporated, spoiled by my annoyance with Lucian and his stapler.

It was the large, grey-haired woman, the one who had been in the hot tub first last night. She came out wrapped in a flowery, cotton dressing gown and gave a huge sigh of contentment. I narrowed my eyes and gave her a look.

She fumbled about in her pocket and drew out some cigarettes and a lighter.

Then she saw me. Her face broke into a broad smile; she looked a bit like Helen Mirren on a really bad day.

'Hello!' she called across, '*Kaliméra.*'

I don't think so sunshine.

'*Kaló apógevma,*' I replied frostily.

Grey-haired woman gave a snort of laughter and lit her cigarette.

'Oh dear. You've lost me there love. I just used up all my Greek.'

'I said good afternoon.'

Her face lit up. 'Ah, you're English too! That's great news. Hey Anita, Juliette, come out here! We've got a new friend!'

She came across the patio towards me, followed by her two

companions who emerged blinking from their house, both similarly attired in dressing gowns and flip-flops.

'Blimey, Kim. It's a bit early for this isn't it,' said the blonde one,
who was still wearing traces of yesterday's blood-coloured lipstick
and, by the looks of it, only one of her false eyelashes. It gave her a
slightly Malcolm McDowell look which was a bit worrying.

The grey-haired woman took a deep puff of her cigarette and
began the introductions. 'This is Juliette, I'm Kim and that remnant
of an accountant is Anita.'

'I'm Sophia.'

The third woman, a brunette I had last seen wrapped in a
Union Jack flag, came forward and gave me a little wave. She was an
accountant?

'I'm going to be retired soon,' Anita confided, 'soon to be taken
away from all those spreadsheets and sedated.'

'Are you on holiday too, Sophia? How long are you here for?'
Juliette asked pleasantly, shading her eyes from the sun with one
hand.

'A month,' I said, wondering why they couldn't tell I was
annoyed. I sounded annoyed to me.

'You lucky cow!' said Anita.

'And you?' I said, hoping they would say they were only there
for a weekend.

'Two weeks,' said Kim cheerfully, 'two weeks of fun and frolics!'

My heart sank. It was no good, I couldn't wait every night for a
fortnight to be woken up by their antics. I would have to say
something.

'God, my head is splitting,' Juliette groaned, 'anyone got any
paracetamol? I can't find mine.'

Anita and Kim shrugged at each other and Juliette looked at me
hopefully.

'You don't have any do you?'

'Actually, I do,' I said.

'I couldn't borrow one, could I?' Juliette said.

'No you can't *borrow* one but you can have some,' I said.

Juliette laughed – apparently, she hadn't cottoned on to the fact that I was infuriated – and she rubbed her temples with her fingers, displaying an impressive manicure of silvered nails.

I got up and went into the house to find my first aid kit. When I returned the three women had opened the gate between our gardens and were sitting around their table with the parasol raised.

'Come on in neighbour,' Kim said, waving me in.

I went through the gate and handed over the paracetamol packet. Juliette pulled out a chair next to her.

'Join us why don't you? Anita's just made a cafetière of coffee and we've got some chocolate Hobnobs.'

'No thanks, I've got—'

'Oh, come on,' Juliette said encouragingly, 'they're only going to melt in this heat. Let's get to know each other. Us girls need to stick together don't we? Isn't this just a gorgeous place? Kim and I haven't been here before. Anita did a stop-off on a cruise with her husband a few years ago. She said it was worth a visit and we were all in need of a break and some time to ourselves. What with – you know – one thing and another.'

The other two muttered their agreement. I wondered what was behind all that. Perhaps I wasn't the only one getting away from my problems. No, I didn't want to get involved, I wasn't going to be distracted by biscuits or juicy gossip.

'Look, about last night,' I said, not sitting down and trying not to look at the Hobnobs. 'You might be here to lark about and of course there's nothing wrong with that, but honestly I have *work* to do and being woken up at two-thirty is not what I need.'

All three of them pulled *oops* sort of expressions and exchanged glances.

I drew on my reserves of indignation to make my point as forcefully as I could without actually being aggressive about it.

'I mean I know you're on holiday, and that's fine and good for you, but I'm not and from the noise you were making it's a wonder the police didn't come out and arrest you.'

'Ooh, I'd like to see them try,' Juliette muttered with a snort of laughter.

'Me too' Anita agreed.

'Well, I'm just saying,' I said rather feebly.

'Sorry Mum,' Kim said in the sort of voice a teenager would use, 'for waking you up.'

She was looking decidedly raddled and hungover this morning. Well that's what you get when you knock back wine all night.

The other one, the accountant, Anita, smothered an actual laugh.

Juliette took two of my paracetamols, washed down with her coffee and a jerk of her head.

'If we woke you up—'

'Well yes you did actually,' I said, trying to sound properly annoyed, 'and then I was awake for hours.'

'Sorry Soph,' Juliette said, 'you should have come and joined us. Come over this evening and you can have a go in the hot tub. It's fabulous and there is plenty of room.'

I hated being called Soph. Her casual use of it made me crosser than ever.

'Sophia,' I said.

They didn't take any notice.

'Just as well there's plenty of room, I've put on over two stone since Stewart left,' Kim said.

'That means there's more of you to love,' Anita said, hugging her.

'You're such a comfort,' Kim said, pulling a face. 'God, I'm hot already.'

'Look, I'm serious. I do have work to do,' I said, 'I'm sure you won't be so noisy now you know that.'

I realised I sounded incredibly pompous and now I didn't know how to get out of it. So I just turned back to the gate, walked through it and closed it with a defiant click.

Behind me I heard Juliette murmur, '*told off, told off*' and the other two giggling like kids. Honestly, how childish.

5

I went back into my house feeling rather unsettled. It wasn't often I felt the need to take a stand like that. Perhaps now though, having had all those heated discussions with Lucian, I was able and entitled to have an opinion. Even so, I hadn't expected to have to deal with something like this on my holiday at all.

It certainly was a hot afternoon, Kim was right. The sun had risen into a cloudless sky and the sparrows had retreated into the shrubbery. I went inside, enjoying the cool of the thick stone walls. I stood at the open door like a headmistress, listening. There was just the muffled sound of their conversation and the occasional stifled laugh. I bet that was directed at me.

For a moment I was a bit disconcerted; they had someone to laugh and chat with and I didn't. There are good things about being on your own, but it's a very fine line between that and feeling lonely. At that moment I felt a bit like the kid left out of the gang at school for no real reason. But I wasn't a kid, I was a fully-fledged adult who had made the decision to come here on my own, and I'd better get on with it.

I had a drink of cold water and reluctantly picked up my laptop.

When I logged on there were two emails from Lucian with suggestions and comments about things I might look out for when editing My Book. I didn't reply to either. I was still a bit fired up.

Then I took a deep breath and opened up the file with his work in it.

I stared at millions of words and occasional blank spaces where he was planning to put pictures and line drawings that had been done to liven up the dull text. I scrolled up and down and then something caught my eye.

I sat and stared at it.

Dedication
    For Gina – my chief supporter.

Not for *Gina My Wife* then?

Would this be the same Gina who, three weeks ago, had flung Lucian's clothes and shoes out of their bedroom window onto the driveway? The same Gina who had deliberately tipped a glass of wine on the keyboard of his laptop as he sat there typing? The Gina who had (allegedly) hurled all the knives in the wooden block at him, one at a time while he cowered behind the open fridge door? How typical of him that, even now, her importance as his wife of thirty years and the mother of his four children had been down-graded to her belief in him. God, what must that poor woman have had to put up with over the years? I felt an unpleasant pang of guilt.

But hadn't I also been his supporter over the years? Listening to his worries, consoling him when something bad happened, cheering him when things went well. Phoning people he wanted to speak to about some minor detail of Templar history, badgering the facilities department and IT support for him when his computer crashed.

I don't know how long I sat there looking at the words and

thinking about that, about my part in the production of this book. I knew I was being unrealistic and petty and I didn't want to feel like that. Outside, the sun was bright and it was a lovely afternoon.

I could almost see Lucian's face in front of me, superimposed on the screen. That classically handsome face, the noble profile. I could almost hear his well-modulated, rather seductive voice with its impeccable delivery. The man who probably believed that unless the American President or Bill Gates was also present, he was the most important person in any room.

I knew better now, at last.

Underneath that charming, pleasant, expensively-suited exterior beat the heart of an untrustworthy and amoral rat. I could almost feel pity for... what was that girl's name? The one Gina had found him with in the marital bed that never-to-be-forgotten afternoon when she had returned home unexpectedly instead of going to see her sister in Cornwall for the weekend.

Poppy, that was it. A second-year student in his tutor group who had gone to his house for some extra tuition involving champagne and furry handcuffs.

Why had he even told me those details? Did I really need to know? Just so he could show off to me what an exciting, desirable man he was? How other, younger, women like blue-haired, skinny-legged Poppy in her swirly miniskirts and Doc Marten boots also found him irresistible.

Silly little trollop.

But hang on, who was I to condemn her? I realised in a moment of horrible clarity that I had been no better than Poppy. I had been just as foolish. And considerably older.

I tried to work out some excuses for myself. Well, at least I had never been to their house, never even seen their bedroom and never in my life considered handcuffs. We had always met at my place, when Lucian would sneak in after dark through the back door, keen not to be seen by any of the postgrads who rented the upstairs rooms in my house.

He used to come creeping in clutching a folder of notes as an excuse in case anyone saw him. Bringing his favourite white wine and sometimes chocolate truffles from the shop near the Bodleian Library. He would sit next to me telling me all about the trials of his day, eating my lovingly prepared meals, telling me how clever I was, how well I looked after him. How thoughtful I was. And I'd fallen for it, month after month. Not quite realising how thoughtless he was. And later I'd accepted his excuses, his denials, his easy lies. Because at the start it had seemed exciting, I'd felt needed and even desirable.

Oh, but he weaved a good tale. He was unhappy in his marriage; he had been for years. He thought Gina was having an affair; Gina didn't understand him, but how lucky he was that I did. That I was dependable. That he could rely on me.

Because it had always been about *him*, hadn't it? And he evidently didn't have a type, he was pretty indiscriminate. Poppy was perhaps twenty, or twenty-one. I'd been fifty-five when our affair started. How pathetic of me to accept his attention. To behave like that. I could see now I'd been lonely and vulnerable after Peter had died, and Lucian had swooped in, sensing an opportunity. Like a shark after an injured penguin. Not that it's any excuse for my behaviour.

My devotion to him had been balm to his wounded soul when he was passed over for a heady chance of promotion that would have taken him up onto the High Table of the university, to greater influence and the possibility of a mention in the New Year Honours list, I saw that now. I would comfort him with things like steak bearnaise, Gruyère soufflé, individual beef wellingtons.

He'd talked about a time for us when his four children would be off his hands, when he could be free – whatever that meant. I didn't have any of my own, but I thought children were always there, whatever their age. Needing beds and money and food at times when you thought they were independent.

Anyway, I shook myself out of my memories and closed my laptop. I didn't owe Lucian anything, least of all more of my time.

But on a more positive note, I was here now, I was actually away on a long holiday for the first time in years. I'd plonked my letter of resignation on his desk, taken all the annual leave owing to me and booked a flight to Rhodes. Agreeing to work on his book was the last flare-up of my years of loyalty to him. I must have been mad.

I was independent, I was financially secure, I was healthy, I was alive. I would not spend my time thinking about him and regretting what I had done, the time I had wasted, the friends I had mislaid.

* * *

I went and had another shower, just because I could, and then I pulled on my grey linen dress. There in the drawer was my new tankini. I pulled it out and looked at it thoughtfully. I don't really know why I had bought it. Maybe I'd thought I would go to a beach and have a dip. However, I didn't have a car, so how I would get to the gorgeous Anthony Quinn beach or St Paul's Bay with its cool beach bar? I suppose I could get a bus.

I'd imagined myself there having a Shirley Valentine moment, sitting by a rough wooden table with a glass of rich Boutari Naoussa and a fabulous view over the sea and some dazzling gin palaces belonging to Russian oligarchs. Google Earth had a lot to answer for.

I put it back in the drawer. It was a rather sedate garment actually, black with a modest gold trim on one shoulder strap. The sort of safe thing most older women would buy, darting into Marks and Spencer one lunch hour, wanting something practical but nothing that would make them stand out from all the other older women. All of us worried about our cellulite and the crepey skin on our necks.

Perhaps I should have been more adventurous like Anita and bought a leopard print one? No, one small step for this woman for the moment, my giant leap for womankind would have to wait for a bit.

I went downstairs and did a bit of general tidying up and then tried getting stuck into my new paperback. After a couple of pages my attention wandered and I looked around. I felt comfortable in this place already, it seemed to suit the new me with its simplicity and lack of bric-a-brac. My house in Oxford contained an excessive amount of clutter, I had to admit. Perhaps when I went home, I would have a clear out. I didn't need all that stuff after all. Silly things that I had kept for no good reason. Peter's books on physics and engineering that I would never read, his chair by the fire that no one sat in any more.

Worse than that, the bits and bobs which reminded me of Lucian.

Underneath my bed I kept a silly shoe box lined with tissue paper, full of menus and a couple of programmes from when we had seen unfathomable student productions and recitals, even a sugar sachet from the café where we had shared our first clandestine coffee. A cocktail napkin with a heart drawn on in biro that I'd kept after a concert at Blenheim Palace we'd attended with his department staff one summer. I'd thought I was happy that day, but I wasn't. Not really. I was just amazed and grateful for the attention.

Why, *why*, when I was intelligent, educated, comfortably off and secure, did I need a man's approval to make me feel better about myself? Particularly that man?

I looked at myself in the mirror in the hallway. I was okay, not too wrinkled and hag-like, perhaps the expensive cream was working after all. My hair was silvery grey, but in good condition and well cut. I had a wardrobe of nice enough clothes; I still had a decent figure.

I had a lot to be grateful for; I didn't need him, I didn't need anyone, I just needed myself.

Was this mindfulness? I'd better look it up.

6

After a few minutes I took the discarded laptop and put it firmly back into its bag. Work? For Lucian? I didn't think so. I was going to think about this time in Rhodes in a completely different light. Perhaps the three women next door had the right idea; I was going to enjoy myself. I wasn't quite sure how, but I'd give it a good try.

I closed my book too; I wasn't really getting into it. There were too many characters and too many of them were in dubious relationships with each other that made me feel uncomfortable.

I went back upstairs and pulled out my make-up bag and applied some mascara and some more moisturiser. Then I brushed my hair and smiled at myself in the mirror. It felt better to smile. I was aware I hadn't done that much proper, happy smiling recently. Today was indeed the first day of the rest of my life.

As I went downstairs, I heard some loud knocking on my patio door. It was Juliette. She was now wearing a flouncy dress printed with llamas that was possibly a size too small, but hey, in the grand scheme of things, who cared? She certainly had the bosom for it.

'There you are. I just wanted to apologise again. On behalf of all of us,' she said.

Happily, she had replaced her missing eyelash and looked very glammed up for what I assumed was essentially an evening in the garden.

'Well thank you,' I replied calmly, 'I appreciate that.'

'We were just so excited to be here, and I suppose it got the better of us.'

'It's okay,' I said, wanting to forget my earlier bad mood.

'Well no, it's not okay.' She spotted my discarded paperback and picked it up. 'How are you getting on with this?'

'Not very well,' I admitted, 'I can't get through the first chapter.'

Juliette grinned. 'Me neither, and it had all those rave reviews didn't it? We had it for our book club. Some of the members were saying it was the best thing they'd read for years. I thought I must have been reading a different book, I thought it was rubbish. Anyway, we wanted you to come over for a drink in our garden, to say sorry.'

'You didn't need to do that,' I said.

'Come on Soph... sorry, I mean Sophia. Come and have a glass of wine with us. You don't want to spend all your time on your own, do you? Like I said, us girls ought to stick together, don't you think?'

I thought about it. To refuse would have been unfriendly and a bit pompous. And then I would have had to maintain my ill humour every time I went into the garden or out to the market and saw them. And I supposed it would be nice to talk to someone.

I relented. 'Well just one.'

Juliette's face broke into a bright smile that revealed some expensive-looking dental work behind her scarlet lipstick.

'That's the spirit! Come on, I'll tell the others, they will be so pleased.'

Not wanting to turn up empty-handed, I grabbed a bottle of wine and a pot of taramasalata and followed her outside and through the gate to their garden. Kim was already sitting there, and the table was crammed with bottles, food and glasses.

In front of me, Juliette gave an expansive two thumbs up gesture.

'Hurrah!' Kim called when she saw me. 'What's your poison?'

'Glass of wine?' I said, offering her the bottle I had brought.

'Nah, you can do better than that,' she said, pulling a face. 'I've looked for Greek cocktails, we had a few last night, as you probably know. Try a Sexy Greek.'

'I'd love to try a Sexy Greek,' Juliette growled, 'just give me half a chance.'

Kim gave a small hyena laugh; she was already slugging ouzo, ice and orange juice into a glass which she garnished with a slice of orange. And a cherry on a stick.

'There you go,' she said, 'get that down you.'

'Well, I'm not sure,' I said.

Anita came out of the house looking rather downcast.

'I've just had Rick on the phone.'

'Husband,' Kim mouthed.

'He can't find any clean pants for tomorrow. Honestly, I've only been away five minutes. Hello Sophia, so pleased you could join us. Sorry about last night.'

Juliette snorted into her drink. 'What did you say to him?'

'I asked if he expected me to come home and look for them and then he got arsey and told me not to get funny, and I told him he could always use the washing machine and he said which one is that and I said,' she took a large gulp of her drink, 'I said it's the white thing in the kitchen under the sink.'

'You'd think he could find it then,' I said.

'Actually, that's the dishwasher,' Anita said, 'I wonder if he'll realise.'

Everybody laughed, me included, and Kim pulled her down into the chair next to hers and pressed a drink into her hand.

'You're supposed to say something when you drink ouzo,' Juliette said, 'I read it in a book.'

'Bloody hell, what's this?' Kim coughed, pulling a face.

'No. You say "*yia mas*",' Anita said, ignoring Kim. 'It means "to our health". See, I knew that degree in classics would come in handy one day.'

We all held our glasses up and shouted '*yia mas*' together. My drink tasted very strongly of aniseed and liquorice. I didn't much like it.

'That's horrible,' Juliette said, pulling a disgusted expression, and tipping her drink into the flowerbed, 'let's have a gin instead.'

So we did. Kim had bought a big plastic bottle of gin in duty free and also a book of cocktail recipes. She flipped through the pages and then stopped, stabbing her finger at the page.

'I think we'll have a Fog Cutter.'

'What's that?' I asked, rather suspiciously.

'Gin, brandy, Bacardi, orange and lemon juice, almond syrup – well we haven't got that one – and sherry, we haven't got that either, we'll have to rename it.'

Kim took the cocktail shaker in the middle of the table and added various things which she then shook up and decanted into a tumbler.

We passed it round.

'That's better, we can call it a Rhodes Reviver,' Juliette said cheerfully as she passed me the drink.

I held up the pot I'd brought. 'I've got some taramasalata, we should soak up this alcohol, shouldn't we?'

'Good idea. Help yourself to some of those stuffed vine leaves. I've got some breadsticks,' Anita said, going back into the house to fetch them.

They spent the next part of the evening coming up with new and occasionally disgusting drinks, until I gave in and opened my red wine. Above us, the sky darkened, and Anita took Kim's lighter and lit some candles.

'The three of us went to university together. In London. That's how we met. We've been friends ever since and we decided when all of us passed sixty that we would form the Old Ducks' Club. Kim is the baby, she's only sixty-three, Anita is the oldest, she's sixty-five—'

'Oh, shut up Jules,' Anita said, 'I'm nearly sixty-six and the prospect is depressing me horribly. I'll have to give up work and then I'll be stuck at home with Rick and his seed catalogues and his endless search for a denture fixative that works.'

'—and I'm sixty-three as well. So how old are you?'

Juliette turned her white smile on me. I hesitated; I wasn't used to being asked my age. Wasn't that rather rude?

'I'm sixty,' I said at last. Well, I would be in a couple of weeks.

Juliette clapped her hands and tapped me ceremonially on the shoulder with a breadstick. 'Excellent! Then I formally invest you as an honorary member of the Old Ducks' Club.'

She raised her glass, as did the other two, and I felt I had no option than to raise mine and clink with them over the table. It felt rather nice actually, to be accepted so easily.

'Marvellous,' said Anita, slapping her palm on the table and making the bottles rattle. 'Now, tell us all about yourself Sophia.'

The three of them turned their interested faces to look at me.

'Well, I live in Oxford where I have been for over...' I had to think for a moment. I was feeling decidedly fuzzy, '...forty years. God is it really forty years? Where did that go? I've just resigned from my job as researcher and assistant to a history professor.'

'Ooh, professor. So didn't you enjoy it? Will you miss it?' Kim asked, pushing her grey hair back off her face. 'Golly, it's still hot. Or am I having a late flush?'

Would I miss it? Probably I would. I'd loved being a part of the university, seeing the students come and go, turning from kids into graduates. But Lucian, would I miss him? He had been such a big part of my life in recent years. Almost the only part. I'd allowed him to take over, dominate my thoughts and my actions. I must have been out of my mind.

'Oh, you know,' I said noncommittally in the end.

'Got any kids?' Kim asked.

'No, no kids,' I said.

'I have two, both in their thirties, and I love them to bits, *love 'em*, but they are both back home at the moment and they are driving me round the bend,' Kim said. 'It's why I'm here. They both have good jobs, Simon has just been promoted, so I'm really proud of him, but it's like the pair of them drop ten years when they walk through the front door. Shoes all over the place, wet towels on the beds, no food in the fridge. I thought I was all past that. And now I'm divorced from their dad they pretend they have come home to *look after me*. That's a joke.'

'Perhaps they should get a place of their own?' I suggested.

'Wouldn't that be nice,' Kim said.

'So, what will you do next, Sophia?' Juliette asked, 'I mean, got another job lined up?'

'Well no, not really.' I took another stuffed vine leaf; I didn't much like them back in Oxford, but here they tasted marvellous. 'I haven't thought about it.'

It was true, I hadn't. I was in the fortunate position of owning my own house and having some investments. I had the prospect of a decent pension too. I supposed I'd just seen myself doing nothing particular.

'Well, you probably have thirty years left, you'll have to do something, or you'll die of boredom,' Juliette said cheerfully.

This brought me up with a shock. I suppose she was right. I hadn't really taken that on board.

Juliette laughed. 'Anita's retiring soon, sometimes she goes on as though her life is over and she's going to turn into Whistler's mother sitting in a rocking chair with a lace cap when we all know that's not true these days. Although I'm a new grandmother and that's made me feel as though it might be an option.'

I looked at Juliette's unlined face and artfully highlighted hair. She didn't look sixty-three, that was true. Perhaps she'd had some work done. I lifted my chin; I was aware my neck was sagging a bit and the expensive cream from the airport hadn't had time to work yet.

'How lovely,' I said, 'how old is the baby?'

'Twins, three months old. Kya and Keira. They are gorgeous of course and I love them to the moon and back, but I'm not flipping old enough to be a granny.'

'Well you are actually,' I said.

Juliette leaned forwards and looked at me, her heavily mascaraed eyes looking a bit woozy and slightly alarming.

'Aha. I *know* that, but in my head I'm not. In my head I'm thirty and it's only when I look in the mirror and see my mother looking back that I realise I'm not. Scary to realise my next significant birthday will be when I'm *seventy*. By then the twins will be in school!'

'Isn't every birthday significant?' I said. 'I mean, the alternative is worse.'

Juliette pulled a thoughtful face. 'True, I s'pose. That's one way of looking at it. But when I was a kid, I wanted to be older... this isn't really what I expected.'

Well join the club, I thought.

'So are you married, Sophia?' Kim asked.

'I was, for twenty-three years.'

'Divorced? Did the dirty on you? All men are the same, absolute bastards,' Kim said, giving me a sympathetic look. She pulled out another cigarette and lit it.

'Well, widowed actually,' I said. 'Peter died eight years ago.'

Kim's face fell dramatically. 'Oh God! I'm so sorry, I didn't mean—'

Juliette interrupted her and put one silver-tipped hand over mine. 'Take no notice Soph, the ink on Kim's divorce isn't quite dry yet and she's in a bit of a mood. We came here to cheer her up amongst other things. Anita needs to think about what she's going to do next once she's been chucked out of the tax office to spend all her time with her husband and I need to have some fun to convince myself I'm not past it.'

I realised with surprise that I was starting to like them, and I was now past the point in our acquaintance when I was going to be able to remain cross about last night.

'So, what did you all study at university?' I asked.

Anita answered first. 'I did classics which is why I now work in the tax office. There's not much call for an in-depth knowledge of Greek philosophy in Kidderminster.'

Juliette was next. 'I did music and did have ambitions to be a classical pianist.'

'So why didn't you?' I asked.

'I wasn't good enough,' she said, 'and I got pregnant with my daughter five minutes after I graduated. Although when I was a student I did date a chap who went on to play at Carnegie Hall. That's my only claim to fame, which is a bit rubbish really isn't it?'

'Impressive. The piano?'

'Triangle – no don't laugh – *and* other percussion things. We broke up because he kept washing his *parts* in my bath.'

'*What*?'

Anita spluttered into her drink and flapped a hand.

Juliette laughed until she nearly choked and Kim had to slap her on the back.

'His drum bits. Don't be so *rude*! I'd come back to the flat desperate for a bath and it would be full of random pieces of metal soaking in washing powder. His cymbals and occasionally his hardware. And then he used to dry his stuff on my tea towels.'

'Dirty boy,' Kim snorted, breaking out into the now-familiar laugh.

The others joined in and I did too; they really were rather funny.

It had been a long time since I'd had a proper heart-to-heart with other women; what is popularly known as a *girly chat*, although I don't think any of us could accurately have been described as girls any more. For the last few years I'd been too busy keeping my phone, evenings and weekends free in case Lucian could get away to see me. What a fool I'd been.

'And I did applod... appli... applied maths,' Kim said, stabbing the table with a finger.

'That's really difficult sums to you and me,' Anita said *sotto voce*.

I raised my glass in Kim's direction. 'Impressive.'

'I started off as a teacher and then when I had the kids I did some private coaching and at the moment I'm a receptionist in a medical practice. So now I count patients and medical waste bags for a living. It's riveting stuff.'

'Still, it sounds quite interesting,' I said.

'Well not really. I'd like to have been a supermodel,' Kim said, momentarily glum. 'Not now obviously, but I did look okay back in the day. Don't look like that Anita, I did. Don't you remember? I had a Biba cocktail flapper dress once; I must have been an absolute twig. Now I am developing an unhealthy interest in comfortable

shoes and winter vests. My greatest excitement is three for two in
the Cotton Traders sale.'

Juliette and Anita gave a groan and Anita pretended to play a
violin.

'Oh stop it, Kim. Just because Stewart did the dirty on you
doesn't mean you have to sink into a decline. You're in your prime,
we all are.'

Juliette half stood up and slapped her hip before falling back
into her chair.

'Prime rump too!'

Kim shook herself and pointed a finger at Juliette. 'You're
asslutely right, that's defeatist talk.'

Juliette looked at her watch.

'Hey, it's nearly midnight! We were going to go out weren't we?'

Anita and Kim groaned.

'I can't.'

'We'll go out tomorrow night.'

They turned to me.

'You can come too. You're with the Old Ducks now and our
motto is seize the day. *Carpe Diem*. What's that in Greek, Anita?'

'*Ádraxe ti méra*! I think,' Anita said with a flourish.

'Well there you go then!' Juliette said.

I'd been almost prepared to have a jolly good row with my new
neighbours, now it seemed I was expected to go out with them. This
was very unexpected.

* * *

'So go on then Soph, tell us why you're here. What's this work
you're supposed to be doing?' Juliette said a short while later.

I was definitely tiddly but still felt the need to deflect their
attention.

'Oh, you don't want to hear about that, s'not very interesting,' I said, 'I'll tell you 'nother time.'

Unfortunately, this made the Old Ducks even more interested.

'We'll be the judge of that,' Kim said, 'it will be more interesting than Rick's pants.' She lit another cigarette and puffed smoke into the night air. 'God, I love smoking.'

'There's never been anything interesting about Rick's pants, and the way things are going lately, there never will be,' Anita said gloomily.

Juliette tapped the table with one silver talon.

'Now here's something interesting – I mean *really* interesting – I noticed in the supermarket. Greek dishwasher tablets are called *Magnum*. Now that might be confusing.'

'I liked Magnum, back in the day,' Anita said, slurping her latest drink. A vodka concoction I believed. 'Tom Daly, with that moustache, he was lovely.'

'I think Tom Daly is a diver,' I said, trying to think straight.

'No! Tom... Tom... I can see him. Moustache, nice smile, curly hair, Hawaiian shirts...'

'Tom... Tom...'

We sat around the table trying to remember.

'If we had a laptop, we could google it,' Kim said.

'That's cheating,' Juliette said firmly.

'I've got one,' I said.

'Ah yes, this work you're supposed to be doing that isn't interesting?' Juliette said, reaching for the red wine.

By then I was definitely over the limit and my resolve not to talk was somewhat weakened.

'I was supposed to be editing my ex boss's latest book.'

'Ooh what's it about? Something exciting?'

'Has it got any rude bits?'

I tried to remember. 'S'bout the Knights Templar.'

Their faces fell.

'Still, it might be interesting,' Anita said kindly, 'all that fighting and armour... and... y'know, stuff.'

'Yes, if you're a history geek with no life,' Juliette said.

'Oh, he had plenty of life,' I said, 'in fact, a bit too much. That was the trouble.'

'Tell,' Juliette commanded.

I sighed.

'I had an affair with him for five years,' I said.

Everyone gasped and looked at me, eyes wide and mouths open.

'I didn't think you were the sort to do that,' Anita gasped.

Well thinking about it, neither had I.

'I assume he was married, and the wife found out? I will *try* not to think less of you,' Kim said, raising her vodka-and-something in my direction, 'seeing as I've been in the same position, but from the other side of the duvet, so to speak. D'you know I caught Stewart with the tart in the back seat of my car? *My car!* He was parked in Tesco car park. I mean it was after closing time, but even so.'

'What did you do?' I asked.

'I waited until he'd pulled his trousers down and then took a picture on my phone and sent it to his mother.'

'You *didn't!*'

'I did. Maureen was always convinced her darling son was perfect and everything was my fault. I thought it was time she found out the truth. She's not spoken to me since.'

'Well you can't really blame her,' Juliette said. 'I think we should have some music, don't you? I feel like dancing. I've got hits from the sixties and seventies on my iPad, I'll go and get it. Don't say anything interesting until I get back.'

'We'll just bitch about you,' Kim called after her.

Juliette stumbled off to the house and Kim and Anita topped up their glasses.

I looked at them over the table; Kim, grey-haired and slightly overweight, dressed in a blue dress and cardigan. Anita, darker-haired, in jeans and a yellow T-shirt that was already splashed with red wine. Rather strangely, I felt quite fond of them already. Perhaps it was the alcohol.

'I really ought to go to bed,' I mumbled.

No one said anything so instead I ate some breadsticks and a few crisps. I realised that perhaps I didn't want to go to bed after all.

Juliette came back with her iPad and fiddled about with it for a few minutes.

After a few seconds, the music blared out, and she started dancing.

'Better turn that down,' Anita said, making exaggerated shushing noises and flapping her hands. 'Remember there's a woman in the house next door trying to work.'

'You can't beat the sixties for good tunes. Beatles, Stones, Herman Goering...'

'Herman's Hermits you twit,' Anita said.

'I know I'm just being daft. That's what my Dad used to call him.'

'The first pop star I remember was Petula Clark. She had a sort of pixie crop. I thought it was marvellous. My mother said it looked as though she cut her hair with nail scissors,' I said.

'Ooh this, now this is one of my favourites. Tommy James and the Shondells, "Mony Mony". I watched this on YouTube the other day, massive sideburns...'

'Do you know, I'm getting sideburns,' Kim said, 'look...' She pulled her hair back, 'I think it's the hormones. I have all these curly hairs in front of my ears. Like Bruce Forsyth on the Generation game. D'you remember that?'

'...and they had terrible ruffly shirts... So how did it end?'

'"Mony Mony"?' I said, confused.

'Your affair?'

'Oh, Gina, his wife that is – *Gina My Wife* he used to call her. I don't think she knew about me, but she did find out he was shagging one of his students. And then I found out about that because Lucian told me. I was so angry.'

'Angry?' Kim said, pulling a face. 'Who were you angry with? The student? Him? What right did you have to be angry with anyone? My sympathies are with the wife. I know what it feels like.'

'You're right,' I admitted sadly, 'I suppose I was angriest with myself, for being such a fool. And hypocritical. And wasting so much time on him.'

'I should think so too,' Kim said. 'What a dirty sod! Surely that's an abuse of something? He must have been a lot older than her, he was in a position of... I can't remember.'

'Quite. Anyway, I ended it and said I was resigning and all he could say was I'd promised to edit his book, and like a muppet I agreed, but said I'd come here to do it.'

'You must be mad.' Juliette held up a hand and hiccupped, 'I call a special vote of the Old Ducks, Soph should not under any circumstances edit his badgering book. All in favour?'

'Aye!' the others shouted.

'Unless, *unless* you really mess it up good and proper,' Kim suggested, leaning slightly to one side as she lit another cigarette. It was a good thing her chair had arms to keep her in place.

Anita liked this idea. 'Yes, change all the words like "grail" to something else. Like...'

'Like sandwich. The quest for the Holy Sandwich,' Juliette suggested.

'He'd notice...'

'Or quail. The quest for the Holy Quail. Subtle, see?'

Juliette turned up the music to full and, in the enclosed courtyard, it was quite loud. After a bit we all decided to go in the hot tub and although Juliette was happy to pull off her dress and get in wearing her underwear, I went off to wrestle myself into my tankini. I was probably not in any sort of state to go in a hot tub, but all of a sudden it seemed a *really* good idea.

When I came back, the music seemed even louder and the three of them were in the hot tub warbling along at the tops of their voices to The Carpenters and 'Close to You'.

I got in with them. The water was lovely and warm; I realised the night air was actually quite chilly now, perhaps the alcohol had numbed me to it.

Juliette had found a bottle of Prosecco while I was away and was taking a slurp.

'Do you know the Bishop of Norwich?' Anita asked her rather pointedly.

'No, should I?' Juliette said, confused.

'It what my Dad used to say. He was in the Navy. The correct response is *he's a terribly nice chap, but he never passed the port either.*'

'Ah.'

Juliette passed her the bottle.

'What did the earwig say as he fell off the table?' Kim said.

She looked around at our momentarily confused faces.

'Earwigo.'

Kim broke out into her familiar hyena laugh and we all joined in; well it did seem quite funny at the time. She was laughing so hard she almost slid under the water. Juliette grabbed her arm and yanked her back up.

I rested my head back on one of the hot tub cushions and wondered what Lucian would say if he could see me now. Drunk and giggling at just about everything.

I hadn't been this drunk in years, not drunk and happy anyway. Drunk and crying possibly. Drunk and despairing definitely. Drunk and happy was better.

I closed my eyes, singing along at the top of my voice with the others.

Suddenly there was a shout.

'*Ti sto kaló...* What the hell do you think you are doing?'

We stopped yodelling along to 'The Lion Sleeps Tonight' and Juliette nearly dropped the bottle of Prosecco into the water.

There was a man standing in the garden with us.

Kim carried on *aweem away-ing* for a few seconds until she realised the rest of us had all shut up.

It was the man with the silver hair and the Greek name, Theo thingy, and he didn't look at all happy.

'This terrible noise,' he said, coming a few steps closer.

'S'not that bad,' Juliette replied, outraged, her head wobbling slightly, 'I was in the school choir I'll have you know. We won flipping prizes.'

'I cannot have this level of noise, it is unacceptable,' he said angrily.

We all looked at him for a few seconds until Anita let out a snort of laughter. I sank down in the water a bit.

The music changed to 'Jive Talking' and Kim tried singing a few tentative *j j j jives* in his direction to see if he would join in. But, of course, he didn't.

'You must stop with this noise. It is past one o'clock; people are trying to sleep.'

One o'clock? How did that happen? I thought.

My head was feeling a bit wobbly too at that point.

'Last night was bad enough but I was prepared to overlook it. I am surprised at you, ladies,' he said and then he looked straight at me, 'surprised and disappointed.'

I sank lower still until my chin was resting on the water.

No one said anything. Juliette pulled a face at me.

'It's her fault,' she said, splashing me.

'Me? You can't blame me,' I said indignantly, splashing her back. I wasn't sure it came out that coherently.

Juliette smothered a laugh and I wanted to giggle. I also wanted to get out, but I wasn't sure I wanted to with Theo there looking so stern. I pulled my tankini top down and then, realising my bosom was making a break for freedom, pulled it up again.

'Perhaps we'd better get out,' I suggested.

'Yes, indeed you might get out,' Theo agreed.

'We can't until you go,' I said, trying not to slur.

'Why not?'

'It's against the law. The Court of Human Rights. The Hague.'

'Is that the same as William Hague?' Juliette asked, waving her tumbler.

'He went bald, he had lots of hair once. Bad career move in my opinion,' Anita said. 'You can't take a politician seriously when he looks like a baby in a suit.'

The iPad started playing '50 Ways to Leave Your Lover' and Anita started crying. Very loudly.

'Rick once called me moany,' she sobbed. 'I wasn't moany, I just wanted him to take the bins out. Without me asking.'

'Tom Selleck,' Kim shouted suddenly, spilling Prosecco down herself.

7

I woke up the following morning very confused. I was lying on top of the bed, still in my tankini. There was a damp towel over my legs, and it felt like there was someone hammering on my skull with a tiny pneumatic drill. I also seemed to have swallowed the contents of a well-used cat litter tray in the night.

I gave a quiet, sad groan.

And then another, slightly louder one. God, that really *hurt*.

I needed a pint of water and a cup of tea. At the same time.

I tried three times to sit up and failed. My core strength wasn't what it should be. Eventually I rolled off the bed onto my knees and hauled myself up with a chair. What had I been thinking? What on earth had I been drinking?

I yanked off my tankini which took some time as the little golden decoration got caught in my hair. I stumbled around for a few seconds with the top over my face, bumping into things. Eventually I found my dressing gown then I dragged myself to the bathroom.

I peered at myself in the mirror. My face looked grey and a bit drawn and my father – famous for his terrible puns – would have said my eyes looked like two rissoles in the snow. I slapped on a bit of the magic moisturiser, wondering if it had the power to cope with this challenge. Probably not. There are limits.

Then I went to the top of the stairs and swayed a bit. The kettle was downstairs, and I wanted to be downstairs, but I needed to be careful otherwise I'd find myself in a heap at the bottom with a broken leg or concussion.

I crept down very slowly, clutching on to the bannisters. Someone was making strange little whimpering noises. I was half way to the bottom before I realised it was me.

I got to the kitchen without incident and greeted the tea bags with a low cry of joy. I needed the biggest possible mugful, but they were all the same size, so I made two.

I felt like death. Never again. Absolutely never again would I touch ouzo, gin, vodka or Prosecco or anything with a cocktail umbrella. Maraschino cherries. Oh *God*.

I sat on the sofa and drank my two mugs of tea, breathing slowly and steadily to quell the waves of nausea. Was it better with my reading glasses on or off? I tried it. Each was equally as bad.

What time was it? I peered at my new Fitbit, also bought at the airport as I had intended to clock up a lot of steps during my stay here, tone up my muscles and possibly lose the extra half stone that had crept on over the last few weeks. Uncontrolled biscuit eating and solitary wine drinking had done me no favours.

It was almost midday. I couldn't believe it. My usual wake-up time was six-thirty.

Perhaps I needed to eat something. What did people usually do in these circumstances? I thought of a full English breakfast and made cheek-inflating, nauseated noises.

No. Thanks.

The thought of orange juice was also too much to bear; I didn't care how much vitamin C was in it, it would be like drinking battery acid. A prairie oyster, with a raw egg. *Bleurgh. Quick, think of something else.*

Toast. Always a failsafe. Maybe.

I made another two mugs of tea. Had I been indiscreet last night? Had I said too much about myself? There seemed to have been a lot of soul baring and discussion going on. Well, from what I remembered. And quite a bit of group savagery regarding men-we-had-known and things-they-had-done. What we should have done about it. Things we could have said at the time and hadn't.

At least I hadn't got all maudlin and tearful with them, which I sometimes had recently. Really, I was too old to be behaving like this. Although if I was honest it had been fun. Still, if one of the students had turned up to my office looking like I did this morning, they would have received short shrift.

Short shrift. That was a funny saying wasn't it? I mean what was long shrift and come to think of it what was a shrift in the first place? I'd have to Google it.

I lay down on the sofa, slowly and carefully so as not to disturb my head too much. I could have done with some paracetamol; I knew I had some somewhere. Then I remembered Juliette had them. I'd forgotten to take them back. Perhaps they were still outside on the table in their garden.

I got up again and opened the back door out to the patio. It was another bright (very bright) day. I went back inside and found my sunglasses. And a sun hat.

Outside, the garden next door was a scene of devastation. The table was exactly as we had left it. Bottles, half-empty and empty. A very full ashtray. Glasses and plates, the remains of the food. I put my hand over my mouth and took a deep breath. No paracetamol then.

I went back inside and lay down with a low, regretful groan. Never again.

* * *

I was woken up some time later by the sound of knocking. I still had my head pillowed on the cushions; one of them was a bit damp, I must have been drooling. Bleary-eyed, I saw Kim on the other side of my patio doors. She looked as bad as I felt. She gave me a little wave and held up the box of paracetamol.

'Afternoon, I thought you might need these?'

'I do and thanks,' I said. I felt a bit better now, maybe toast was a good idea after all. 'Everyone okay?'

'Sort of. Well, I haven't seen Jules yet. But I did hear her complaining as I came downstairs so she's still alive. It was a good night wasn't it?' She grinned.

I gulped down two tablets with some cold tea.

'I think so,' I said, 'from what I remember of it.'

'Oh well, if we can't go mad occasionally at our age then it's a pretty sad lookout,' Kim said, 'although it's been a very long time since I did.'

I nodded my head carefully. 'Me too.'

'My son Simon is always drooping about the house at the weekend complaining he's tired. I tell him if he went to bed before three in the morning and stopped playing with some chap in Houston on his Xbox, he might not feel so bad and be able to do his own laundry. That idea you had about them getting their own place is worth thinking about.'

'I sometimes wonder how young people afford it all, mobile phones and nights out on the razzle.'

'Ha! Their parents pay. You wouldn't believe the number of times my two have come to me over the years, complaining about having no money. And they both earn as much as I do. But Gemma has all the gear, some of it's designer stuff too. I used to shop at Miss Selfridge when I was her age. Or C&A, remember them? God, the shoulder pads could have had someone's eye out when I look at the photos. Well, better go, I'll see you later. I need coffee.'

I'd read once that it takes about three hours to metabolise a large glass of wine. Based on my memory of the night before, I'd probably be over the limit for three days. Possibly longer. Good job I didn't have a hire car.

* * *

By late afternoon I'd showered, got dressed and had another snooze in front of the television.

Three very glamorous and excitable women were talking about something that necessitated a lot of hand waving and laughter. *Ándres* – that was men – and *plastiki cheirourgiki*, which I assume meant plastic surgery. I was never going to go down that route, although Juliette did look good for her age, and I guessed she'd had something done. Perhaps I would ask her.

I went back in front of the mirror, relieved to see I now had some colour back in my cheeks. I pulled the skin back from my face, two hands in my hair. Did that make me look younger or did I just look like a woman in a wind tunnel, trying to imagine herself with a facelift? Did I need one?

It was sad really. The things women did to themselves. All that stuff about Botox and fillers. Tattooed eyebrows and lipliner. Boob jobs and bottom lifts. Liposuction and photoshop and waist trainers. Diets and fads, years of despair. Why did whole generations of women feel like this? Never believing we were good enough. Never gaining our own approval. Why?

Men didn't do that did they? They probably didn't ever give it a thought. Older men like Lucian assumed they were still irresistible and appealing. They didn't seem to have any trouble attracting young girls like Poppy, skin as clear as a child's, throwing on crazy, mismatched clothes and still looking great, while older women like me bought overpriced moisturisers and expensive bras and stared in the mirror, doubt in our eyes.

* * *

'I've brought you a cake,' Juliette said, peering cautiously around my patio door an hour later. She held out a paper bag which I took. By this point I was starving but didn't know for what. Cake seemed a good option.

'Thanks,' I said, 'what is it?'

Juliette flopped down onto the chair opposite me.

'No idea. I just pointed at a few and gave the nice man some money. I think its honey and orange. Feel okay?'

'I think so.' I took a bite; it was sweet and delicious, exactly what I needed.

'That was a great night wasn't it?' she grinned. 'Just what we all needed.'

'A few hours ago I would have said not – thanks for this, it's wonderful,' I said, munching.

'Well, we can spend the rest of our lives being sensible and behaving ourselves. I don't think one night of excess can hurt.'

'As long as it's just one night,' I said.

Juliette laughed. I looked at her, wondering if she had gone under the knife or whether she was just...

'What do you think of cosmetic surgery?' I asked.

'You mean have I had any?' she said, arching one eyebrow.

'Well... yes, I suppose so.'

'Of course I have. Don't be daft!' She ticked off the answers on her fingers. 'First, I had a brow lift, my varicose veins done, my teeth, a bit of Botox, then later on, a full lift and a boob job. Why?'

'I just wondered. You make it sound like a shopping list.'

I ate some more of my cake.

'You don't approve, do you?' she said, wagging a finger at me, 'you think I'm letting the team down, pandering to society's obsession with youth?'

'It doesn't matter what I think. I'm curious to know why you had it all done, that's all. And did it hurt?'

'I did it for me. Well mostly for me. Actually, that's not quite true; my ex and I used to work at the same company, and we still did after the divorce. He was always criticising me and making little digs, although he knew what I was like when we got married. But, of course, it got much worse when it came to the financial wrangling. He told the judge I shouldn't get what I was entitled to as I had no idea how to manage money. That I would just fritter it all away. Mercifully, the judge was a woman and didn't agree. You could tell what she thought of him by the way she looked at him. So once the settlement hit my bank account, I did the full lift and the boob job so he could see where some of the money had gone at the Christmas do. Now that *was* a good night. He wasn't happy. But I was. It was a great feeling. Doing something for me. He called it selfish, of course. And yes, it did hurt. And when I had my varicose veins done my legs looked like someone had battered me with a baseball bat. Fancy doing something similar?'

'God no, I wouldn't dare. It sounds terrible.'

She laughed. 'We'll see shall we. Nothing hurt me as much as what Gary did and at least I had something to show for it other than stretch marks.'

8

By the evening I was fine again. And, presumably, sober. I went out briefly to the little supermarket at the end of the road, feeling slightly nervous that one of the Old Ducks would spot me and invite me round for a 'little drink'. I didn't think my liver could take it. And they were talking about 'going out' tonight. No way José.

Instead, I went to bed early. They woke me up of course, at about ten-thirty. They were back in the hot tub, knocking back wine and chatting reasonably quietly. How did they do it? They were made of tough stuff, that was true. But this time I wasn't irritated or glaring out of the window at them. In fact, in a funny way, as I fell asleep it felt nice to know that they were out there.

* * *

The following morning, I was awake at six-thirty, feeling great. I even felt like cooking again. Perhaps I would make something for the Old Ducks next door, as a sort of peace offering for my bad start with them. If they had decided I was friend material perhaps I was, and maybe I should make a bit of an effort.

Downstairs, drinking tea, I opened my laptop. There were six new emails from Lucian, each one more agitated than the last. His book, his publisher, his terrible workload, what was I doing? He'd expected to hear from me, why hadn't he? Gina was being unreasonable about everything; none of his children were talking to him. Like I should care? I realised I really didn't.

Underlying all of this was a heavy dollop of what I believed was called transferred guilt. By which I meant he was trying to make me feel guilty for abandoning him in his days of need.

I sat and thought about this for a while and realised I felt no guilt at all. Nor was I likely to. What Juliette had said had resonated within me. This time was for me. I came here to physically get away from Lucian and his domestic dramas and do the work I had promised I would. But now I was here, I could see my past life and choices rather more clearly. I was actually starting to enjoy myself. Well, apart from yesterday's hangover.

Having come to that realisation, I needed to do more than just wander around the old town, buying bread and wine. I had assumed I would be closeted in the house working on Lucian's manuscript, perhaps going to the Palace of the Grand Master and the museum, checking a few facts or dates. Well, I was blowed if I was going to do that now.

I took out my guide book and the tourist map of the island and spread it on the table. Then I googled Rhodes' top tourist attractions. There were so many places I could go and some good suggestions on how to get there. I'd have to look up bus timetables.

I found out Lindos was a pedestrianised town, supposed to be pretty with its own acropolis. There was St Paul's Bay, Kallithea Springs, there were boat trips and stunning walks. That sounded like a good starting point. I would not stay indoors with a boring book on ancient battles, dead popes and obscure facts.

There was a knock on my front door.

I opened it and was more than a bit surprised to see Theo standing there.

Working on defence being the best form of, well defence I supposed, I started talking.

'Look, I'm sorry, okay? I know we were making a row the other night; I know we were behaving badly. We were probably breaking all sorts of by-laws, and if we were then I apologise. Thank you for not calling the police. I really don't know what prompted it, but I suppose...'

He tilted his head to one side, listening. He was in his usual jeans and linen shirt attire with what my mother would have called 'Jesus sandals' on his bare brown feet. He really was extremely attractive, in the way men sometimes are when they are comfortable with themselves. I bet he didn't give cosmetic surgery a second thought.

I shut up and gulped a bit.

'Are you okay?' he said.

Hmm. What did he mean by that? Was I okay; in other words, was I recovered from my hangover? Or did he mean was I completely bonkers, one banana short of a bunch?

'I'm fine, I mean... well I was a bit... you know. Just fine thank you.'

'Good.'

'Good.'

So what exactly do you want?

'I thought, as you don't have a car... you don't have a car, do you?'

I actually looked around me in an incredibly foolish gesture as though there might be a car hiding somewhere in the house.

'No,' I said at last, 'no I don't.'

'Good.'

'Well, if there's nothing else?' I said, preparing to close the door.

'I wondered, hmm... *tha itheles na deis*... if you would like to see somewhere?'

'Where?' I asked, a bit confused.

He pulled a thoughtful expression. 'Oh, maybe Tsambika Monastery. There is a wonderful view from there. Or Kallithea Springs?'

How weird. That was absolutely what I had been thinking about doing. Was he psychic?

Or hang on, perhaps the house was *bugged*, and he had been listening in.

I'd seen the Bourne Trilogy; I knew how phones and houses and laptops could be accessed. For example, once, I'd been just *thinking* about buying some new garden furniture, and the next day my Facebook feed had been filled with advertisements for cane chairs and barbecues.

Were there cameras too? Hidden in the table lamp perhaps or in that little statuette of the Colossus on the bookshelf?

I stood for a moment open-mouthed at the horror of all the possibilities.

'It was just a... *sképsi* – just a thought.' He gave a little shrug.

'Why?' I asked, playing for time.

'Why not? Just a kindness. This is a beautiful island and I thought you might like to see something of it, that's all. I meant no harm.'

'No, I didn't think you did, I just wondered how you knew that was what I had been thinking...'

His face lit up. 'So, you would like this?'

I thought about it. 'Well yes, but I don't actually know you, do I?'

'I live two doors away from you. You have my business card. I have no police record. I own this house and the one your friends are in,' he said.

'They aren't actually my friends. Well, I suppose... I mean I didn't know them until a few days ago. We just met because they were making such a noise, and I complained.'

'I thought so,' he said, 'you didn't seem to be of them. Of their group.'

'I've got to know them, they are nice women,' I bristled defensively. 'They have come here for a break from their everyday lives, problems. There's nothing wrong with that.'

'I understand perfectly. They are women with family. Men, children, family can be problems.'

Well ain't that the truth?

'But—' What was I trying to say here?

That because some friends behaved like gap year students on a bender and not like responsible adults it didn't mean they were to be condemned? Although I too had been critical to start with. It somehow seemed more acceptable now that I had become one of them. Hmm. My parameters for acceptable behaviour were becoming rather fluid.

'Your problem is that there are many beautiful places to visit and no easy way to get there,' he said. He fixed my gaze with his beautiful dark eyes. It shouldn't matter that he had beautiful dark eyes. Lucian had lovely eyes, grey and expressive. Look where that had got me.

'There are buses, or taxis,' I replied.

His face lit up and he gave me a broad smile.

'Then I will be your taxi. I have a day free. I have a car. I know the roads and the best places to park, and you won't need to worry about the tip. I am trustworthy, I am a retired man with a lot of free time, I like these places. They deserve to be seen.'

'Well—'

Despite my reservations, he was so nice, so friendly, that the idea was beginning to appeal to me.

'Tell your friends next door where you are going. And that you will be back later on. You have a phone, they have phones.'

He held out his hands in a gesture that said, *so what's the problem?*

I was torn. I had, after all, come here for some time on my own. I didn't want to spend all my time with the Old Ducks, however much they made me laugh in a way I hadn't for a long time.

'So, if I called for you in—' he looked at his watch, '—an hour? Would that be suitable? Please, if it is not, then say. My time is my own. I can fit in with you.'

'Yes,' I said, feeling independent and a bit daring, 'I suppose that would be fine.'

'*Éxochos*. Excellent.'

I closed the door in a bit of a daze. What had just happened?

Anyway, I thought I'd better do as he had suggested and tell my neighbours where I was going.

And I was going to knock up something nice for them too. What could I make? I wanted to do something Greek. Something I could prepare quickly and cook when I got back from my trip. I did some web searching on my laptop and came up with chicken and potatoes marinated in lemons and garlic, with some rosemary (which I had in the garden) and olive oil. I nipped out to the shops at the end of the road, bought everything I needed and then started work. It sounded ridiculously easy and it was. Fifteen minutes later the chicken and its marinade were assembled and ready. When I got back all I would need to do was dump it on top of some onions and potatoes and shove it in the oven. I couldn't wait.

* * *

Twenty minutes later I had changed into my cream linen dress, told my neighbours to expect something nice for their evening meal, and was sitting in the passenger seat of Theo's car with the warnings of the Old Ducks ringing in my ear, including a self-defence manoeuvre Juliette had learned at judo.

It was a lovely car too, dark green, a classic soft-top MG. I knew that because it was green and it had a badge saying MG on the front, not because I'm a car geek.

I tied a silk headscarf over my hair, feeling very Grace Kelly-ish, and we sped off down the road, away from the harbour. I spotted another big cruise ship which had just docked. People were streaming out towards the town carrying bags and maps. I felt quite childishly pleased with myself for not being one of them. I was almost a local. Well, for the time being anyway.

'We'll take the 95, Rodou Lindou,' Theo said after he had cleared the usual city traffic of vans and trucks.

I'd imagined the two of us driving along beautiful roads, winding through the countryside, like Cary Grant and Grace Kelly in that Hitchcock film in the South of France. Possibly seeing girls dressed in traditional costumes smiling as we passed them, even a colourful elderly man with a donkey waving at us. The man, not the donkey.

The reality was a bit disappointing actually, pretty much the same as any dual carriageway in any country. There were blocky blocks of flats and uninteresting groups of shops and petrol stations and any number of building sites. I didn't know if the pedestrianised town of Lindos was pretty or not because we completely bypassed it, sweeping onwards past coach parks and new hotels with swimming pools next to the road, until suddenly our route swept and curled down towards the wonderful blue sea. And then there was a secluded bay where a yacht was slowly moving out beyond a tiny white chapel. I expect it was filled with laughing girls in bikinis, taking Instagram poses and pouting. The yacht, not the chapel.

'St Paul's chapel. Only built in the 1950s, but very popular with Greek couples for weddings,' Theo said, slowing the car down to make the turn.

We hadn't actually had much of a chance to talk during the journey because driving in a car with the roof down was noisy. But he had pointed out landmarks and occasionally places he had lived or worked. It seemed he had been a builder for most of his working life before he turned to property development.

'Building is a young man's game; property was my hobby but then – well it became more interesting and certainly a lot easier.'

'This is such a beautiful place,' I said, as the noise from the car engine faded away. I was awestruck by the bay in front of me.

There was a sweep of sparkling clear sea, a little beach with just a few holidaymakers sitting on sunbeds, some under the shade of parasols.

'In the summer it is so much busier,' he said, 'this is the best time to see it. Easy parking too, I told you I knew the best places.'

The parking spot would have done it for me; it was overlooking the most mouth-watering view. The sun was bright and warm, it had only taken us about an hour to get here but it was so different from the north part of the island.

Theo led the way down a path to the rock-strewn beach. I took my time; I didn't want to risk any more damage to my knee followed by an afternoon spent looking for a support bandage.

In England there would have been a hot dog van and a café selling kites. Here, there was a taverna, built on top of a rocky promontory a stone's throw from the glistening, turquoise sea. There were rough wooden tables and chairs, a large, glass-fronted chiller filled with beer and wine, a few palm fringed parasols. It was exactly what I had hoped for.

'Are you hungry?' he said, 'I thought you might like to have lunch here?'

'Oh, yes, that would be wonderful,' I agreed enthusiastically.

'You're sure? I can take you somewhere else if you prefer. They do a lot of fish here. You're not a... *chortofágos*... vegetarian? If you are then—'

'No, not at all, this looks ideal,' I said.

I was impressed that he would think of this, that he would want to take my feelings into consideration, I wasn't used to that.

We walked along the edge of the sea to the café where we sat at a table perfectly situated on the rocks, in the shade. We could see a few people swimming, a boy with a scuba mask and flippers. There was a woman in a black (of course) swimming costume, huge sunglasses and a big straw hat who was up to her knees in the sea looking out at the horizon. She looked a bit like Joan Collins but probably wasn't. Her husband was even older and was leaning on a stick, shouting at her to come out of the water. From what I remembered, Joan's husband was significantly younger than she was and probably never shouted at her. Anyway, I reckoned Joan Collins would more likely be on a yacht somewhere, being amusing and drinking champagne, not turning her back on her husband with a face like thunder. I could have been wrong. Even screen legends had their off days.

'Now then, to start with, what will you have to drink?' Theo said.

'I'd like some sparkling water, please,' I said.

He looked a bit surprised. 'Okay.'

I laughed. 'I'd like to reassure you I don't make a habit of binge drinking.'

'Binge? What is that?'

'Um... drinking so much you get blotto, wasted, plastered,' I said. I fished in my bag for my little dictionary and looked it up. '*Methysménos.*'

'Ah yes, I see,' he said with a little smile.

I felt a bit silly then. Should a woman of my age get blotto at all? Well, on the other hand, why shouldn't she? It was my money and my holiday. There was no age limit to being daft. There was proof of that in the papers every day.

A young Greek god wearing an apron round his waist in a very cool way meandered up to our table and handed us two menus. Then he shook Theo's hand.

Theo ordered something and they had a rapid-fire chat. The Greek god wandered off again, gazing appreciatively at a young woman in a white bikini who was wading languorously out of the sea in full Ursula Andress mode, minus the knife strapped to her thigh.

Sparkling water was brought; I gulped down half a glassful gratefully. Driving in a soft-top car is fun but a bit dusty.

'The food here is very good,' Theo said encouragingly, 'they have scallops if you like them?'

'Love them, I'm just not that good at cooking fish,' I said, grateful he hadn't recommended anything with tentacles. Or the eel, which I had just noticed on the menu in front of me. I didn't think I could bring myself to put that in my mouth, and if I had, it wasn't good manners to spit the food into a napkin when one is being taken out for lunch.

'I recommend the prawns too if you like them. Although the steak is always very good, it's up to you. My treat.'

We discussed that for a few minutes as I didn't think it right that the taxi driver should go without a fare and then pay for my food too.

I carried on reading the menu, thinking hard. I was going to be sophisticated and Greek and take my time with this meal. I was going to savour it and appreciate the flavours, not race through it, desperate to get to the desserts as I usually did. But I had already noticed they served panna cotta, one of my absolute favourites.

'Prawns would be lovely,' I said at last, 'thanks.'

Greek god came back and exchanged a bit more rapid-fire conversation and some laughter with Theo who paused and introduced us.

'This young man is Alexis, my nephew,' he said.

Alexis shook my hand and gave me a glorious smile.

'*Kaló apógevma kyria*. Good day, madame.'

'*Kaló apógevma* to you too. I can see the resemblance, Theo,' I said, 'he looks like you.'

'His mother is my younger sister, Hera. She is a lawyer. Alexis is also a lawyer, but he loves the ocean too much for his own good, don't you? When the winter comes, he will be back in the office.'

Alexis made a dismissive noise and laughed.

'I don't blame him,' I said.

Alexis fished his notepad and pen out of his apron pocket, took our order and wandered off again.

Theo turned back to me. 'So Sophia, tell me about yourself.'

'Oh dear, what do you want to know?'

He threw up his hands and laughed. 'Why do you say this? *Oh dear*? As though there is nothing interesting to tell.'

'Perhaps because there isn't,' I said.

'Nonsense, a lovely woman like you must have a story to tell.'

He thought I was lovely? And he was prepared to say so?

My word, the Greeks certainly knew how to chat up a woman. Not like Lucian, who had romantically caught my attention five years ago by asking if I would go and buy him some Night Nurse during my lunch hour because he thought he was coming down with man flu. Which of course he did, leaving tissues all over the place and giving me piteous looks for sympathy, which I foolishly – instead of telling him to man up – gave him. With the benefit of hindsight, it was downhill all the way from there.

The starters arrived quickly, three plump and luscious scallops served on their shells with a dash of rich jus and a lime wedge. They smelled and looked wonderful.

Theo called Alexis back over.

'We should have just a small glass of very chilled, very dry white wine with this don't you think?'

Despite my preference for red wine, I thought this was an excellent suggestion.

'Good idea,' I said, trying not to shovel the food into my mouth as fast as I wanted to.

Slowly, be elegant.

He was right, it was like a little zing of delight to mix the two things.

'So, tell me what brings you to Rhodes,' he said. 'You booked very suddenly.'

Of course he would know this. After all, he owned the house.

'Last minute decision,' I said, 'I had some work to do for my ex-boss, and I could do it just as well here as back home. I needed a break.'

'And is that going well? The work I mean?'

Hmm, no not really seeing as I've given up on it.

'Oh not bad,' I said vaguely, 'you know.'

'Why are you doing work for your ex-boss I wonder,' he asked thoughtfully.

I shook my head, not looking at him. 'It's a long story, not very interesting.'

'My guess is you are like me, not doing any work at all,' he said, and he grinned.

'Well, no not really,' I admitted with a guilty laugh.

He raised his glass to me. 'Good for you, *kyria*.'

We clinked glasses across the table and his eyes met mine.

I swear to God, a little frisson passed between us. A tiny bolt of attraction. Well, I didn't know if he felt it, but I certainly did. That was very inappropriate. I hadn't really expected that at all.

9

We were there for hours. I didn't think I'd ever spent so long over a meal. But it was really lovely, and the setting couldn't have been bettered.

There were boats in the bay and people on the beach to watch. Several couples lying on sunbeds, fingers busy on their iPhones; girls in complicated, stringy bikinis flouncing about and sending sly glances at the various waiters and attendants. A group of young men plumping up cushions and sweeping the sand off the board-walk terraces, something that seemed to take a long time and frequent cigarette breaks. What a life.

I wondered how things were back in Oxford. I bet it was still raining. I had three postgraduate students renting rooms in my house; they were all sensible – one might almost say dull – which suited me just fine. They didn't seem to communicate much with each other never mind the party-loving undergrads.

But in my absence, had they taken advantage with all-night parties and more outrageous friends I didn't know about? Would I get home to find empty bottles in the shrubbery and drugs and knickers stashed down the sofa cushions? Thinking about Nigel and his obsessive interest in fruit flies, I doubted it.

'So, you are avoiding doing any work? Will your friend be annoyed?'

'He's not my friend,' I said, investigating my last prawn.

'Ah, you were arguing with him that day you arrived? I remember.'

Oh God, he *had* been eavesdropping. What had I said? Had I been shouting or swearing?

'Well, maybe a bit. He didn't believe me when I resigned, and he didn't believe me when I said I was going on holiday either.'

'You are a woman with strong feelings about this I can tell. You were angry.'

'I was angry with myself, I think,' I admitted.

I picked up a tender asparagus spear and dunked it into the aioli.

'Are you married?' I said, keen to turn the conversation away from me and onto him.

'I was,' he said.

'So you're divorced?'

He shook his head. 'Elena died. We had been married for thirty-two years, happily married. We had one daughter, Olympia. She is a doctor; she lives in Australia with her husband Mark.'

'I'm sorry, you must miss her,' I said, 'you must miss them both.'

'Of course, but *den peirázei* – never mind. I've got used to it. Olympia has a good life; I have a good life. That's what matters.'

'Have you got a picture of her?' I said.

'Of course.'

Theo pulled out his phone and scrolled through it for a few seconds before handing it over.

'There,' he said, 'that's the latest one. They live in a place called Wollongong, just south of Sydney. She is on the beach of course;

they always seem to be on the beach. That's Mark and that's their little boy Alfie.'

I looked, Olympia was sitting wrapped in a towel, leaning against her husband while their son stood behind them, his hands on their shoulders. Olympia was gorgeous, dark glossy curls tossed by the sea breeze. Bright sparkling eyes just like her father's. Mark was a hunky sort with a craggy, interesting face, and the little boy was angelic with a head of blonde curls. They looked like a poster family for life in Australia.

What must it be like to have the most important person in your life living on the other side of the world? I tried to imagine it. No number of friends or family would quite make up for that, surely? And a grandson too, how awful to miss out on him.

'She's beautiful,' I said, 'she looks so happy.'

'This photo is of their house; it overlooks the sea. They have the most marvellous views. And they surf. They have a good life; I'd rather they weren't so far away but there you go.' He looked at the photo for a few seconds. 'As long as they are happy. That's all I care about.'

He put his phone away and bent his head over his food; he'd ordered a rather beautiful fillet steak with tiny new potatoes. I looked at him, his lean intelligent face, his thick silver hair. I supposed Juliette would call him a fox. He had probably been a real heartbreaker when he was a young man, he probably still could be. Was that my cue to be careful? I knew what damage heartbreakers could do. I wasn't going to allow that to happen again. But at that moment, Theo just seemed like a genuinely nice man to me, content with his life but sometimes, like just now when he had looked at photos of his daughter so far away, with just a hint of sadness in his eyes.

He looked up suddenly and caught my curious gaze.

'And you are married, Sophia?'

'No, I mean I wouldn't be here alone on holiday if I was,' I said. 'Peter liked holidays when he could be persuaded to take them. When we were first married he liked a big holiday every three or four years rather than lots of short ones. But that all changed. He died eight years ago.'

Theo briefly put one hand over mine, warm and friendly.

'I'm sorry,' he said.

I pulled away and picked up another asparagus spear.

'This is good,' I said, nodding at the food in front of me, 'really good.'

'Are you a good cook, Sophia?' he asked.

'Not bad,' I said with a laugh in my voice, 'but I'm a bit hit and miss when it comes to fish, which is why this is such a treat.'

He looked confused.

I picked up my little dictionary.

'*Merikés forés kalés* – sometimes good and sometimes...' I shook my head.

He smiled. 'Ah I see. I will cook for you one day. We will catch a fish and cook it on my boat.'

Boat?

He had a boat. That was rather exciting, well of course it depended on what sort of boat.

'That would be *kalós*. That would be good.'

He clapped his hands. 'You are learning Greek.'

'I don't know much,' I admitted.

He said something then, a long sentence that I didn't understand. I looked at him, puzzled.

'I'll tell you one day,' he said, 'if you will come out on my boat.'

Now this did remind me of *Shirley Valentine* and all that business with *my brother's boat*. Perhaps I was being too accommodating.

'Well maybe,' I said.

At that point my phone pinged with a text message, it was from Kim.

Everything okay? Do I need to call the police?

I texted back.

Everything is fine. See you later.

'Your friends checking I have not behaved badly?' Theo said.

'Something like that,' I admitted, flushing a bit at being caught out.

'I told you, I am trustworthy. You are quite safe. Now, I would like some panna cotta, what do you think?'

What did I think? I thought yes please, that's what I thought.

* * *

The sun was dipping down behind the hills surrounding the bay by the time we finished our coffee, and the evening was suddenly chilly. I pulled my jacket on, and Theo leaned forward to help me. There were lights in the canopy above us now and candles in glass lanterns on each table, which made everything look rather magical.

It was almost romantic, not that I was a particularly romantic type, but I could see how in the height of summer a wedding here might have been rather glorious. Flowers everywhere, the lights glowing in the summer evening, a bride trailing her exquisite lace veil carelessly in the white surf...

My wedding to Peter had been very straightforward in comparison. A short ceremony in the registry office with my mother, a few friends and Peter's parents. Followed by a table for ten in a hotel where my mother had twittered on, horrified by the prices, all through the meal. Had I always been the sort to be satisfied with so little? Didn't I deserve more sometimes?

Theo put the car roof back up against the chill on the journey home, so I didn't feel particularly glamorous and Grace Kelly-ish this time, I was just aware how small the car was alongside the trucks and lorries coming the other way.

We drove back through the evening the same way we had come, taking a small detour very briefly so I could see the famous *Anthony Quinn* beach further up the coast. That was gorgeous too, not so big but the same smooth water and a couple of the usual gin palaces, anchored out in the bay. There were lights shimmering in the windows. Perhaps the frisky, pouting girls I had imagined on board had put on some clothes and were playing Scrabble or doing the washing up. Perhaps not.

'Thank you for this,' I said as we reached the outskirts of the town, 'I've had a lovely day. And a splendid lunch too. I wish you would let me pay towards the meal; you've done all the driving.'

'Not at all. We have discussed this already. I told you there was no need. It's my pleasure,' Theo said. 'I've enjoyed it too. I'll tell you a secret; I've talked and laughed more today than I have in a very long time. And I'm proud of my homeland, I'm glad to show it off to you. It feels to me as though you can appreciate how special it is.'

'I do,' I agreed. 'It's wonderful.'

The streets of the town all looked very pretty with the fairy lights and candle lamps illuminating the pavement cafes.

'How splendid it all looks,' I said. 'So beautiful.'

'It is. But things will start to close at the end of October. Soon the local people will take a break, the holiday flights will cease, and the season will be over for another year.'

'That's a bit sad,' I said. 'Does it get cold here in the winter?'

'Oh yes, 10 or 11 degrees, and rain, we have flooding sometimes too. But sometimes it can be warm. Then in the spring, ah! The flowers, the wild flowers are wonderful, everywhere is so green and pleasant again.'

'It sounds lovely.'

He parked the car and turned to look at me.

'Perhaps you will return and see them?'

Again, that little, unexpected sparkle of attraction that was so disturbing. I was very nearly sixty; I was grey-haired and, at the moment, unemployed. Men didn't look at women like me in that way, did they? I was one of the invisible ones, fading into the background.

'Perhaps I will,' I said, trying to sound casual.

We got out of the car and walked back towards the little alleyway where we both lived; we reached my door first and stopped.

'Thank you for being my taxi,' I said.

'*Méchri tin epómeni forá, fíle mou,*' he said.

'What does that mean?'

'Until the next time, my friend.'

He took my hand and gave a little bow over it. Now that was definitely romantic. No one had ever done that to me before.

I'd made four new friends in the space of a few days; life was definitely looking up.

10

Less than five minutes after I arrived back, the Old Ducks were outside my patio doors, hammering on the glass.

I rolled my eyes and let them in.

'Are you okay?'

'Did he behave?'

'Did he kiss you?'

'Are you going to see him again?'

They sat down, Anita placing a bottle of red wine in the middle of the table.

'Now then, don't hold back, tell us everything,' Juliette said.

'Absolutely everything,' Kim insisted. 'Every disgusting, titillating detail.'

I turned on the oven and then busied myself finding wine glasses and Anita unscrewed the top from the wine bottle. I turned to find them looking at me almost hungrily.

'I'm going to be a great disappointment. There are no disgusting or titillating details. We went to St Paul's Bay...'

'I've heard that's lovely,' Kim said.

'It was. There is a taverna on the beach and we had lunch.'

'And?'

'And I had scallops and prawns and he had scallops and steak. Then we both had...'

'We don't care about that!' Juliette said. 'Did you like him? Did he kiss you?'

'Yes, I liked him and no he didn't kiss me,' I said. 'Honestly! Talk about nosey.'

'So you didn't need my judo move?'

'No, I didn't.'

'And are you going to see him again?'

'Well I expect so, Kim. I mean, he only lives a couple of doors down.'

Juliette sighed in exasperation. 'Kim means are you going to *see* him again? You know, *see him*.'

I shrugged carelessly. 'I've no idea.'

'Be careful, you don't know him at all, and you know what men are like...' Kim said.

I definitely wasn't going to mention the fact that he had a boat.

'Kim's right. You need to be really careful,' Anita agreed, taking a sip of her wine. 'A friend of mine had a relationship with someone she met in Sardinia, on holiday, and when she went home, he wouldn't leave her alone. Kept ringing her up, asking for money so he could fly over to Birmingham to see her.'

'Who was that? What happened?' Kim said, round-eyed. 'You hear about that sort of thing all the time. Men are the pits, honestly they are.'

'It was Pat, you've met her, ginger Pat. Works in my office. Quite a big girl, bouncy you know. Good fun but not the sort to inspire a mad passion, I'd have thought. She had to block him in the end. She was petrified he was going to just turn up on her doorstep with his suitcase. She'd gone off for her friend's hen week, they stayed in a hotel with a view over the sea. She said it was really lovely. What her husband would have said if an Italian waiter had appeared out of the blue, heaven only knows.'

I assembled the chicken and potato dish and stuck it in the oven.

'I don't think that's going to happen.' I washed my hands. 'Theo was just nice, friendly. Pleasant and polite.'

'That's a bit disappointing,' Juliette said, her mouth turned down. 'Were you playing hard to get?'

'I wasn't playing anything,' I said.

I took my wine and had a sip.

'We had a good day too,' Kim said. 'We went shopping and then to the tourist information centre and found out about boat trips. You can go out snorkelling and have a buffet lunch...'

Juliette looked mutinous. 'I'm not going snorkelling, my highlights would probably turn green.'

'...or go to Symi Island. It's supposed to be lovely. Picturesque and charming.'

'Just like Theo,' Anita said, with a wicked smile. 'He sounds picturesque and charming.'

* * *

An hour later we sat outside, with my new tablecloth on the table and a sensational meal in front of us. I couldn't quite believe how something so simple could be so delicious. The Greeks evidently knew what they were doing. I just added a green salad and some bread and that was all we needed. That and some more wine of course.

'This is incredible,' Juliette said, mopping up some of the lemony sauce with some bread, 'I want the recipe.'

'It's just a few things chucked in together,' I admitted, 'really easy. I'll definitely make this again.'

'I bet it won't taste the same at home,' Anita said, scooping up some more potatoes from the dish.

'Probably not,' I said. I'd been thinking much the same thing.

'Well thank you for this,' Kim said. 'That's the best thing I've eaten for ages.' She raised her glass. 'To the chef!'

The others clinked glasses and I felt happier than I had for a long time. It certainly beat toast and peanut butter any day.

* * *

I went to bed that night thinking about Theo and feeling quite girlish and silly. I ran through our conversations, remembering his expressions and how he had laughed. Theo had asked me out, taken me for lunch, asked my opinions and listened to my answers. He had been pleasant company, there was going to be a next time...

Was there going to be a next time? Or was that just part of the charm offensive that would see him emailing me about how he was having problems with his bank and asking for money, swearing undying devotion and turning up on my doorstep?

No, he wouldn't do that.

He wasn't that sort.

Was he?

He had houses and a boat and a cute car. His clothes were clean and stylish. He wouldn't want to just land on a woman who had rented out her spare rooms to three introverted postgraduates who lived on biscuits, toasted sandwiches and Pot Noodles.

Land on me. There was another thought for me to wrestle with.

I meant *land on me* in the physical sense. Would he expect that? Didn't all men expect that at some point?

I had loved Peter, but he had been a true academic who was so immersed in the details of his research that he often forgot about meals and Christmas and coats in the winter and for a large part of our marriage forgot about sex too. But that was okay, sort of. I got used to it.

Lucian had been the opposite. Sex to him was a sort of award, I think. A notch on his mental bed post. Proof to him that he was important and clever in the most intimate way. I assumed he also enjoyed it, he said he did. I did too, but was that the sex or the excitement or the unexpectedness of it all? I wasn't sure. What I did know was that I wasn't going to fall for a smooth-talking charmer again. Not even a tall, silver-haired, dark-eyed one. With a boat.

* * *

The following day I didn't see Theo at all, or the day after that. I was shocked to realise how disappointed I felt.

I'd assumed too much. In my innocence, I'd thought he would be round to see me again, perhaps drop in for coffee, that he might... Oh well, life was full of disappointments. I shouldn't have been surprised. Maybe he had just been kind, curious, at a loose end that day and looking for something to do. Perhaps he had exhausted all his interest in me.

Even if Theo wasn't around, the Old Ducks were out and about in a noisy, laughing group. I went with them walking around the town, going up onto the ramparts at the top of the wall and marvelling at the wonderful view. We went to the beach which was huge and covered in sunbeds and parasols. We went to see the new Colossus of Rhodes sculpture on the sea front. I thought it was a bit disappointing to be honest and looked like a cross between an eye and a man doing 'head shoulders knees and toes'. Not a patch on the one-hundred-foot-high statue of Helios with no clothes on that used to be at the harbour mouth before it was destroyed by an earthquake.

We shared lunches and bottles of wine and we laughed a lot.

We bought sunglasses and T-shirts and took photos of each other and selfies of us all where we always seemed to be laughing. What a change this made to the way my life had been recently.

I thought I was beginning to glimpse the person I had been many years ago. And I rather liked that person. I could laugh, I could make other people laugh, I could voice opinions and people didn't scoff. I could be me.

My phone had lots of new pictures of us. In the garden, on the beach, one where an American tourist had offered to take our picture outside a café. The four of us had huddled together with our wine glasses raised and shouted *Yia mas!* as she took the picture. I'd looked happy, like a normal woman out for the day with her friends. Very different from what I had been not so long ago; someone who was permanently making excuses, lying to myself, someone who was anxious about the simplest things. That was what my relationship with Lucian had done to me. It was time to wise up.

Each day I made them some new meal; perfect peppers stuffed with pork, chickpeas and rice; moussaka rich with tomatoes, aubergines and nutmeg, smothered in béchamel sauce.

'Oh golly, that was delicious,' Anita sighed happily as she pushed her empty plate away one evening. 'You could do this cooking malarkey for a living. Where did you learn to cook?'

'From books,' I said, 'like most people. And the television.'

'I watch all the TV cookery programmes,' Kim agreed, 'I love them. Hairy Bikers, Bake Off, Jamie Oliver, and I can't cook like that. Do you know, one evening I was watching Nigella slinking around her improbable kitchen like she does. You know, caressing the saucepans with her eyes and getting steaks from her local butcher and almost seducing him in the process, and she was wearing one of her cashmere cardigans, which of course we all do when we are cooking. And all the fairy lights were on along the shelves and she was making some casserole or other with about a thousand different ingredients—'

'All of which she already had in her uber-cool pantry?' Juliette added.

'Exactly. And I realised I was watching her doing all this culinary magic while I was sitting on my sofa in my disgusting old dressing gown eating custard out of the tin. I mean, how ridiculous is that?'

'I like cooking,' I said, 'I had a lot of time when Peter was alive because he was always working. And he liked the things I gave him, he appreciated it.'

'I should think so,' Juliette said. 'My ex didn't realise until we had divorced that meals didn't always come in foil trays.'

Kim stood up and went to perch on the garden fence, lighting up a cigarette.

'I used to try with Stewart, but then one day after we'd been married for about a year, I realised he didn't know or care what he was eating as long as there was enough of it. One potato more than a pig, I used to think. I hope his new partner knows how to cook, because Stewart certainly didn't.'

Once our meals had gone down a bit and the others had cleared everything away, we went for a dip in the hot tub. It was a great way to spend the evening, just relaxing and chatting.

We had a discussion about how much hot tubs cost, and I wondered whether it was worth having one in my garden back home. Thinking about the weather there when I'd left, it didn't seem a good idea at all. I couldn't imagine myself sitting out there on my own between the recycling bins and Nigel's bike, drinking Strawberry Daiquiris in the rain.

* * *

The day after that, the Old Ducks next door decided we were going out for the day. We didn't have a car and Kim didn't fancy a long journey on a bus because she was prone to travel sickness so we decided to take a boat trip. Juliette wanted to meet some Greek people. I think she meant she wanted to cast eyes over some Greek men, although, as she admitted, any nationality would do, seeing as I had 'snared' the only decent-looking man for miles.

'I have not snared, nor have I set out to snare anyone,' I said indignantly.

'Perhaps that's the secret,' she said, 'play it a bit more aloof.'

The other two laughed.

'Like to see you try, Jules, I bet you couldn't even spell aloof, never mind do it,' Kim said.

We were only a short walk from the harbour, so that morning, after a couple of false starts when Anita had forgotten her new sunglasses and Juliette wanted to change her lipstick (no I couldn't quite understand the importance of that either), we took the ferry from Rhodes to Symi Island.

It was quite a smart ferry, not too full and the sea was calm. Even so, Kim stayed up on deck, her eyes fixed firmly on the horizon.

When the harbour came into view, it looked as though we were sailing into a film set, designed by Disney, with row upon row of colourfully painted houses with red tiled roofs and white gables rising up the hill from the harbour. It was absolutely delightful. The water below us was as clear as crystal, shimmering in the sun.

Juliette had spent much of the journey engaged in conversation with a short, rather elderly man wearing a panama hat and a bemused expression. Juliette was in full 'laugh at everything he says' mode, which had apparently won her several beaux over the years. Possibly this latest conquest of hers was wondering why he hadn't tried his hand at being a stand-up comedian if he was that amusing. Eventually we docked in the harbour and dragged her away; I rather think he was relieved. His daughter certainly was.

When we left the ferry, we walked along the side of the harbour, past an artistically placed anchor and several rows of mopeds and motorbikes until we came to a square lined with tavernas, each with their own canopy. It looked lovely, the perfect setting for our mid-morning coffee and, after a brief discussion, ice cream. We sat in the shade, watching the people passing us, holiday makers, shop workers, a group of bored-looking young lads who completely ignored us.

'We'll have to go home soon. I wish I could do this forever,' Anita said, tucking in to her coffee and chocolate gelato with a dreamy expression. 'Wouldn't it be great?'

'Wouldn't you get bored?' I said. 'Wouldn't you miss your family?'

She took another spoonful. 'Nope, I don't think I would. And I bet they wouldn't miss me. I wonder if Rick has even noticed I'm not there and is still clogging up the dishwasher with his pants and not knowing where to put the dirty dishes.'

'Perhaps he just shoves them all in together?' Juliette suggested. We all pulled disgusted faces.

'And what would you even do here?' I asked.

'No idea. Perhaps I'd run a B&B. That little house over there, with the blue ironwork balcony and the flowers. I'd only have to work for half a day giving them breakfast and I wouldn't have to work all year because things shut down in the winter.'

'I think you have a romanticised view of running a B&B,' Juliette said. 'Doesn't everyone pinch the towels and smoke out of the windows?'

'And make a racket in the garden in the evening, getting drunk and singing...' I added mischievously.

'Ooh, who would do that?' Kim said, 'I'll come and help you,

Anita. I bet you any money that when I get home the kids will have left the washing baskets overflowing, and the food cupboards will be empty. I was going to have a wager with myself how long it would take them to ask what's for tea. I bet I wouldn't even get to put my bags down. I've been thinking, it's my fault for letting them get away with it.'

'You're an enabler,' Juliette said, 'I've been telling you that for months, ever since they moved back in with you.'

'Why did they move back in anyway?' I asked.

'Gemma said she wanted to save up for her own flat and Simon broke up with his girlfriend. She said he didn't help around the house enough. I should have turned him around and sent him packing. And if Gemma didn't spend so much on clothes and make-up and nights out with her mates, she might have a chance to save something. I've decided I'm going to charge them rent when I get home. Or even better, see about getting them both to move out. They will be outraged. But I'm going to be retiring soon. I should be taking things a bit easier and enjoying myself, not running around after them.'

'Too true,' Anita said.

* * *

When we'd finished, we walked on, up steps lined with flowerpots, through pretty streets, past shops selling touristy things, hats and keyrings and footballs. There were tavernas getting ready for the lunch trade, and several of the young and attractive waiters called to us – much to Juliette's delight – trying to entice us in. We dragged her away from all of them.

When we did decide to stop for lunch, there was a lot of discussion and disagreement about where we would go. Kim wanted to sit outside in the sun, Anita wanted the shade.

Eventually we found somewhere that we could all agree on, that combined the right food with enough choices to suit us, plus menus printed in English and a view of the little fishing boats in the harbour. It was lovely. Juliette had been persuaded by a rugged-looking, bedroom-eyed Turkish chap who evidently had been to the same flirting academy that she had. She beamed up at him as he pulled her chair our for her. She was quite shameless.

We sat down, feet aching, and Juliette ordered some cool white wine.

'Goat meat in lemon anyone?' she said doubtfully as she scanned the menu.

'Spicy meatballs,' Anita said, 'or possibly stuffed aubergines...'

Eventually we decided on our choices and sat down to wait. The town was busier now, people were leaving offices and shops looking for their lunch. It was all very relaxed and pleasant.

And then suddenly I saw him. I was so surprised that for a moment I didn't say anything. I didn't have to.

'Hey, isn't that Theo?' Juliette said rather too loudly. 'Over there with that blonde woman in the white jeans, by the ice cream seller.'

Of course, everyone swivelled round to look. I could feel my cheeks flushing. With what? Embarrassment? Annoyance? What right did I have to feel those emotions? None at all. I took a deep breath and a sip of my wine and calmed down. But I carried on watching him. We all did.

He went to sit slightly turned away from us at the next taverna just down the street from ours. The blonde, who was tall, willowy and wearing some huge, stylish sunglasses, sat down opposite him, her back to the harbour, so evidently, she wasn't interested in that. What she was interested in was Theo. There was a lot of hair flicking and arm touching going on.

'He looks like he's having fun,' Juliette said, a bit more quietly.

I reckoned even she could tell I was upset. No, I had no right to be upset. I was uncomfortable. So, he could take me out and pay me attention one day and then a few days later move on to the next woman. Perhaps that was where he had been. It was everything I had dreaded, another man who was prepared to mess me about. Well, I could stop my foolish daydreams and fantasies about him. Stop building him up into something he wasn't.

Kim – bless her – moved her chair to block my view of him and his companion, and I smiled.

'It's fine, honestly, Kim, I'm really not bothered,' I lied.

She leaned back in her chair and listened for a few minutes.

'I can't hear very well but I bet she's American. She looks American, doesn't she? Well, I think... I think he's a... a... I'm trying not to be rude,' she said at last, 'I did warn you. Men are all the same.'

'It's fine,' I repeated. 'It's absolutely fine.'

We ate our meals and then had coffee and all the time Theo and the blonde were laughing away, obviously enjoying each other's company. It was all very disappointing. And yet why should I care?

11

Eventually the time came to return to the harbour and take our ferry back to Rhodes. It had been such an enjoyable day, and yet tinged with a dissatisfaction that I couldn't really express. And of course, the other three were laughing and chatting away as though nothing had happened. Which it hadn't, not really.

I kept a low profile to start with, wondering if Theo was going to be on board the ferry with us, but he wasn't. Perhaps he was staying the night. Laughing and drinking ouzo with the blonde, possibly American, woman.

We reached the harbour as the evening was starting to darken. Juliette had passed the time flirting with some random crew member who was serving drinks behind the little bar. This was so successful that we ended up with a free round of shots.

'It's Souma, it's made from figs apparently, so that's one of your five a day, isn't it?' Juliette said with a wink at the barman.

'Absolutely madame,' he agreed, winking back.

'I don't think so,' I said.

We downed the shots together. It was very strong and slightly

sweet, and I almost fell off my bar stool. Juliette's enamoured
barman laughed and offered us another. We wisely declined.

Walking back along the harbour and into the little alleys, we
were hungry again, and there was no way we were going to be
cooking anything. We stopped at a little taverna we were passing
and bought some gyros – the most Greek form of fast food. Something like a kebab but, to my way of thinking, better. It tasted
marvellous.

'Hot tub!' Juliette shouted as we reached home.

'Oh, I don't know,' I said. I wasn't really in the mood this
evening.

'Come on, we'll be going home before you know it; you can have
all the peace and quiet you want after that can't you?' Anita said.
'You'll be able to think of us, battling through the rain, dealing with
our dirty washing, while you'll still be here, thinking *well I'm glad
they've gone.*'

'I won't think that at all,' I said, and I surprised myself, because I
knew I would really miss them. Their chatter, their laughter, the
way they enjoyed life.

We'd had fun together, we still were. My stay here would have
been very different if I hadn't met them.

'Then we'll see you out the back in ten minutes,' Kim said, 'and
no excuses and no looking at your emails from that sod back home
either. Promise?'

'Promise' I said.

We went back into our respective houses and I hurried upstairs
to find my tankini which was drying on the side of the shower
screen; it must have been surprised to have been used so much.

* * *

'Right, we are going to be sensible this evening and just stick to one drink,' Juliette said.

By the time I arrived in their garden she was already in the hot tub, holding a tumbler of red wine. She was wearing an orange zebra print swimming costume and her blonde hair was pinned up on top of her head with a jazzy red clip. I felt quite dull in comparison.

'How do you manage it Juliette?' I asked as I clambered into the warm water.

'Grab a tumbler. Manage what?' she said.

'Always being so – so up. You're positive and colourful and optimistic all the time. You're full of...'

'Don't say it,' Juliette cackled. 'I know what I'm full of. And I'll let you in on a secret. I'm not actually that person at all. I used to be probably the shyest person you'd ever meet, but life's too short isn't it? To let yourself be dragged down. And I can tell you have been in the past.'

'Oh, I don't know,' I said, holding out my tumbler for her to fill.

'Don't argue, I've been there,' Juliette said, shaking her head, 'been messed around, lied to, disappointed so many times. And then one day – just after I realised what a rat I'd married, how my marriage had failed, how I had hardly any self-confidence and that I was about to lose my home – I saw a photograph of Elizabeth Taylor, and a quote, *"Pour yourself a drink, put on your lipstick and pull yourself together"*. And I thought, nice one Liz. That'll do for me. So that's what I did. First, I started using lipstick. And then I had my first facelift. See? I still don't look like Liz Taylor because she was absolutely glorious wasn't she? But it did iron things out a bit. You know, the droopy eyelids.'

'I'm not having a facelift,' I said, 'not after what you said about it being painful.'

'Then don't have a facelift, have a life lift instead, have a brain lift, have a good go at life lift. That's my advice. It might all end in disaster but at least you will have tried.'

'Yes,' I said thoughtfully, 'I think I will.'

She gestured at my black tankini. 'And start buying colourful things, it'll make you feel better. At our age, you get ignored a lot.'

'Well that's true.'

'People can't ignore you if you're wearing yellow or shocking pink or – I don't know – peacock feathers.'

'They just think you're crazy,' I said.

'Yes, but then they do actually *see* you and some of them remember you. I realised I spent my youth moaning because I didn't have hair like Farrah Fawcett, I wasn't cool like Cindy Crawford. But looking back at old photos, I was okay. Quite okay actually. And then it struck me, when I'm eighty-five I want to look back at the way I was when I was sixty-five and think, hey I wasn't bad, I did my best. I didn't give up.' Juliette turned and shouted. 'Come on you two, we're already halfway down our first glass and we're talking serious stuff here.' She turned back to me. 'And remember, someone is out there holding their breath and waiting for you to fail. Make sure they suffocate, that's what I say.'

Anita and Kim came out and climbed into the hot tub.

'Sorry, we got distracted. We were talking about Stewart and Rick,' Anita said, 'and wondering if Kim's voodoo doll is working yet.'

I gave her an incredulous look. 'You actually have one? Where from?'

'The internet,' Kim admitted, slightly abashed. 'You can guess where I stuck the pins.'

'Kim!' I said.

'Oh well. The pins didn't work, his new partner has just had a baby, poor little cherub, having him for a father. Gemma and Simon are horrified. Stewart keeps whining, *don't turn the kids against me*, and I say I don't need to, you do that perfectly well on your own.'

'Forget him, that's my advice,' Juliette said, waving her tumbler so that red wine splashed into the water. 'Tomorrow is another day. And I keep telling you, just because Rick is becoming a grumpy old man, doesn't mean you have to join him.'

'How do I change a man who only gets excited about his compost heap?' Anita grumbled.

'Hmm, difficult one,' Kim said.

'Drape yourself across it in your best underwear?' I suggested, surprising myself.

Kim looked at me, mouth open and then laughed. 'You've changed!'

'Well, maybe,' I said.

'So what are you going to do when you get home?' Anita asked me. 'New job? New man?'

'No new man, that's for sure,' I said. 'I've learned my lesson. The more I think about it, the more awful I feel. I've been so thoughtless, and I can see that now. I'm no better than the silly little students who run after Lucian and hang on to his every word.'

'Worse actually, because you knew he was married,' Kim interrupted, 'if this is the moment to be honest. And you're definitely old enough to know better. And you probably dismissed the wife as the problem, when in fact he was the problem and so were you.'

I let this sink in. It was true, I had behaved really badly.

'Yes, I suppose you're right.'

'You were just as much an enabler with him as I was with my flipping kids, so I'm not much better. Letting them get away with it. I can't tell you how much I've enjoyed being away from everyone back home. It's given me time to think a bit. Take stock.'

'And you, Anita. You're retiring soon and what then?' I said.

The wine was going down very nicely; I was beginning to feel better about the day and forget about Theo and what he might be doing over on the island.

'I'll have to do something,' Anita sighed, 'or I'll go mad and you'll read about me in the papers. *We can't believe it; she always seemed such a nice person. All that running around the garden in her knickers and then battering her husband with a leaf rake like that was so completely out of character...*'

Everyone laughed at this image.

'I need to do something too,' Kim said, her eyes distant and unfocussed as she tried to think of the options, 'something new and exciting.'

Juliette interrupted. 'You should give up smoking Kim, that would be a good start. You know it's not good for you, and you're only doing it to annoy Stewart and he doesn't even live with you any more. Dance classes,' she added, 'I'm going to go to ballroom dance classes. I love *Strictly*, I'd love to find my Anton du Beke. So charming and elegant.'

'I bet he lies around in jogging pants eating crisps all over the sofa when he's not on TV,' Anita said.

'But with a shirt and tie,' I insisted, holding up one finger. 'I'm not going to have anyone dissing Anton du Beke.'

'Of course.'

'I feel like going dancing,' Juliette said, holding out her glass for a refill. 'Let's go out tomorrow night. When we were at the tourist information, they told me about a place just around the corner and up the next street which opens at ten o'clock. There's live music sometimes, what do you say girls?'

'Ten o'clock at night?' I said, thinking this was usually my bedtime.

Juliette nodded. 'Funnily enough, yes. Come on, let's do it. Old Ducks on tour, before we have to go back to the daily grind.'

'I haven't been to a night club for—' I thought about it, 'over thirty-something years!'

'Then it's about time you did,' Anita said. 'What's the worst that can happen?'

We bickered about the details of this for a while and in the end Juliette won. She also offered to lend me something to wear. Scary.

'No miniskirts,' I said firmly.

'I don't know why not, your legs are okay,' she argued. 'I think you'd look good in my orange thing with the sequins.'

'Hmm,' I said doubtfully, not having seen the garment.

'Remember what I said about that person holding their breath?' she said with a stern look. 'Now somebody better get out of the tub and fetch another bottle.'

* * *

The following morning, I was up early and went down to the bakers as usual, bringing back a box of goodies for everyone. I might have been a good cook but making that sort of thing was a skill too far for me. I'd tried making croissants once; it had taken me a long time to clean up the baking sheets and all that burnt butter.

I didn't expect to see them much before late morning, because one drink had led to another and I hadn't got to bed until after eleven o'clock. I'd left the others still sitting in the garden, Kim thinking about giving up smoking while she smoked yet another cigarette, Juliette practising her dance moves and Anita covered with a blanket, asleep on one of the recliner chairs.

Just as I had settled myself with a book, a mug of tea and a croissant, there was a knock on my door.

It was Theo.

I felt my stomach clench. I'd almost managed to park my annoyance with him; now it all came flooding back.

'Oh, it's you.'

'*Kaliméra*,' he said. 'Good morning Sophia.'

'*Kaliméra*,' I responded coldly. I didn't invite him in.

'I thought I would come to see if you were okay,' he said. 'I haven't seen you for some days.'

'No, well, you've been busy, haven't you?'

He looked innocent. 'Busy? I suppose so. And you? And your friends next door?'

'We've been busy too. In fact, I'm busy at the moment.'

I have an urgent appointment with a croissant. Do you know how hard they are to make?

'I wondered if you had managed to get out again, somewhere new?'

'Yes. As a matter of fact, I did,' I said. 'I've been to lots of places.'

He waited for a moment, expecting me to elaborate I expect, but I didn't. We stood and looked at each other and then he frowned and held up a hand.

'You are angry with me? You seem angry. I don't know why.'

'Do I? I said unhelpfully. 'Oh well.'

'Sophia—'

Sometimes I know when to keep my mouth shut and sometimes I don't. What had Juliette said? *Pull yourself together*.

'I'm busy,' I repeated.

'Perhaps I could take you out again? To the Acropolis or Kamiros?' He was looking so handsome and so thoroughly trustworthy that I almost weakened. Could I be wrong about him? Were all men the same underneath their good manners? And thinking about it, what did he expect from me?

'No thank you,' I replied, rather more firmly than I had intended.

'Kallithea Springs? There are many things there that you might like.'

'I don't – I really have to go.' I started closing the front door.

'Then maybe—'

'No thank you,' I said and shut the door.

I sat with my tea and my croissant and hugged my knees. I felt rather foolish and regretful now. I'd never been any good at being rude to people. And when I was, I nearly always ended up apologising, which didn't really help.

I didn't think he could be in any doubt about my mood, although most men I'd known needed to have just about everything spelled out to them in words of one syllable before they understood.

Women did that when they were annoyed, didn't they? We were to blame too. We were fools to ourselves sometimes. We used these little phrases that didn't actually agree and yet didn't provoke.

No, it's fine. I don't mind. It's up to you.

If you say so. It doesn't matter. Forget about it.

Do you think so? It's okay. Whatever.

Why did we say things like that? It was so passive. And then afterwards, when men took us at our word, we'd get annoyed with them for not divining with their non-existent sensitive side, what the actual problem was.

I wasn't going to say things like that any more.

Wouldn't it be better to just come out with it in the first place? To say things like, *No, I don't want to watch the football because I can't stand it. Umpteen overpaid men kicking a ball, spitting and falling over.*

Actually, you look terrible in those trousers even though they are your favourite brown cords. Unless pantomime horse is the look you're going for?

Yes, I do want to watch Mary Berry making another cake and no it's not the same as all the other cakes she makes because this one has cinnamon and sultanas in it.

We've been married for twenty years, surely you know I don't like pineapple on pizza. Or on anything else for that matter.

12

What was it that Anita had said about our trip to the night club? *What's the worst that can happen?*

That was tempting fate, wasn't it? It was the sort of comment that was just begging for karma to come up and give you a slap on the back of the head.

In retrospect we could have guessed it would end in tears. But it did start quite well.

Juliette's *'orange thing with the sequins'* turned out to be proof that one of us was slightly colour-blind. As far as I was concerned it was quite a nice apricot shift dress, decorated with sequins around the neck and hem, and as I was a few inches shorter than she was, it was a reasonable length too which was a surprise.

The three of them were very excited and insisted on doing my hair up with some sparkly clips and a lot of hair spray and then Juliette got a bit carried away and stuck some of her spare false eyelashes on my eyelids. They were decorated with little flecks of glitter too which made me wonder if I looked a bit like a drag artist, but the others insisted it was just a bit of fun and why not. Looking at myself in the mirror – three different shades of eye shadow, sparkly blusher on my cheeks – I could think of a few reasons why not, but I didn't want to be a party pooper, so I didn't protest too strongly.

Meanwhile, Juliette was getting very hyper at the prospect of a night out. She was dancing around the bedroom singing 'Lady in Red', decked out in what looked to me like a purple dress, which she had coordinated with scarlet shoes and a straw clutch bag. She was right when she said people would notice her.

Anita and Kim were both in black, brightened up with colourful sparkly scarves and dangly earrings, and all of us had applied enough make-up to audition for roles as pantomime dames.

At eleven o'clock, after sharing a bottle of Prosecco and giving Juliette the time to reapply her lipstick, we tottered out of the front door on our unfamiliar heels and along the cobbled street towards the square and the unparalleled delights of the Hot Potato nightclub.

As we rounded the corner, we could see an encouragingly long queue waiting by the entrance; everyone was chattering away and nearly everyone was young enough to be our children. Still, nothing ventured.

I did wonder if perhaps the burly doorman with his black suit and mirrored sunglasses (why?) would cast an incredulous look at us and send us home, but no, we were waved in with almost a smile and a friendly *kalispéra kyries*.

Inside it was *dÿo gia éna* hour, which meant two for one, or happy hour. We found a table and tucked our handbags underneath it. Juliette went up to the bar, which was wooden and quite rustic, as though the place was really a pub in the daytime, and the only change now was the lighting, which was, of course, quite dim.

I'd gone to a few nightclubs back in the day and nothing much seemed to have changed in the last forty years. It was as noisy, crowded and unattractive as the ones I remembered; the floor was just as gluey. The only difference was the lighting, which, over the dance floor was now pulsing to the beat of the very loud music. I hoped none of us had any sort of undiagnosed tendencies toward fits.

The drinks were brought to our table on a tray by a pretty girl who, like the harassed and sulky-looking barmaids, was dressed as a French maid complete with a lace bow in her hair. The owner must have bought a job lot. She dumped down a sticky tray holding eight tall glasses of various luminous concoctions decorated with straws and paper cocktail umbrellas.

'Gosh, what are these?' Anita shouted over the noise.

Juliette shrugged. 'No idea, the girl behind the bar just said *October special*? and I said okay. Anyway, cheers!'

We clinked glasses over the table. I didn't have a clue what I was drinking. It wasn't unpleasant; it was sweet, synthetic, highly coloured and the sort of drink that somehow makes you feel thirsty. Perhaps that was the idea. The Hot Potato was doing a roaring trade anyway, with girls dashing all over the place with loaded trays, their lace bows slightly askew.

Funny, I thought, *this sort of thing is going on all the time while I am sitting at home watching* The Repair Shop *and blinking back tears at the emotional reveal at the end.*

Tourists and, presumably, locals crowding in every night, quaffing huge drinks, eating limp fries and calamari rings from plastic red gingham bowls. By this time, I would usually have been in bed and asleep. So yes, it was good to do something so out of character. We attempted a few dances, which really consisted of shuffling from foot to foot around our handbags, mum dancing, I think you'd call it. Like the embarrassing dad dancing you see at weddings, but more sedate. The drinks were finished and replenished, more young people came in and the music and the chatter became louder.

At the tables next to us were some gloriously pretty girls dressed like floozies, in sparkly, skin-tight dresses and vertiginous shoes which, undoubtedly, they would regret before the night was out. Where did they buy these things anyway? There must be a lot of trendy shops somewhere, perhaps in the more modern parts of the town. Had their parents seen them before they'd left home?

I watched them for a minute, saw how they scanned the club, flicking their hair, looking for the boys who would make their night. Nothing new there then, except all of them were glued to their iPhones, the ghostly light from the screens illuminating their glowing drinks. Some of them looked awfully young. I hoped it wasn't a school night.

'Good evening lovely ladies.' A man came and bent over the table, leaning on the back of my chair and Juliette's.

He looked a bit mafia special to me in his black shirt and leather trousers, but Juliette rose to the occasion and flashed her smile at him.

'You are having a lovely evening, lovely ladies?'

'Lovely,' I said, wondering if he did sarcasm.

He didn't.

His smile broadened. 'I am Stavros. This is my place, my club, you are most welcome.'

'Well, thank you,' Juliette drawled, arching her eyebrows at him.

'You would like drink? I will get you proper drink, not this rubbish,' he said with a dismissive sweep of one hand over the laden table.

Anita and Kim looked at me and the three of us were obviously equally suspicious. The place was full of attractive girls, why was he bothering with the four of us?

He snapped his fingers at a passing French maid who gave him a sullen, sideways look that spoke of intense dislike, and within minutes, the table was cleared, and five new glasses and two bottles of wine appeared in front of us.

Stavros pulled up a chair and doled out the drinks.

'We will drink to the future, to friendship and to life,' Stavros said.

I'd seen him open the bottle, so my assumption was that we were okay drinking it. We probably wouldn't end up bound, gagged and drugged in the boot of a car.

Perhaps I'd binge-watched too much Netflix in the last few months. It was awful what went on, especially near the White House. I'd watched NCIS. There couldn't have been many marines left, the rate they got dispatched. And in so many different and innovative ways. You'd have thought someone would have investigated that.

Stavros took a good glug of his wine and shouted at us as the thumping beat of the music was ramped up to maximum.

'Now tell me lovely ladies,' he yelled with a broad smile and the glint of gold from his molars. He waved his fists from side to side, 'You like dancing?'

Juliette was next to him and probably now the only one who could hear him; they soon started shouting at each other like old friends while the rest of us knocked back the wine which, to be fair, was rather good and certainly better than the luminous cocktails.

As the evening progressed, Juliette and Stavros ventured onto the dance floor and shook a tail feather baby. You had to give it to her, Juliette was certainly game for a laugh. And a nifty little mover too. It was certainly impressive how her enhanced bosom coped with it. I hadn't thought about that, but it was a bonus. When I'd once tried running, I'd had to invest in something that was like a straitjacket two sizes too small.

Although there was a universal dance style of jumping about and holding hands in the air with the young crowd, Juliette was giving it her best moves and even doing a bit of hand jive that the local kids seemed to find hilarious and tried to copy. There was nothing new under the sun was there?

They ended up with a circle of whooping young people and us, of course, surrounding them and clapping, something both Juliette and Stavros seemed to find very enjoyable judging by their triumphant smiles and hugs.

'Good grief,' Anita shouted over the noise, 'what is she like?'

The DJ, a sweaty youth with acne, realised the value of pandering to his boss and the music continued into some classic fifties and sixties hits. Spurred on by her success, Juliette then had a go at a jive.

I'd give him his due, Stavros did his best, but the heat in the bar and the activity was obviously getting to him and he was positively glistening with sweat. In fact, it was dripping off his nose. It looked as though he had been wearing eyeliner, which was now smeared over his face. It was impressive but not in a good way.

Kim, Anita and I went back to our table and poured out some more wine. Some of the trendy types eventually got fed up with the display of old people having fun, and started wandering off to the bar, complaining. Swift to sense this, the DJ reverted to the pounding beat of whatever young people like these days. What was it called? Gunge? I wasn't sure.

Mercifully, Juliette and Stavros needed a break by this time, and she came back to our table and threw herself down into her chair, blotting at her face and her neck with some paper napkins. Stavros stumbled off behind the bar and into the back rooms of the building, presumably for some oxygen.

'Well that was great!' she shouted over the noise, 'I'm whacked.'

'You were having fun,' Anita yelled back.

'I was, that's more like it. You should come and join me when I get my breath back.' Juliette fanned herself with a beer mat and gulped down her drink.

Several of the young people came wandering up to look at her, occasionally giving her the thumbs up or just shouting *Hey trelí giagiá.*

Juliette looked well pleased with herself.

'Listen to that, they've got a nickname for me,' she said, happily, raising her glass to them in salute, '*trelly yaya!*'

Everyone within hailing distance cheered.

Anita leaned over to me.

'They are calling her crazy grandma,' she shouted in my ear. 'Better not tell her that.'

I sneaked a look at my watch; it was nearly two in the morning. We'd all had a dance, some questionable drinks and Juliette had been the centre of attention, so perhaps it was time to go home?

Stavros came back. He'd washed off the eyeliner, changed into a new shirt and was holding a bottle of champagne.

He popped the cork off with a cheer and the champagne foamed all over the table. All the watchers applauded.

'Champagne for my lovely lady! My favourite lady of the whole year!' he shouted, and sloshed some into our glasses, on top of the dregs of our other drinks.

'Woohoo Stavros,' Juliette cheered, downing it in one.

She was going to be sorry in the morning, that was for sure. Is this what she did at home in Sutton Coldfield?

'Such fun!' Stavros said jubilantly, 'so busy tonight, so busy! So much fun! The gods sent you to us this evening!'

'Which god was that then? The Greek god of crazy old women who should know better?' Anita said.

'We are closing soon, lovely Jilia,' Stavros said, 'you and your friends come for little drinks with me and some friends?'

'Not a chance,' I shouted.

Unlike Juliette, I didn't like the sound of this.

'Yay,' Juliette yelled, and Stavros topped up her empty glass.

'Juliette, we need to get home,' Kim said.

'Nah! Let's get this party started,' Juliette carolled back.

'There is no way we are going to let you go off with these people,' I said.

Juliette pouted. 'Spoilsport! It'll be fun.'

One of us needed to have some sense.

'Where's your handbag?' I said.

Juliette looked around vaguely. 'Stavros picked it up off the floor when we were jiving. I dunno where he put it.'

'Oh great, you need to find it. The house keys are inside.'

Stavros looked thoughtful then stumbled off for a bit and eventually came back with Juliette's straw bag.

'What a lovely lady, a lovely lady who makes my club so amazing,' he said, patting her face, 'you come back again. Come back and see me again, I find you best table, best drinks. No October specials.'

I reckoned he was drunker than she was. Perhaps it was an occupational hazard if you owned a nightclub?

It took quite a long time to get out of the Hot Potato, because Juliette's many new admirers wanted to hug her, and give high fives.

'*Hey trelí giagiá...*'

'I love young people,' Juliette slurred happily. 'They're so... young.'

Outside, the cold night air was shocking, and it was drizzling with light rain. I began to sober up and shivered, realising my feet were really killing me. The heels weren't doing my knee any favours either. Anita and Kim had already taken their shoes off. As we picked our way down the cold, wet street, Juliette stopped, held her head and leaned against the wall.

'Coming,' she shouted at our retreating backs, 'I just need a moment.'

We stopped to wait for her, I wouldn't have put it past her to double back into the nightclub and then we would never get her home.

Two men and a woman were catching us up. They didn't look much like clubbers to me, and they didn't look at all as though they were having an enjoyable evening. They reached Juliette and stopped.

They were obviously talking to her and she was laughing. Until the moment when one of them took hold of her bag and looked inside. At this point we assumed she was being mugged and the three of us hurried in her direction.

The newcomers were gabbling at her in Greek and holding something up in front of her face. Juliette lashed out and tried to grab her bag back and succeeded in whacking one of the men squarely on the nose. There was a great deal of yelling and we added to it, rushing up shouting and trying to form a protective group around her. It was useless, we were rapidly moved out of the way without ceremony and pushed up against the wall while the other man who wasn't bent double trying to stem the bleeding turned Juliette around and put her in handcuffs.

'It's not mine! It's not mine! It's a mistake,' Juliette shouted as she was led away, her stilettos skittering on the cobbles.

Anita came to the rescue. As much as she was able to.

'What are you doing? *Ti káneis? Ti káneis?*'

The woman in the party gave us a sour look and a sweeping glance.

'*Astynomikós. Tsántes.*' She flashed a wallet at Anita.

'She wants our handbags,' Anita said, her voice trembling. 'They are the police.'

13

I'd only been in a police station once and that was a few years ago in Oxford during freshers' week when I'd gone to hand in a mobile phone I'd found in my hedge. Even that encounter had made me feel uncomfortable and ever so slightly guilty.

I could never understand how in police dramas on television people were so offhand and rude with the various detectives and sergeants. They'd turn their backs and, in some cases, even walk away when they were being questioned. And in *Midsomer Murders*, when the one who seemed the obvious culprit for pushing a farmer into his combine harvester or throwing a rich old lady down the stairs said *I didn't do it*, it was always true. He'd always got an alibi. It was a bit of a giveaway.

I wouldn't dare behave like that, and certainly not if it was someone who looked like John Nettles. I'd *want* him to take me in for lengthy questioning and possibly dinner afterwards.

Not that I would murder anyone anyway. I'd be like a rabbit in the headlights, probably cry and claim ignorance or possibly admit guilt when it wasn't true. Even traffic wardens evoked a shudder of dread in me if I was honest. And if a police car was behind me when I was driving, I was *more* likely to swerve across the road or speed through sheer terror. Perhaps it was just my generation.

Anyway, the police searched our bags and sneered at us in Greek for a few minutes and then Juliette was hustled into the back of a police van along with several other miscreants. Her face was white, and she was still shouting.

The rest of us were waved off with some angry words and, as Anita said, told to clear off and behave ourselves.

'We'll come and get you,' I shouted at the police van, hoping Juliette could hear us, 'don't worry.'

'Get her from where?' Kim said. 'We don't know where they are going. And it's not like they're taking her to a party or anything, we can't just be on the lookout for balloons on the gate.'

'How are we going to get into our house?' Anita said. 'Oh God, Juliette's got our house keys.'

'Come to mine, we'll sort something out. Oh, poor Juliette, she must be terrified. What did she do?'

'I think they found something in her bag,' Kim said, her teeth chattering with nerves.

'What?'

'I don't know! I don't know! She kept shouting *it's not mine*. What are we going to do?'

At this point I thought we all needed to calm down. 'Let's get home, and we'll work something out.'

Back at my house, we sat on the sofa and I made us all some coffee.

'What are we going to do? We are supposed to be going home soon. The flights are booked and everything,' Kim wailed, 'we've got to get her out of there.'

'Will they put her in prison?' Anita asked, her eyes wide and frightened. 'Oh help, I wish Rick was here, he'd know what to do.

He'll be absolutely furious if he finds out. He told me I'd get into trouble.'

Anita burst into tears and Kim put a consoling arm around her.

'Then don't tell him, Rick doesn't need to know. I'm certainly not going to let Stewart know. He'd make a three-course dinner out of it.'

'But I always tell Rick everything, he always tells me everything. And he's so honest. Even when he nudged a car in the car park, he insisted on leaving a note on the windscreen and he hadn't done any damage at all,' Anita said miserably.

'We're not in trouble, Juliette is,' I said. 'We need to get help.'

'Where from? Who can help us?'

'I don't know. What do people do when this happens? Should we ring the British consul? Anyone know where it is?'

I opened up my laptop and did some speedy searching. I was rapidly sobering up.

'There's a vice consulate in Rhodes. What does that mean? Appointments only. The main consulate is in Athens.'

'They won't take her to Athens, will they?'

'I don't know,' I said, panicking.

'We need to get her out of there. This has to be a misunderstanding,' Kim said. 'I think I'm going to be sick.'

She did look rather green.

'Bathroom's upstairs,' I said.

* * *

We drank our coffee and rang Juliette's mobile phone a few times in case she was able to answer it, but it went straight to voicemail. Perhaps it was turned off or out of charge. Or perhaps the police had confiscated it?

We needed some advice. We needed legal help.

Ah yes. Relief washed over me as I suddenly remembered something.

'Theo's sister Hera is a lawyer,' I said. 'I've just remembered. We met her son Alexis on our day out. He was working as a waiter but he's a lawyer too.'

Kim and Anita looked up hopefully.

'I think on balance Hera sounds like the better bet than the waiter. Where does she live?' Anita said.

'I don't know.'

'But we know where Theo lives,' Kim said, her eyes alight with hope.

I knew what this meant, we would have to go around to his house and wake him up. No, *I* would have to go and wake him up. We couldn't all hang around outside his front door like carol singers.

My heart sank. Oh, for heaven's sake. And the last time we had met I'd been rude to him and given him the brush-off. Now I was going to have to back-pedal and ask for a massive favour. And what if Hera was the sort of lawyer who only did house conveyancing or wills? She might not know how to handle the problems of a sixty-something woman who had been apprehended drunk outside a nightclub with something suspicious in her bag. Or perhaps it was someone else's bag. That Stavros had picked up by mistake. Perhaps that was why Juliette was shouting, *it's not mine*? Of course! What could it have been? How could we prove it? Maybe I could be the one to help.

'You need to go round and wake him up,' Kim said firmly. 'He won't mind if he realises it's an emergency.'

'This is definitely an emergency,' Anita agreed. She stood up and dragged me to my feet. 'Go now, quickly! Hurry!'

I considered putting my shoes back on, but somehow I couldn't manage it. Perhaps my feet had swollen what with all the unexpected pounding.

Instead, I limped barefoot out into the dark lane while Anita and Kim watched me from the doorway as though I was going to knock on the door and run away. Honestly, I might have done that when I was six...

I knocked and stepped back to look up at the windows. All the lights were off. Well of course they were, it was three-thirty in the morning.

I knocked again, rather louder this time. Still nothing happened.

Perhaps he was out. Perhaps he took sleeping tablets and was in a drugged stupor.

'Knock harder,' Anita called in a hoarse whisper from her place on the doorstep.

Oh well.

I took both fists and hammered for about thirty seconds on the door.

A moment later a light came on in the upstairs window and a few minutes later a light showed downstairs.

I felt a thrill of relief. Thank God he was in anyway.

I heard a key being turned in the lock and the door opened.

Theo stood there in a cotton dressing gown, his feet bare on the stone flagstones of his hallway.

'I'm sorry,' I gabbled, 'I'm sorry to wake you up but it's an emergency.'

He blinked, obviously confused, and ran one hand through his hair. 'Sophia, what are you doing?'

'It's Juliette. We went to a nightclub. She really wanted to go, and she was dancing and perhaps we drank a bit, but the owner... she was dancing with the owner, Stavros, and he was making a big fuss of her and he...'

'Sophia, slow down. Take a deep breath and tell me, what is the matter?' Theo said.

I obediently took a deep breath.

'Okay. We went to a nightclub, and when we came out Juliette was arrested.'

His eyebrows shot up. 'Why? What did she do?'

'The police stopped her and searched her bag, but she said it wasn't her bag, and they must have found something because the next thing she was in the back of a police van and I think she might have broken the policeman's nose, because he was bleeding. Then they put her in handcuffs, and they searched our bags too but there wasn't... we don't know where she is or what to do.'

Theo ran one hand over his face and blinked a bit.

'Where was this?'

My mind went blank. Nightclub.

'Something to do with vegetables,' I said.

'You didn't go to the Hot Potato, did you?' he asked.

'Well yes, we did,' I admitted.

He made an exasperated noise.

'*Gia ónoma tou Theoú*. For heaven's sake, Sophia. Come inside, it's cold on the doorstep.'

I gave Anita and Kim a wave and stepped inside.

His house was quiet and dark apart from the light which shone down the stairs.

'Now sit. Tell me what has happened?' Theo said, switching on a table lamp. 'Before you start, I would tell you that establishment is a terrible place. I can't think why you went there of all the places you could have chosen.'

'The tourist information people said it was...'

'The police are always waiting outside to catch people. Usually young people, they don't usually pick up... never mind. It seems on this occasion your friend was one of them.'

'Oh God, what can we do?'

'Calm down, I will telephone Hera. She will know how to deal with this.'

'I really feel awful about this, Theo. Really, I do. I didn't know who else we could call on. And you did say Hera was a lawyer, although of course she might just do straightforward things like notarising things and dealing with tax...'

'Hera will know what to do,' Theo repeated firmly. 'Where have they taken your friend? To the police station I expect?'

'Is there a prison?' I said. 'They won't have taken her to prison, will they?'

'No, be calm. There is no prison on Rhodes, the nearest one is Kos. And I'm sure they won't be taking her there in the middle of the night. She will probably be in a holding cell.'

'*Oh God.* Does that mean she will have a police record? Will she have to go on some offenders list?'

My knowledge of criminal activity and consequences seemed rather sketchy all of a sudden, despite binge-watching *Vera* and *Inspector Lewis*. They filmed a scene of *Lewis* around the corner from my house once. It took them absolutely hours with trucks and lighting and loads of people milling about with cameras and cups of coffee, and when I saw it on television it lasted about twenty seconds. God, why was I thinking of such ridiculous things now?

'Be calm Sophia, it will be alright. Let me phone Hera now.'

'Tell Hera I'm sorry,' I said, 'we're all really sorry.'

'It won't be the first time she has been woken in the night for something and it won't be the last, I'm sure of that. Stay here.'

He disappeared upstairs, presumably to fetch his mobile phone and returned a few minutes later.

'Hera, *sygnómi gi aftó...*'

I sat, silently perched on the edge of my seat as he rattled away, apparently explaining the problem and asking for help.

What must they both think of us? I flushed with embarrassment. A crowd of middle-aged women behaving like teenagers,
getting stopped and searched by the police in the dead of night.
And one of us being led off in handcuffs after hitting a police officer. How absolutely shameful.

There was a long pause and I could hear someone on the other
end of the phone talking equally rapidly. Theo laughed. Oh good
grief, they were laughing at us. And who could blame them?

Then Theo talked some more and then he turned to me.

'How old is your friend Juliette?'

'Sixty-five? Sixty-four? I'm not sure. Sorry I can't remember.'

He relayed this information and then chuckled again.

'*Éxochos, éxochos.*'

I knew what that meant; excellent.

What was Hera saying, what was she prepared to do, and what
would it cost us?

My blood ran cold. Did travel insurance cover this sort of
expense? What sort of fee were we agreeing to? What if we couldn't
afford it? What if Juliette was taken to Kos or Athens, how would we
get her home again? Would we have to appeal for clemency to the
Prime Minister and write to our MPs? Would we all end up in the
newspapers?

I could just imagine the headlines.

OAPs in drugs ambush.

Elderly holidaymakers arrested in nightclub after drunken brawl.

English woman taken to Greek prison in handcuffs, 'I've let my family
and my country down,' said the grandmother of two, 'I'm ashamed of
myself.'

There would probably be pictures too, of Juliette in an orange
prison jumpsuit or maybe something from her university days

when she had been in the orchestra. I'd seen some of her pictures on her Facebook page; most of them were of her with a drink in her hand. That wouldn't help.

I was aware Theo had ended the phone call.

'Right,' he said, slipping his phone into his dressing gown pocket.

'Right what?'

'Hera is going to sort it out, don't look so worried. It might take some time though.'

'But what can she do? What will she say?'

'Hera is a lawyer; the local police know her. She will sort it out. *Irémise*. Calm down.'

I stood up. 'What shall we do? Do we need to go and talk to them?'

Theo put his hand on my shoulder. 'Go home, go to bed, it may take Hera some time.'

'You're sure it's going to be okay?'

He bent and kissed my cheek.

'My poor friend, cheer up.'

'Oh, one other thing?' I said.

He raised his eyebrows questioningly.

'Have you got some spare keys for their house? Juliette had them in her handbag too, and the police took it.'

He walked over to a row of hooks, took one set of keys and handed them to me with a comical look.

'Now *that* is serious,' he said. 'I'll have to get the locks changed.'

14

I went back to my house where Anita and Kim were still sitting on the sofa, looking worried. They glanced up hopefully as I came in.

'What's happening?'

'He's going to get his sister on the case. I just hope she can do something to help,' I said.

'So what did he say?'

'Theo? He rang his sister and told her what had happened. I think she's going to track Juliette down and try and sort things out.'

'Perhaps she can get her out on bail,' Kim said, 'but how much would that be? I've been thinking about that. We might have to club together to pay it. And how long will it take? We're supposed to be flying home on Saturday. If she's out on bail how can we get her out of the country?'

'I don't know. I don't know any of those things,' I said.

Wow, I was so tired, I could hardly keep my eyes open, but there was no chance any of us were going to sleep.

'I got some spare keys for your house from Theo,' I said, handing them over, 'so you could go to bed if you wanted to?'

'No chance,' Anita gave a huge yawn, 'much as I might want to.'

'I'll make some more coffee, shall I?' I said.

'Good idea.'

I went to make a big cafetière of coffee and found some biscuits in the cupboard. It was going to be an even longer night than any of us had realised. How long ago that all seemed now. Juliette fussing about with my hair and make-up...

Remembering that, I went to look in the mirror and gave a little scream. My reflection was horrific. Both of my sparkly clips were missing so my hair – well-sprayed with hairspray at the start of the evening – looked as though I'd been in a fight and lost. My dark red lipstick was faded in the middle and smeared over my cheek, so I looked as though I had been punched in the mouth. On top of that one of my sparkly false eyelashes was now re-attached to my *eyebrow*. How on earth had that happened? I looked like some sort of bizarre Picasso painting. One he would probably have left in an attic somewhere.

'Why didn't you tell me I looked like this before I went around to see Theo,' I said.

The other two looked vague.

I pulled off my false eyelashes and dumped them in the bin, I wouldn't be needing them any time soon.

'Do you think Juliette is okay?' Kim asked as I put the coffee tray down on the table.

'You've known her longer than I have,' I said, 'what do you think?'

'She seems very resilient, but she wasn't always like she is now, underneath it all...' Anita said. 'You know she's had a lot of knocks. Alcoholic father, crappy husband, her daughter was only ten when Gary left so she was a single parent, she's always pretended everything was okay, but I don't think it was. She had to give up her music career, just as she was getting somewhere. She got pregnant at the same time she graduated and, in those days you had to get married, so they did. She got a job at Gary's firm doing something dreary which must have been soul-destroying. And then she found out he was screwing around the typing pool and had been for years.'

'Poor thing,' I said. I felt both sympathetic and guilty, because let's be frank, I'd been part of something horribly similar.

'I think she covered it up, how hurt she was, by developing this mad, outrageous character. All the cosmetic surgery, crazy behaviour, dating.'

Kim added, 'And then she became a granny. And she was thrilled, don't misunderstand, and she dotes on those little girls, but – well it made her realise that perhaps she was getting on. Old.'

'We all are,' I said. 'Death and taxes. Can't avoid either.'

'Oh aren't we cheerful?' Anita said. 'God my head really hurts, any one got paracetamol?'

I thought about it. 'You've had all mine.'

'Water then.' Anita got up and ran a glass of cold water. She stood at the sink to drink it. 'I think I'm about ready to go home if I'm honest. I mean, I've had a great time, but I could do with a few early nights. I'm even missing Rick and I never thought I'd say that. I'd feel safer if he was here.'

'Nor did I,' Kim said, 'seeing as you've been telling us he's the most boring man on the planet.'

'Well, he is, sometimes,' Anita said, 'but I've been thinking. Let's be fair, he has a lot to put up with being married to me. My house-keeping for example. It always looks as though there's been a mili-tary coup in the bedroom. And the laundry pile has its own micro climate it's so huge. I should have that sort of thing sorted out at my age, shouldn't I?'

'Mere details,' Kim said. 'Rick could do it just as well as you.'

'Suppose so, but he's very good at doing the garden and stuff.

And the recycling bins. He washes them out every week. With hot water and washing up liquid.'

'Good God,' I said, 'it's never occurred to me to do that.'

We sat drinking our coffee in silence for a few minutes, then Kim looked at her watch.

'It's five o'clock. What do you think is happening? Do you think Hera has arrived yet? Do you think she's arguing with the desk sergeant and telling Juliette to say *no comment* to all the questions?'

'I've no idea. How long do these things take anyway?'

'Do you think she's being questioned? Do you think it's like it is on television; nice cop, nasty cop and someone thumping the table? Or do you think she's just sitting in a cell in the dark?' Anita said.

We shrugged.

'Well, do you think we should phone her daughter?' Kim said.

Anita shook her head and then held onto it with both hands. 'Oh flip, I shouldn't have done that, it really hurts. No, we shouldn't tell her. Not yet, she can't do anything.'

'Wouldn't your kids want to know if you were in trouble?' I asked.

Kim pulled a face. 'Probably not. I can just imagine Gemma's reaction. *Honestly Mum, you're so embarrassing...* And my son would just want to know what's for tea.'

'Aren't we allowed to be embarrassing?' I said. 'It's just because we're older. What age do we have to morph into sensible, law-abiding sexless people? I feel as though I've been that for most of my adult life. Except for the Lucian thing, which was so totally out of character that looking back, I can't really understand it.'

'So why did you do it?' Kim said.

I thought about it. Remembering our stolen meetings, coffee in dark corners with him, countless wasted and lonely weekends, Christmases, birthdays. The promises of 'something' later, when his children were older, married, independent, who knows. There never was going to be anything, was there?

'I had a long, happy but rather ordinary marriage. After Peter died, I was so lonely, and life just seemed so dull and final. I think I was just desperate for something exciting in my life. Before it was too late. Pathetic,' I said.

'So now?' Kim said.

'No idea. Go back to Oxford and buy a cat I expect,' I said, rather glum at the prospect.

Although that didn't come out right. I liked cats. I'd wanted one for years. Lucian and Peter had both been allergic to them of course, which is why I hadn't already got one. I would get one when I got back home. Possibly two.

'But you can do anything now!' Anita said. 'You don't have any responsibilities, you have your own home, you're healthy. You've no idea how lucky you are.'

'I'm going to go back and give my two kids a month's notice,' Kim said suddenly. 'Sophia is right. There's no reason why they can't have their own flat. If nothing else, it's not good for either of them to be back living like teenagers when they are both in their thirties. They can jolly well go out and find somewhere else to live. Even if they have to move in together. I'll even pay their rent for the first month. The first three months if that's what it takes.'

'That's a bit drastic isn't it?' Anita said. 'You'll be on your own.'

'It's not much fun being alone,' Kim said. 'It soon becomes lonely. I know what it's like. Why do you think I'm so mad at Stewart? But at the same time, it's not right for my kids to be living with me, they need to get their own lives sorted, stand on their own feet, not hang around mum all the time kidding themselves I need them there, because I don't. I don't think what Sophia did was right, but I understand how she felt. I'm going out the back to have a cigarette.'

'I thought you were going to give up?' Anita called after her.

'I am, just not tonight,' Kim shouted back.

Kim pushed open the patio doors, letting in a blast of cold early morning air which was rather refreshing. I realised we were still all sitting around in our night club outfits; it really didn't seem right to be dressed up like this when we were all feeling so depressed.

'I'm going to get out of this dress and have a shower,' I said. 'Tell me if anything happens.'

Anita nodded, and leaned her head back on the cushions and closed her eyes.

'Poor Jules,' she said.

* * *

I scrubbed off all my make-up and showered, pulling on some trousers and a sweater. We might need to take some things to Juliette later on, and I wasn't going to turn up in a sequinned dress and heels. Not unless I wanted to look like a sad old git.

Which I didn't.

I watched myself in the bathroom mirror as I brushed my hair. It's funny how you never actually see your own face as others do, because the image is always reversed. And most of the time, whilst I could see my reflection of course, I didn't actually *look* at myself. So, what did I want to look like? Sixties to me had always meant old, but now I was nearly there myself, was I old? Of course I wasn't. Did I look old? I just looked like me. It felt strange to realise some people would say I was the same age as old people. Inside I didn't feel old at all, not now.

This holiday had turned out to be a surprising make or break moment for me. I'd come here thinking one thing, and now I felt completely different. At least it had given me time to think. It seemed there were differing paths ahead of me, ahead of all of us really. To rage against it all like Juliette, find a path through it all like Kim, or gear up and make the best of it like Anita.

I put on some more expensive face cream, wondering if it had the power to undo the damage done by several late nights and too much alcohol. No, it didn't. I still looked a tired wreck. But a clean wreck. I did feel a bit better. I wondered if there was any news about Juliette.

Downstairs, Anita was asleep on the sofa, snoring gently, her mouth open. I went outside and found Kim sitting at the table in my garden, still smoking.

'You're going to kipper yourself if you carry on,' I said, pulling up a chair next to her.

'I don't care,' she said, 'I've enjoyed this holiday so much, well until now of course. I looked forward to it for months, I had to get Gemma and Simon on board, stock up the fridge, make sure everything was organised and now it's almost over. Now I've got to go back to a house that will be in chaos, Stewart swaggering around like some sort of stud because he has a new baby. Well let's hope he's a bit more involved with this one than he was with the other two. Then I'll return to a boring job in the health centre when I could have helped NASA calculate the next moon shot once. I could do really difficult sums once upon a time, but it took all my efforts and patience to get my son through GCSE maths and now he barely knows how to add up without a calculator. What does that say about my mothering skills?'

'Oh come on, you did what you had to do,' I said. 'I bet your kids would say you're a great mother.'

'I'm average,' Kim said, lighting another cigarette from the stub of the first. 'Like most mothers I'm betting.'

'Children are such a blessing,' I said in a pious voice.

We looked at each other and both burst out laughing.

'You daft beggar,' Kim said, wiping her eyes. 'I need to shake things up at home, I can see that. I'm turning into a burning martyr, moaning about everything, complaining I have to do everything and not asking for help.'

'Good idea,' I said.

'The number of times in the last few months I've heard myself saying, *oh for heaven's sake, give it to me, I'll do it*. Whether it's taking the recycling out or unloading the dishwasher—'

'At least yours won't be full of Rick's pants,' I said.

'True. What a ghastly thought. But is it better to have *someone's* pants clogging up your dishwasher?'

'Thanks for that,' I said. 'I'm never going to be able to unthink that image.'

'When I get home, I'm going to try internet dating and I'm going to advertise myself to offer maths tuition. The younger generation seem to be taught so badly, there has to be someone out there who needs to know their tables.'

'Good idea.'

15

Dawn was breaking over the garden and still we heard nothing about Juliette or what was happening. Anita and Kim went back to their house to shower and change, and then they came back to my place.

'Any news?'

'Nothing,' I said. 'I would have told you if there was.'

'We can't just sit around and do nothing,' Anita said. 'I feel absolutely terrible. We should have stopped her; we should have done something.'

'What would you suggest?' Kim said. 'You know what Jules is like. And we could hardly take on three police officers. We'd all be in a cell together if we had.'

'But... something. It can't be too hard to find out where she's been taken, surely?' I said.

'We could go back to the tourist information place,' Anita said, 'and say, excuse me, our friend was arrested last night for possible drug possession, hitting a police officer and drunkenness. Any clues as to where she might be or what's going to happen to her? No, I don't think that's going to get us anywhere.'

Kim started crying again. I put an arm around her, and she sobbed into a tissue.

'What are we going to do?'

'Cheer up. I'll go and knock on Theo's door again. It's nearly eight o'clock. I'll ask if he knows anything,' I said.

'Good idea.'

I found some shoes and went up the street and rapped smartly on Theo's front door. Nothing happened for several minutes. I was beginning to wonder if he was out when the door opened.

He was still in his dressing gown.

'I'm sorry. Did I wake you up again?' I said.

'Yes but it's fine. Is there any news of your friend?' he asked, ruffling his hair with one hand.

'Nothing, we were hoping you might know. I'm sorry I woke you up.'

'You've apologised enough, it's fine. I'll ring Hera; come inside. I'll make some coffee.'

His house was much bigger than the one I was renting; the door opened into a wide room furnished with pale furniture and several brightly coloured tapestries on the walls. He motioned me towards a chair and went to make coffee.

'I hope she's not too annoyed about all this,' I called.

'*Min anisycheíte*. Don't worry,' he called back, 'these things happen.'

'Do they? Not to me they don't,' I said.

He came back out of the kitchen with two mugs of coffee. I wasn't much of a coffee drinker as a rule, and I had drunk so much of it in the last few hours that I didn't want any more. But I took it anyway. Being here with him, in his space, felt somehow calming, better. I drew comfort from him even though he had nothing particular to tell me.

'So you haven't heard from Hera? I said.

'Nothing, but as I told you, it would take her some time to get there.'

'Oh, I'm sorry, I didn't realise.'

'Please stop apologising,' he said. 'You asked me for help, that's what friends do.'

Were we friends? I suppose we were. He seemed to think so. But I'd been angry with him, hadn't I. I'd been rude. Perhaps real friends could cope with that.

'Is there anything I can do? Where is she, do you know?'

'I assume she will be at the main police station. It's not a dungeon.' He gave me a little smile.

I had a mental image of Juliette sitting on the edge of a concrete bench, still in her purple dress and red stilettos, looking up at a grimy window and crying. No, perhaps they would have taken the shoes away in case she used them as a weapon. Could you commit suicide with a stiletto?

'Her friends – we – are so worried about her.'

'Of course. Look, I'll phone my sister, shall I?'

'Please.'

I sipped my coffee. It was hot and too strong, but I hardly tasted it. Theo talked at speed to his sister and even chuckled a couple of times.

I had been an only child; how would it feel to have a sister or a brother I could laugh with? I didn't have anyone really, I realised. No partner, parents, children. I had cousins and friends of course, but I'd been lazy about keeping in touch with them recently. I'd been so preoccupied with Lucian. There was no one close to me who I could confide in or ask for advice in difficult matters.

How did someone my age start again, making new friends? Perhaps these last few days had been a refresher course, showing me that I was okay really; people wanted to talk to me, I could talk to them. There was nothing wrong with me after all.

I realised I had talked more about myself with the Old Ducks in the last few days than anyone. Possibly in my life.

Theo ended the phone call and turned to me.

'Right!'

'Right what?'

'She's just been released.'

I gave a scream of delight.

'You're sure? Absolutely sure?'

He nodded.

I darted across the room and flung my arms around him and kissed him.

He kissed me back.

I stood in his arms and blinked a bit with the shock. He grinned down at me.

'You're happy. Then I am happy.'

'I am,' I said, and I realised it wasn't just because of the news about Juliette.

We looked at each other for a few seconds and I honestly thought he was going to kiss me again. Which didn't exactly worry me.

But then he cleared his throat and let me go.

'Hera said she persuaded them to drop all the charges, not even a formal caution. She says your friend seemed to persuade them herself. She's not got *Altscháimer*... Alzheimer's, has she?'

'Good heaven's no, she might be a bit colour blind—' I said. 'Why?'

I held my hands to my cheeks which were hot, I was probably blushing.

Theo grinned. 'In which case she managed to persuade them she was just a harmless older lady who was confused.'

I felt much the same at that moment.

But in a good way.

'So I'd better get back,' I said, 'if she's coming home.'

'Of course,' he said. And he smiled. 'I'll see you soon *o fili mou*. My friend.'

As I walked back down the alley toward my door, a police car pulled up behind me and out stepped Juliette.

'Juliette!' I shouted.

'Sophia!'

We ran and hugged each other. I think both of us were crying.

The police car slowly passed us. There were two officers sitting in the front seats, and both looked at us very closely through the open window.

'Ha! *Taiste tis gátes*. Feed the damn cats,' one shouted.

'What cats?' I said. 'Have you got community service or something?'

'Let's get inside,' Juliette murmured sending him a look. 'I've been pretending to be crazy for the last few hours and it's very tiring.'

'You *are* flipping crazy!' I said. 'I'm so glad to see you! Come on *trelly yaya,* let's get you home.'

We hurried back indoors to screams of delight from Kim and Anita.

'We were worried sick!'

'What did they say?'

'Are you all right?'

'Were you locked in with a lot of murderers and thieves?'

'It wasn't exactly the jail scene in *Chicago*, Kim,' Juliette said, 'but it wasn't very nice.'

'Are you hungry?'

'I need a wee.' She dashed upstairs and after a few minutes came back downstairs looking a bit calmer.

'That's a lot better. I need a shower too, I feel absolutely disgusting,' Juliette said, plucking at her purple dress which was now crumpled and stained. 'I'm still in this red dress and I feel terrible. I'll never wear it again.'

'You've got others, love, you'll bounce back from this,' Anita said, hugging her, 'and that dress is purple.'

'Is it? I need a sleep too; I don't think I got a wink all night. I must look like the wrath of god. There was some woman in one of the other cells shouting all the time, and then someone else would shout back at her and then they would have a screaming match. And then a policeman would come and shout at them both. And it was all in Greek, so I didn't even know what they were arguing about. But I think the language was pretty ripe so maybe it's just as well.'

'Did they question you? Was there nice cop nasty cop?' Kim asked.

'Did they bang on the table?'

'There was a man in uniform with a wart on his nose who needed a bath and a change of clothing,' Juliette said. 'He looked as bad as I felt. It can't be much fun dealing with drunks every night.'

'Did he speak English?'

'A bit, and to be fair he was okay. Just kept asking my name and did I know what was in my bag and I just said it wasn't my bag and I wanted to go home.'

'Poor thing!'

'And they gave me a cup of tea, which was nice I suppose. Although it was too strong and not hot enough. And I was desperate for the loo, but I wasn't going to go there, in case they were watching me. I just kept thinking about the Sahara desert and hot sunshine to take my mind off it.'

'Brave girl,' Anita said. 'I'd have been petrified. And then what happened? And what was in your bag anyway?'

'No idea. They didn't tell me. And I kept saying it wasn't my bag. Nothing happened and then I was just waiting for ages. And then I could hear this new woman and she started shouting at the man with the wart. Well not exactly shouting but speaking very loudly. And then she came in and you'll never guess who she was...'

'Theo's sister, the lawyer,' I said. 'I went next door and woke him up and he got in touch with her to come and save you.'

'Yes, Hera something that ends with -opolus. She came in and said to me *you are confused, yes?* In a really meaningful way that sort of said, *act like a dotty old woman*, so I did, and I kept saying I had to get home to feed my cats. And then she said some stuff in Greek to warty man, and he did some shrugging and then she got a bit sharp with him.'

'Oh dear, this sounds awful,' Anita gasped, clenching her fists to her mouth. 'Have you got cats?'

'No, that wasn't the point!' Juliette said. 'That was my get out of jail free card, literally. I was petrified.'

I supposed women of our age had that sort of fear of authority which young people just didn't. All those protesters standing up to riot police and chucking rocks at police cars. I could never do that and I didn't condone it obviously, but it says something doesn't it?

'And then every time she looked at me, I said the bit about my cats again and in the end he just ripped up this bit of paper and did some sighing, and then she said I was going home. And I said I didn't know how to get home and she got the policeman to get a car for me. And I think he was shouting that he wasn't a taxi service and she looked at me and I did the cat thing again and the next thing, I was in the back of a police car and – well here I am. I've never been so relieved.'

We all had a good group hug and Anita and Kim did some happy-crying and we all mopped each other up and I made some tea and opened another packet of biscuits, because that's what English people did in a crisis wasn't it?

'Yes, but you'll never, ever guess who the lawyer was, that's what I was saying,' Juliette said.

'Who?'

'That blonde woman we saw Theo with, that day we went to Symi Island. Remember? The one at the café, and you thought he was flirting with her. That's why it took her so long to get to the police station because she had to catch the first ferry over to Rhodes. She says there's never any point just phoning them because – well I don't know, but I can guess. She lives there. On Symi.'

'Oh good grief,' I said, shock washing over me like a cold shower, 'and I was so rude to him.'

'She was absolutely lovely, not American at all, I don't know why you thought that Kim. And she looked so glamorous, even at six-thirty in the morning. Marvellous lipstick. I should have asked her what it was. I'd have been scared of her too, except she was there on my behalf. Anyway, she was going to see Theo later on this morning after she'd done some legal stuff, you might even meet her if she hangs around. Do you know those rude kids in the nightclub were calling me crazy grandma?'

'Yes we did,' Anita said.

'Why didn't you tell me? Blooming cheek!'

I wasn't really giving Juliette my whole concentration. He had kissed me. Was that a sort of *yay she's out* hug and a congratulatory kiss or something more? I wasn't bright enough to understand the subtleties of men. My recent history proved that.

16

Juliette and the others went back to their house at that point. It was breakfast time and never had four women been in more need of carbohydrate-laden products. So I went up the road to the bakery and brought back a huge bag full of pastries and tartlets to share. And even that was a lovely feeling, that I was doing something nice for my friends.

Juliette had a shower and changed out of her party finery and then had a nap, bouncing back thoroughly refreshed just in time for late elevenses. We sat out in their garden with mugs of tea and coffee and the baked goods heaped up into a bowl in the middle and we talked it all through again.

As with all tales that are told and retold, details were exaggerated, added and elaborated on until eventually we all started to laugh again. And strangely enough, I began to feel as though my life really was tipping back onto its axis. That after months, no, years of self-doubt and not knowing where my life was going, I had it in me to be okay after all.

I could make new friends; perhaps when I went home I could catch up with my old friends. I would contact my cousins in Scotland. I could talk to new people and who knew, maybe life had more to offer me than I had thought.

And love? What did I think about that?

Perhaps that saying about youth being wasted on the young was true. And perhaps love was too. But why were all of us, in our own way, looking for love? We were certainly past wanting or expecting children, all of us were educated and financially secure unlike many people our age. What were we, what was I, looking for?

Juliette was looking to keep a hold on her youth, Anita had realised that she was stuck in a fossilised marriage and in my opinion was angry with Rick as a result, but at the same time she was definitely missing him, that was the thing to come out of this, and Kim was just fed up with being lonely and at the same time having no privacy and being taken for granted.

Was this what happened to women when they were considered too old to be models, sports stars or that new thing that I didn't really understand – influencers? Did we just become someone's wife, partner, mother, someone's carer? Not actually important in our own right?

I didn't want to be valued because someone else occasionally needed me to do something. To be someone's helper or childminder, someone's relative, a woman who could help out when everyone else was busy.

What about me and what I needed? Did women like me want love or just companionship? Could I have both? Could I fall in love again? Was that even possible?

Juliette had an idea.

'I want to say a proper thank you to Theo and his sister. Hera, isn't that a brilliant name? Let's take them out for dinner, the four of us and them. Tonight.'

'They might be busy,' Anita said.

'They might not.' I liked this idea.

'Oh, we all know why *you* want to see him,' Kim said. 'Bit of a girly crush is it?'

'No.' I sounded unconvincing even to myself.

'I think he fancies you,' Juliette crooned, in a very silly voice.

'Oh stop it,' I said, then, 'do you think so?'

Kim huffed a bit. 'Well I wish he looked at me the way he looks at you, I wish any man looked at me for that matter. I think I must be past my sell-by date.'

Juliette flapped a hand dismissively. 'Rubbish, remember that saying "never give up, never surrender"? That's my motto. Along with "never get caught" after last night. So where shall we take them?'

'Shouldn't we ask them first?' I said.

'Good idea. Off you go then,' Kim grinned, motioning me towards the door with her hands.

'So what you're saying is I have to go round and ask him? Can't we do rock, paper, scissors or something?'

'No we can't. You've got to do it. Off you go,' Anita insisted, 'and no snogging.'

'Anita!'

* * *

I brushed my hair and freshened up my mascara before I went round to knock on Theo's door. He answered almost immediately.

'Come in,' he said, 'come and meet my sister. She stayed here after – well you know.'

Now this was a bit scary, but I could hardly just run away. After all, they were the two people I needed to speak to.

Hera was sitting at the dining table with a mobile phone and a pile of paperwork in front of her. She was, as Juliette had said, incredibly glamorous. Slim, with expensively highlighted blonde hair and wearing the sort of clothes that looked simple but were probably massively expensive.

She got up as I came into the room and gave me a smile.

'You must be Sophia.'

We shook hands.

How did she know who I was?

'I've heard so much about you,' she added.

What? What had she heard? Good stuff or bad stuff?

We sat down on either side of the table.

'Coffee? Tea?' Theo said.

'No thanks, I've been drinking coffee and tea all day. I'm sorry to interrupt again but I wanted to ask if you were both free this evening? We would all like to take you both out for dinner. I mean it's short notice and you might have other plans, but—'

'We would love to,' Hera said, 'absolutely love to. I'll stay tonight Theo, if that's okay with you?'

'Of course.'

'Oh, right. That's great. Fine.'

Now they were going to want times and location and I didn't know either.

Theo came to my rescue.

'Remember the taverna where I met you that first time?' Theo said. 'The owner is an old friend of mine and his food is very good.'

'You recommended the dolmades?' I said, remembering.

Theo smiled. 'That's the place. Why don't we go there? Shall we say seven o'clock? I don't think anyone needs a late night, do they?'

'Absolutely not,' I smiled back.

There, that nice little sparkle of attraction again. I wondered if it was just me or if he felt it too. How would I know?

'By the way, what was in the handbag Juliette picked up? Did they believe it wasn't hers? Did they tell you?' I asked.

Hera grinned. 'Once they actually opened it and investigated properly, they found all sorts of things that could never have been Juliette's. A wallet, a phone, even a fake ID card that she obviously wouldn't have needed. And I don't know what the girl who actually owned it thought she was buying but there was a sachet of oregano, herbs... Once they realised that, they knew they were wasting their time.'

'You're kidding!'

'As far as Constantine and I are aware, there is no legal penalty for buying cooking ingredients. Still, it didn't stop them from wasting more time investigating. And delaying the whole thing with unnecessary paperwork.'

'What about the fact that Juliette hit one of them?'

Hera smiled broadly. 'They put that down to an accident, I don't think any police officer wants to admit they have been punched in the face by a woman who is a pensioner and possibly very confused. That would be very shameful for him.'

We talked for a while about Juliette and what had happened, and Hera asked me how I was liking Rhodes. She darted little looks at me and at her brother and there was a funny little smile on her face which made me wonder what it was that she found so amusing.

Having agreed on the details of the evening's event, I went back home wondering what I would wear. I had brought a case filled with clothes for sitting around editing Lucian's book, not going out anywhere trendy. Did it matter what I wore? Did this count as an actual date? Wow.

The Old Ducks were on the patio in their garden. They waved me over through the connecting gate.

'What did he say?'

'Was he there? You've been ages.'

'Did you snog him?'

'No I didn't, Anita! Why are you so obsessed with me snogging him? Yes, he was there and so was his sister, Hera, so opportunities for any sort of lip-locking was limited. They said yes, that would be great. They will see us at seven at a place I know.'

'What was she like?'

'Very nice, very stylish,' I said, 'you know, that sort of elegant casual, *I've-just-slung-on-these-clothes* look that makes you want to kill yourself. Casually tied scarf and flat shoes and a lot of linen.'

'Ah, I know what you mean, and you know if I put the same outfit on, I'd look like an unmade bed,' Kim said.

'Exactly,' I agreed, 'so what are we going to wear tonight? No sequins.'

Juliette's eyes brightened. 'Let's go shopping.'

Anita groaned.

So that's what we did.

* * *

It wasn't easy to start off with; there was a lot of pale linen to be had but it was all very droopy, and I didn't have the figure for crossover bodices and dangling ties. I tended to look as though I was wearing a hospital gown backwards which wasn't the look I was hoping for.

There was a lot of cartoon-embellished wear too and cropped linen trousers which, in my opinion, no woman over twenty and under six feet tall would look good in. But eventually we found a shop that catered for the more mature lady and I bought a dress. It was chic, sea-green and incredibly expensive. Left to my own devices I wouldn't have even tried it on because it had one of those asymmetric hems that look as though the maker was a bit tiddly when they cut it out. But what would I know about modern fashion? Perhaps I should find out. I'd almost forgotten about shopping and the buzz it could bring.

After a light lunch (finishing up the breakfast pastries) we all retired to our own rooms for a nap, because we all needed a rest and were anticipating a late night. Or at least an exciting one. My three friends were going home in a few days and they wanted to make the most of their time left here.

Up in my bedroom, I realised when they did leave I really was going to miss them. Would I actually be lonely here on my own? Maybe. What would I do with my remaining time in Rhodes? I had expected to be most of the way through Lucian's manuscript by now and I hadn't even got past the front page. In fact, I realised that I hadn't really thought about Lucian for days. Not even briefly.

That was a huge surprise to me. How odd that someone who had dominated my waking thoughts for so long could just fade from notice. But even so, having remembered him, I did wonder what was happening back in Oxford.

My mobile rang.

It was Lucian.

I looked at the phone display and sighed very loudly.

You see, it's always dangerous to think too much about some people. Or perhaps I was psychic and knew he was going to ring me? I should have blocked him a long time ago.

Still, I was hidebound by my innate politeness mixed, of course, with curiosity. A dangerous combination.

I answered the call.

'Lucian,' I said, my tone decidedly unfriendly.

'Sophia, thank heavens!' He sounded out of breath.

'What do you want? I'm busy.'

'Busy with The Book I hope.'

Numerous possibilities ran around my mind. In the end I went for honesty because it was easier, and it would annoy him more.

'No. I haven't looked at it,' I said.

'You mean you haven't finished?'

'No, I haven't started. I told you I wasn't going to.'

There was a long pause in which I wondered if we had been cut off, or if he had put the phone down. Except with mobiles, you didn't actually do that.

It used to be quite satisfying to slam a phone receiver down. It wasn't the same to press the red button with an angry finger.

'You've got to be joking,' he said at last, 'I mean my publisher is going to go mad when I tell him. He's ringing me all hours... wanting it back...'

'Oh well, I did tell you I wasn't editing your book. And I haven't.'

'You are really leaving me in an impossible position.' He sounded close to tears. 'And I miss you terribly.'

'Oh well,' I said again.

'Are you still in Rhodes?' he said at last. 'What on earth have you been doing for God's sake?'

Nothing I was going to tell him, that was for sure.

'Enjoying myself. Look I have to go, I'm going out for dinner with friends later,' I said, enjoying how it sounded to say that.

'You haven't got any friends,' he scoffed.

'Well that just shows what you know,' I said, and ended the call.

I realised that much as it might be satisfying to be downright rude to someone, there were better ways of really annoying them. You can teach an Old Duck new tricks.

17

Just before seven we set off for the taverna, which was called *Oraío Fagito*, or, as Anita told us, Great Food. It seemed a long time since that first evening when I had been there on my own, eating at Olympic speed.

The evening was chilly now and we went inside to find Theo and Hera waiting for us. The place was bigger than I thought; it looked like a Hollywood version of a Greek taverna. At the back of the room was a little stage containing a piano, a drum kit and an amplifier plugged into a bass guitar. There were three chaps dressed alike in black flared trousers and red ruffly shirts which was all a bit 1970s, but perhaps the look had come back into fashion?

They were playing some reasonably successful music, the sort one might hear in lifts or shopping malls, but it was all very pleasant. And it wasn't too loud.

There were strings of amber lights, round wooden tables and chairs and colourful cans of tomatoes, olives and peppers on the shelves.

Why did foreign groceries look so much more exciting than ours did at home? They had pictures of voluptuous girls in frilled dresses on them and drawings of cheerful looking young farmer types holding up tomatoes the size of footballs. I wondered idly if I could take some home with me and then realised the problem with baggage allowance. It wouldn't make any sense to lug a gallon tin of passata back, and knowing my luck, the customs officials would be suspicious and make me open it. And then I would be faced with travelling back to Oxford on the coach with the open can and my luggage and there would be bound to be a couple of sharp bends and sudden stops, and by the time I got off the bus it would look like *Nightmare on Elm Street*... oh well, never mind.

'Welcome, hello,' Hera said, and she stood up to greet us all, giving me two unexpected cheek kisses. 'Come and sit by me and tell me all about your day. Theo, you can sit on the other side of Sophia. Juliette! I hope you are recovered!'

Juliette went to give her a hug and started thanking her for all she had done. Before we had come out, we had discussed how big Hera's invoice would be, and when would be the best time to broach the subject. I didn't think this had been the time, but Juliette, conspicuous in her pink top and white trousers, couldn't hold back.

'Please send me your bill, I'll let you have my address.'

Hera pulled a funny, thoughtful face.

'This evening will cover it, Juliette, don't worry. I quite enjoyed winding Constantine up, he's had it coming for a long time. Now, shall we order some wine?'

Theo came over and also gave me two kisses.

'Good evening my friend.' He held me out by both hands to look at my dress. 'You look wonderful.'

'Thank you,' I said, biting back the urge to tell him about our shopping trip earlier that day and voice my doubts about the asymmetric hem. It was a compliment and I was just going to accept it for once.

Anita and Kim had vowed off the demon drink earlier that day, but seemed to have forgotten about that, and soon the six of us were toasting each other in carafes of local red wine which were deposited on our table by our waiter.

Who was that waitress who had been here that first evening? Blonde, Australian. God, my memory was not what it used to be.

Cass, that was it. I wondered what had happened to her; perhaps she had gone back to filming perfume advertisements.

'So, Sophia, how are you now?' Theo asked, leaning slightly towards me to talk. Juliette and Hera were getting on like a house on fire at the other side of the table, and Juliette was back to her old self again, outrageous and loud. I had to admire her spirit.

'I'm fine thanks. I don't know how to thank you. I don't know what we would have done without you. And Hera of course.'

'It was nothing,' he said. 'I was happy to help. Now your friends are going home but you are not, you will be able to get on with your work?'

'I don't think so,' I said. 'I'm not doing any of it.'

'Good, then maybe I can persuade you to come out on my boat?'

'Oh I don't know,' I said with a smile.

He touched my hand with his for a brief second.

My heart did a little samba; he was looking exceptionally good, in a light linen jacket and dark jeans. How nice to see a man of his age could be so stylish and hadn't hung onto the cords or slacks of his youth or, even worse, tried to embrace baseball caps, a straggling grey ponytail and logoed sweatshirts. I turned my attention to the menu that had been placed in front of me. The words danced in front of me too. I was feeling very excited; for a moment I wondered if I would be able to eat anything at all, but those croissants and tartlets had been a very long time ago, and I was very hungry.

A huge platter lined with vine leaves and containing various dolmades was placed on the table between us, along with bowls of dip, olives and cubes of feta cheese. With many exclamations of appreciation, we got going.

'You were right, these are delicious,' I said.

Theo smiled. 'I told you they were. Are these Greek or Turkish? There have been many arguments about that. They are Greek of course! So, tell me what you think of Rhodes, now you have had some time here.'

'I've had fun,' I said, 'I haven't had fun for a long time. I wasn't expecting things to turn out the way they did, but yes, it's a wonderful place.'

'Not like home for you?'

'Nothing like home.'

I thought about 'home' for a moment, Oxford with its golden buildings and spires. The narrow streets and the hordes of tourists, the impossibility of driving and parking which in a way was similar. But here, it was very different.

There was a brighter light illuminating the old stones of Rhodes, warmth, freedom from my routine, new memories. Perhaps it was just the novelty of being on holiday, of being on my own, of doing things just for me. But also, the pleasure of broadening my horizons, meeting new people. The joy of realising that life and fun and opportunities were still out there for the taking.

I was beginning to understand something; this was the sort of escape, the sort of life-changing experience that made people run away from their routine and their lives and take up pottery in the Dordogne or viticulture in Tuscany.

Were there women my age somewhere in Spain or Denmark who yearned to live my life in Oxford? Maybe there were. Maybe there is a little restless seed in all of us when one phase in our lives comes to an end and we are looking for something else, a fresh start, a different face.

Is that what this was?

But I did like it here, in my funny little house, with the baker at the end of the street, the fine cloud of flour patterning the cobbles in the early morning. The sound of a church bell early in the evening, the way flowers grew in unexpected places, halfway up a wall or tumbling out of a stone gutter.

'And will you return?' Theo said.

I avoided the question.

'Tell me some more about your family, about your daughter, about Olympia,' I said.

'She is thirty-three with a husband Mark. They are both doctors and their son Alfie is six. I saw him last year when I went to visit them. He's a lovely boy, always in the sea or playing sport.'

'You must miss them,' I said.

He held out the bowl of feta cheese to me and I took some.

'Yes, but the world is a smaller place these days. And my horizons are bigger.'

'That's a great way to look at it,' I said, 'I was just thinking the same thing. I think my horizons have been pretty small.'

'I have family here still remember, so many cousins and second cousins. My father made a family table as there were so many of us, out of planks of wood. Oh, you look puzzled, but it was beautiful. He was a craftsman, he planed and polished it until it shone. It was big enough for twenty people. It stood under the vine in their garden, where my uncle Nico lives. It is there still.'

'And what do you want to do now?'

He sat back in his chair for a moment and then smiled.

'Oh, so many things; I want to see the Northern Lights, the sky cold with frost, I want to see the Great Barrier Reef, white sand and blue seas in the Indian Ocean, I want to sleep in a bed over the sea and listen to the waves beneath me. I want to remember some things forever.'

He was distracted by Hera at this point who wanted him to

remember the name of some friend who was moving to Symi Island after years in Italy.

I hadn't travelled much at all during my last years with Peter. My husband had come to hate any break in his routine; he hadn't even renewed his passport. And then, of course, he had been ill.

What things did I want to do with the rest of my life, I wondered? Not so long ago I would have thought that I had achieved everything I was capable of, that I was slowly going to fade into old age and unimportance. But I didn't have to accept it had to happen, that was the thing. I had my health and strength, I was financially comfortable, I still had chances. Opportunities, if I was brave enough to take them.

I could still learn new skills, find new friends, grab everything the world had to offer me. I was determined I wasn't going to just give up and spend the rest of my life thinking about what I could have done.

No choice, really, which was the most attractive option.

'Well,' Theo said, as he turned back to me, 'have you thought of something you want to do?'

'Yes, I have. I want to see the Grand Canyon, I want to walk the pilgrim way to Santiago de Compostela with a cockle shell in my hat, I want to see the Statue of Liberty. I want to find out if the Rockies are as impressive as people say they are. I want to see the Norwegian fjords, and the sun rise over the pyramids.'

I stopped, almost breathless, as I saw the world open up in front of me.

'You are going to be busy,' he said with a laugh, 'and those are excellent choices, but first I think you should start with something easier and simpler.'

'What?' I said.

'You should come out on my boat.'

'You are very persistent, aren't you?'

'We have no time to waste, we have memories to make,' he said.
I grinned. 'Then yes, I will!'
'*Éxochos!*'

* * *

It was such a lovely evening. We just sat around eating delicious
food and drinking excellent wine and talking to each other. What
was it about Greek food that was so special? It was true comfort
food, contentment on a plate. The spices, the herbs, the delicious
smells of roasting vegetables, all mixing together to make the whole
experience unforgettable.

Other customers drifted in and the place gradually filled up,
everyone seemed happy and there was laughter in the air. The
shopping mall music continued for a while but then the three musicians took a break, voicing their respectful regret but promising
they would be back soon. They were rewarded with a polite round
of applause.

This was the sort of occasion I had always wanted to be a part of
and never had. Peter didn't much like eating out any more than he
had enjoyed spur-of-the-moment holidays and with Lucian there
was seldom the opportunity; he was always terrified of being seen
by someone who knew Gina. Someone who knew we shouldn't be
together on a wet Thursday evening in Banbury, eating indifferent
food in an out-of-the-way pub.

This was how I should be living my life, out in the open, with
friends and without constantly worrying about being seen, saying
the wrong thing, ordering a main course that would show me to be
dull and unsophisticated. I wasn't going to think like that any more.
If I wanted cottage pie at *The Ritz*, then I would order it.

'So, the police thing really is over?' Juliette asked during a pause
in the conversation. 'I mean the whole thing. I won't get stopped by

the police when I get back to Heathrow? I'm not on some blacklist that I don't know about?'

'Not at all, it's quite clear you must have grabbed the wrong bag, you can go back to buying Italian herbs without fear,' Hera said.

We all laughed and Juliette shook her head. She got up from her seat.

'I'm off to find the loo. Don't talk about me while I'm away. Anyway, do I look like a woman who smokes pot, or dried Italian herbs for that matter?'

'No comment,' Anita said.

'Nice!'

* * *

A few minutes later, I spotted the three musicians finish their drinks and obviously start making a move to carrying on playing for us. At the same time, Juliette came back from the loo. As she passed them she said something to one of them. All three nodded in unison and went back to their bar stools.

The next thing we knew Juliette was sitting down at the piano.

I nudged the others.

'What's Juliette up to?'

Anita turned around in her chair. Her eyes widened.

'Good grief! Is she going to play the piano? I haven't heard her play for years! Kim, look! Juliette's going to play!'

We sat in stunned silence, watching her. We could just see her head over the top of the piano. She didn't look at up, just looked down intently at the piano keys.

And then she started to play. It was surreal. And a wonderful moment.

The first notes were almost too quiet to hear, and almost drowned out by the sound of talking from the diners, but gradually people stopped and turned to listen. She was playing 'Clair de Lune', and she played it absolutely beautifully.

It was about five minutes of bliss. She didn't look up, except at one point she closed her eyes and tilted her head back, enraptured by the wonderful music. I didn't know about anyone else, but I was in tears. Our noisy, insecure friend had this wonderful gift hidden inside her and was sharing it with us that evening. The notes rippled out across the taverna which had gradually fallen into an awed hush. People had even stopped eating to listen. A couple were standing up to film her on their mobiles. Even the bar staff and the waiters were standing, watching and listening.

At last Juliette reached the end of the piece and the last notes faded away.

There was an instant of absolute silence and then people started to applaud. Some stood up, some cheered, some, like me, had tears in their eyes. It was a magical moment. The three musicians, knowing themselves utterly outclassed, were clapping too and one of them patted Juliette on her shoulder. She looked rather overwhelmed by what she had just done.

'My word, what a talent!' Hera said across the table as the noise died down and people started talking again. 'How wonderful to hear that!'

Juliette came back across to sit down, her progress slowed by strangers who wanted to shake her hand and thank her.

At last she reached our table and slipped into her chair, looking rather flustered.

'I didn't know I was going to do that,' she said. 'I haven't played it for years.'

I hugged her. 'Juliette you were marvellous!'

Kim and Anita cuddled her and Juliette wiped away a few tears with her napkin.

'Gosh, I'm totes emosh,' she said.

'You were absolutely terrific. Everyone was spellbound,' I added.

'I really, really enjoyed that, I don't know why I haven't played for so long; I don't even own a decent piano any more,' she said.

'Then surely you must get one,' Theo said. 'You have a great talent.'

'Well, I might,' Juliette said. 'Now everyone, stop looking at me!'

* * *

When we'd all calmed down again, we finished our meal with something called *galaktoboureko* which was a sort of superior custard pie flavoured with cinnamon and lemon. It was fabulous. I would definitely have to find the recipe for that. Then we had coffee and the barman brought us Metaxa on the rocks as a gift from another customer who had enjoyed Juliette's playing so much.

I'd often looked at the Metaxa label and thought it looked as though it would taste of petrol, but it didn't. It was absolutely delicious. Another lesson learned.

Theo had been trying to teach us more Greek words and even in my slightly tiddly state I was doing quite well. I almost didn't want the evening to end, or the week, when my new friends were going home. I'd miss them, and their hot tub.

'What will you do when your friends are home again?' Theo said.

Crumbs. Was he psychic?

'Oh, I don't know,' I said.

I had allowed myself a sort of vague and very pleasant image of both of us on his boat. Although I still didn't know what sort of boat it was. I hoped it wasn't one with sails that needed raising and lowering and messing about with and coils of rope that I could get tangled up in. I've seen enough clips of people being knocked overboard on *You've Been Framed*. Perhaps it was a small motorboat or – worse – a dinghy with oars I would have to heave on. Upper body strength was not my thing.

'When the ladies leave, I have to do some redecorating in their house,' Theo said. 'Just painting and tidying up the living room. You could always come and help me if you wanted to. No pressure.'

This sounded like a good idea. And it would mean I could get back in the hot tub.

'I'd love to,' I said. 'I love decorating.'

'Do you? Well that's marvellous. I'll let you know when I will be starting.'

Hera leaned across him and wagged a finger at me.

'He's a tyrant,' she said. 'He won't stop for anything until he has finished. Don't take any of his nonsense!'

Theo grinned at her. 'Sophia can paint or not paint it's entirely up to her; I don't notice you volunteering.'

'Of course I won't,' Hera said, 'I know what you're like! Sophia, come and sit next to me so I can tell you about him! Juliette you don't mind, do you?'

I swapped places with Juliette who favoured me with an exaggerated wink as she passed me. Hera gave me a smile.

'I just wanted a chance to get to know you,' she said.

Ooh, where was this going? Should I be worried?

Hera ran one finger around the rim of her Metaxa glass and then looked across at me.

'You seem to have had quite an impact on my brother.'

'Have I?' I said rather foolishly.

I was glad the music from the trio at the end of the room had started up again, and that Juliette was talking in her usual animated way with Theo.

'I'm happy to see it,' Hera said. 'He's been alone for too long. He's met a few people over the years, but nothing's really worked out. I don't know why. He's kind, he was a loving husband and father, and he's a wonderful uncle to my children.'

'I'm sure he is, I mean yes he's very kind.'

Hera sipped her drink. 'So?'

'So?' I wondered where she was going with this.

'I get the feeling you are special to him. He has talked about you to me, something which is most unusual.'

'Has he?' I said, wondering if it would be really bad form to ask what he had said. I mean, I wasn't fifteen.

'He has, and I hope you don't mind me saying something. But none of us are children. All of us are middle-aged and hopefully sensible.'

'Yes, that's true,' I said, trying to look sensible.

'Please be kind to him. He is my big brother and has been through a lot. Elena was ill for years before she died. Theo did everything for her, cared for her with much love and when she died a light went out inside him. And Olympia was in Australia with her own life and her own family. He was very alone. There is only so much family can do. Do you understand?'

'Yes of course.'

'I wonder if you have ever been sad and alone? Perhaps you have.'

'Yes,' I said carefully, 'I have. I know how that feels, it's horrible.'

'Then you know it's possible to allow your feelings to lead you in the wrong direction. Perhaps meet the wrong person, cling to someone when they are not the right person, for you or for your life.'

'I know exactly how that feels too,' I admitted.

Well, I did. It crystallised the thoughts I had already been thinking recently about the last few years. In a way it made me feel better and worse at the same time.

Hera sipped at her drink and blotted her mouth with her napkin.

'Then I'll say no more except to thank you for bringing a spark back into my brother's eyes. Even though you have known each other for such a short time, you seem to have something. I hope you will forgive me for speaking to you in this way. At our stage in life, we are looking for different things, aren't we? Not for the promise of children or the sort of new life we create when we are twenty or thirty. But for something else, something different. But a sixty-year-old heart can be broken as easily as one of sixteen. He is my brother and I love him; I want only the best things for him.'

'So do I,' I said. 'He's a very special person. He's taking me out on his boat.'

Hera pressed my hand with hers and smiled.

'Is he? My goodness. That's wonderful.' Her face brightened. 'You and I should meet for coffee soon, or lunch, so I can tell you what a terrible boy he was when he was young, I have many photographs of him, but I'm going back to Symi tomorrow, and eventually you will be going home. I don't know how we can fit it all in before you do.'

I looked across the table to where Theo was shaking his head and laughing at something Juliette had said, and I felt a little jump of affection for him and for my friends and the evening.

'I'll be back,' I said.

She patted my hand again. 'Good.'

What Hera had said resonated with me; we were looking for something different at our stage of life, and of course she was right.

She had started talking to Anita and was slightly turned away from me now. I looked over at Theo again, taking the moment to think.

To think about what I was looking for in my life. I wanted kindness and honesty. I expect we both did. We needed companionship and support and commitment to the future when we would grow old and might face new challenges that people seldom considered when they were young. Was I the one to give those things to Theo? Was he the one for me?

He glanced over and saw me looking at him and he winked at me.

* * *

We paid the bill and left the taverna, walking down the quiet streets towards home. And suddenly it did feel like home to me. As though my years in Oxford were forgotten or irrelevant now. This place, this life, suited me. A mad thought ran around my brain.

I didn't want to leave. There was nothing holding me in Oxford any more, there were memories, my house, regrets and some responsibilities but nothing I couldn't sort out, nothing I couldn't live without.

Foolish; I expected everyone felt that way when they went on holiday, that's all it was. Perhaps the vividness of this feeling would fade when I left, and I'd forget about it once I had settled back into my life. But I wasn't sure I wanted to. Now I needed something else, something completely different.

* * *

'So you are not angry with me any longer?' Theo asked as we slowly walked home, our steps, our stride matching.

'Angry?' I said, playing for time.

'Oh yes, you were angry with me, and you closed the door on me.'

I looked up at him, he was smiling.

'I made a wrong assumption,' I said.

'About what?'

I didn't want to go on talking about it; when I looked at the facts it made me look foolish and immature.

'About me?' he said, filling in the silence.

'Yes, sort of.'

The others were walking faster than we were and were quite a way ahead of us. We could hear them chatting, praising Juliette again. She was laughing and obviously excited.

'What did I do to upset you?' Theo asked, his voice filled with humour.

'Oh look.' I struggled to find the right words. 'I might as well tell you; we saw you on Symi when we went there for the day. You were with Hera, but of course at the time...'

'Were you? I didn't realise that. You should have said hello, I didn't see you at all.'

'We were having lunch.'

'Ah I see. And of course, you thought I was with another woman, you didn't know she was my sister.' He gave a shout of laughter which made the others stop and turn around for a moment. 'What a shame, we could have had a nice lunch together.'

'Yes,' I said. 'I'm sorry.'

'And what was my sister saying to you? Was she telling you what a horrible brother I was? How I took her favourite dolly and put it on the top of the garden shed where she couldn't reach it?'

I laughed. 'No, she didn't tell me that but it's interesting to know! She did say she had a lot of photos of you.'

Theo took hold of my arm and stopped, turning me to look at him. 'You thought that day on Symi I was *se peirázo*... playing with you? Being untrustworthy?'

'Well—'

'My friend, I would not do such a thing, I hope you know that?'

'I think so,' I said, flicking a glance at the others ahead of us who had resumed their walk and were just turning the corner into the street where we were staying.

For a few seconds we were alone together. In the dark evening. He stopped walking and turned towards me.

I suddenly felt jumpy, as though something was about to happen.

I started to babble to cover my nervousness.

'It was a lovely evening. Wasn't Juliette wonderful?'

'She was. And so are you.'

He bent and kissed me, and it was really lovely. It was nothing like with Peter, where kisses and demonstrations of affection had been in short supply, or like Lucian where everything was always tinged with guilt. It was different, it was better. It was the proper way to be kissed.

He put his arms around me and we stood just holding each other in the darkness. His body was warm, deliciously so after the cold evening air. He tasted lovely and he smelled even better. I did like a man who wore aftershave. I kissed him back, and for a moment I felt a bit giddy. It could have been the Metaxa. It probably wasn't.

18

Theo took my hand and tucked it under his arm. Then he bent and kissed my cheek.

'Come on, we must get back or your friends will worry about you,' he said.

Worry? No. Gossip? Yes.

We went the rest of the way in silence, but it was a nice silence, not one caused by disagreement or irritation with each other. A friendly silence.

I felt at ease, happy with myself. It had been an exciting evening and I liked being with him, I liked his company and his conversation. I liked the way his eyes crinkled when he laughed. I liked the way he accepted me for who I was, not for anything else.

Despite that, the familiar little over-thinking demons were nagging at my mind. What on earth was I doing? Only recently, just a few weeks ago, I had thought myself in a tenuous relationship with Lucian. I had thought we had a future together sometime in the hazy, undetermined future and yet now I was kissing another man. Thinking about another man. A man I had known for hardly any time at all. A man who lived thousands of miles away from my home. Who – if it hadn't been for my need to get away from Lucian – I would never have met. Wasn't there supposed to be a decent breathing space between this sort of connection? A time when I would recover from it. Get my wagons into a circle and try again.

I'd been in love with Lucian. Hadn't I? I was beginning to wonder. The feelings I had nurtured for Lucian hadn't been like this.

What was I getting myself into this time? A so-called relation-ship with a man I barely knew, who spoke a different language, ate different food, lived a different life from mine. I knew the colour of his car, some sketchy details about his past and the fact that he had a boat and he seemed to enjoy my company. That was about all.

Well he must like me, mustn't he? He kept seeking me out, being kind to me, talking to me, suggesting trips on his boat. Was he genuine? Was I being a bit hasty?

We passed the baker's shop at the end of the alley, closed now although the scent of delicious things seemed to hang around in the air. I sneaked a look up at him; my word he was handsome. Should that make a difference? Was this going to degenerate into a sort of ghastly middle-aged holiday romance, which ended with promises to keep in touch, the occasional email or text which I would read a hundred times, wondering *what he meant by that*?

But did that matter?

I found him attractive and good company. I liked him. I liked being with him. Wasn't that enough to be going on with? What was he expecting from this? What was I? Did sex come into it at some point?

Well, if it did, he'd better hurry up and make his intentions clear because I rather enjoyed the prospect and I was supposed to be going back to Oxford in just over two weeks. Was that an okay time span to commit to sex with someone? Or was it too quick? Young people seemed to hop in and out of relationships as easily as changing their shoes these days, but I wasn't like that. Was I? Why did this feel so different?

I'd known Peter for a long time before we got married. I'd worked for Lucian for several years before we fell into our unwise relationship. This one was moving with unexpected speed in a totally unanticipated direction. Did this work for people our age?

We reached the front door of my house and mercifully none of the others were hanging around on the doorstep to see what we were doing. Theo kissed me goodnight and hugged me.

'We can go out on my boat on Thursday. The weather will be good.'

I thought for a moment. 'Yes. That sounds marvellous.'

'Good. Until next time.'

Next time. There was going to be a next time.

Well of course there was, we were meeting up on Thursday, we were two doors apart in the same street. You see? I was doing it already; forensically examining his every statement, his every look.

I put on a double dose of the expensive moisturiser that night. It was all very well kissing in dark alleyways, but in the full light of day if he got that close, he might notice my wrinkles if he hadn't already. And crow's feet.

And I needed to get the tweezers out and check my incipient moustache. I think it's to do with hormones or lack of them. I dimly remember my grandmother when I was a child; she could have given Hercule Poirot a run for his money by the time she had died at eighty-seven.

* * *

It was quiet and dark in the garden when I went to lock up. Just the sound of my brain cells jangling with my unexpected excitement.

I went to bed and thought about Theo. Like some sort of daft teenager, I replayed our conversations and kisses. Fancy that; I was nearly sixty and still someone wanted to kiss me. But then why shouldn't they? I certainly wanted to kiss him and I'm sure he was older than I was. Something else I didn't know about him because I hadn't asked. It didn't seem to matter anyway.

The skies outside my window were cloudy, the moon hidden somewhere. In fact, I rather thought it was raining. I opened my bedroom window to check. Yes, it was. That was a shame, it had hardly rained at all since I had been there. Perhaps it would be better tomorrow. It was only a few days before my three neighbours went home. And then what? What would happen? It was very thrilling to wonder.

Funny how there were different sorts of excitement. This anticipation of perhaps seeing Theo again tomorrow, of going out with him on Thursday, didn't feel the same as waking up as a child and knowing it was Christmas Day or my birthday, not like the day Peter proposed.

Thinking about it, that hadn't been exciting at all, he'd been in his study writing some academic paper on some obscure branch of physics. Well, it wasn't actually a study, more of a space under the stairs in the sitting room that he had lined with shelves and row upon row of devastatingly boring books. I had just taken him a cup of tea. He'd looked up and said *I suppose we ought to get married*. I'd been in the middle of sewing a button onto his hairy sports jacket at the time and I went back to my chair by the fire and I'd said, *yes, I suppose we ought to* and that was it.

Why had I agreed to such a half-arsed proposal? Why hadn't I insisted he get down on one knee with an open ring box in one hand and a bottle of Bollinger in the other? I think because I was very fond of him, well I loved him otherwise I wouldn't have said yes. I would have pretended not to hear and gone back to sewing on that button.

Peter was kind and intelligent and on top of that, with the dubious benefit of hindsight – which was always a tricky thing – I'd assumed that no one else would ever ask me.

And Lucian? That was completely different, it had been exciting, and I'd run with it at the time because it was so unexpected. Working at the university where there were literally thousands of young, pretty, clever girls with slim figures and manageable hair, I'd thought I would pass unnoticed. But he had noticed me.

I came back with the bottle of Night Nurse and a box of man-size tissues that day and he'd taken my hand and thanked me. *Thank you*, he'd said, *you're so kind. You understand.* He'd got over his man-flu before anything else happened. I'm not so desperate that I would have kissed a man with a streaming cold.

And Theo? This was very different. However much I wanted to, I couldn't quite think of the right words, and I fell asleep trying. But Theo was the last thought I had that night and the first one in the morning.

* * *

The following day, I was awake early. The rain had gone, the sky outside was washed and clear again. I dressed and went down to the baker's shop and bought a big bag of goodies for us all. We could share breakfast together again. We wouldn't be able to do that soon. That was a sad thought; the Old Ducks were going home. I knew we would exchange details and addresses and vow to keep in touch, but would we? I could see I might be the weak link in the chain, but after all the three of them had been friends for decades so they had managed it.

I went through the garden gate when I heard their back door open and saw Kim coming out for her first cigarette. Her face lit up when she saw me and my carrier bag.

'Is that for us? You are kind. I was just thinking what I really needed today was something gorgeous and calorific. Preferably with added butter.'

'I have one of just about everything,' I said, 'I have diples, bougatsa, various baklava, revani—'

'Did you get those mushroom and cheese pasties?' Kim scrabbled at the bag.

'I got the last two,' I said, 'I know they are popular.'

'You're a star!' She took a bite of one of the pasties. 'There, that's mine now.'

'How old are you?' I said, grinning.

She swallowed her mouthful. 'Wasn't Juliette fabulous last night? She was quite emotional when we got back here. She said it was the first time she'd played in years. So how did you get on? We scurried away to give you two some space. I hope you made the most of it?'

'We had a nice chat,' I said, 'and that's all. Are the others up yet?'

'Getting showered; they will be down in a mo. So, did you snog him?'

'Kim, you're so nosey!'

Kim lit her cigarette and waved a careless hand at me. 'Yes, we all know that. Well, did you?'

'I'm not answering that on the grounds that I might incriminate myself.'

'You did snog him! Excellent work!' Kim did a fist pump with her spare hand. 'I do believe you're blushing.'

'I'm not, it's a warm day,' I said, turning away.

'I don't know why you are so evasive at your age. I mean, we could all see it that first night he came around and told us off.'

'Really? Saw what?' Despite myself I was intrigued.

'Oh Sophia, *please*, even you must have seen it.'

Well no actually, seen what? What did I miss?

'Um...'

'Sophia, you're attractive, intelligent, funny and kind. Why wouldn't he like you? Right, I'm going to get everyone down for breakfast and Juliette will get you talking. She was having a nice chat with Hera last night over dinner. Very interesting. Fancy some coffee?'

'What did she say? Did she say anything about me?'

Kim took a last puff of her cigarette and stubbed it out in the ashtray.

'Ha! How old are *you*?'

* * *

'So, what are we doing today?' Juliette said. 'Not long before we go home, girls.'

The three of them all pulled mouth-turned-down faces.

'I need to buy some little things for my granddaughters, that's the first thing. I keep forgetting. Actually, I haven't bought anything for anyone yet. At this rate I'll be taking them back some horrible sweets from the airport shop that they can't eat.'

'I haven't got anything for my two either,' Kim said. 'I suppose I should.'

'Right then, it's a day for souvenir shopping,' Anita said, 'I could take Rick a bag of Greek compost I suppose, that would fire him up.'

'Or a multipack of Greek pants,' Juliette suggested, eyebrows raised, 'with a picture of the Colossus of Rhodes on the front?'

'Let's stop talking about my husband's underwear,' Anita said as the laughter died down. 'It's too upsetting.'

'Let's talk about last night, and how Sophia and the handsome Theo got on,' Kim suggested with a devilish grin.

'Ooh yes,' Juliette said, 'I was talking to Hera, she said he's had a couple of relationships since his wife died but nothing serious and neither came to anything. And she didn't like them anyway. But she likes you Sophia, so you've got a head start there. Result!'

I could feel my face growing hot. 'Well, that's nice.'

'You really should talk to Hera,' Anita said, 'she might have some inside information.'

'I suppose... and you were marvellous on the piano last night, Juliette. I hope you're going to keep playing?'

'I rather think I will. I'll get a new piano as soon as I get home. I don't know why I haven't done it before.'

'It was wonderful,' Kim agreed. 'So romantic. Perhaps it put Theo in the mood. Did Sophia tell you they had a bit of a snog last night?'

'What?'

'Tell us!'

I got up and refilled the cafetière to cover my embarrassment.

'There's nothing more to tell,' I said.

I was feeling a bit uncomfortable. They were all assuming that the minute they left Rhodes, Theo and I would pounce on each other. Would we? Did I have it in me to pounce? Had I ever pounced?

The other three kept on attacking the pastries, having discussions about who wanted to share a particular favourite with whom, and this degenerated into a *'you cut and I'll choose'* argument. It was like having a load of teens around the table.

'So did Hera say anything else?' I asked at last, unable to stop myself from returning to the subject.

'Aha! You are interested, I thought so,' Juliette said. 'Hera said she thought you were good for him, that he seemed happy.'

I glowed inside with satisfaction. 'That's nice.'

'So, what are you two going to get up to once we leave I

wonder?' Kim said. 'While we are back in England, fighting our way around the supermarket to refill our depleted cupboards.'

'He asked if I would help him paint this place actually, he says it needs a bit of smartening up before the start of the season in the spring.'

'Well that's a new one. Come over to my place little lady, and I'll show you my big roller,' Juliette said in a growling voice, 'and my paint samples. Nice!'

'You could offer to do some stripping for him, or something,' Kim added.

'Or wash out his brushes?'

'You're very rude,' I said, laughing.

'We expect to be told,' Juliette said. 'We all want your email address and everything. Here's my phone, put your number in.'

'And we expect an invitation to the wedding,' Kim added.

'Stop it, now you're being silly,' I said. 'But I am going out with him tomorrow. He has a boat.'

'*What?*'

19

Once we had cleared up, we left the house to go shopping for souvenirs. There were a lot of shops and stalls to browse through. Any number of fridge magnets, bead bracelets and key rings. There were resin statues and monuments, some of them very rude. I didn't realise the ancient Greeks were like that. I mean who needs a resin model of a mooning gladiator? (Perhaps that wasn't actually a genuine antiquity.) Apparently, Juliette's son-in-law did. And a hollow plastic head of Plato, ready to be filled with a pot plant or pencils? Kim bought two. At least they didn't weigh much. They scooped up any number of small plastic amulets and necklaces. Snow globes with an inaccurate model of the Grand Palace inside.

Juliette was thrilled to find some tiny T-shirts with the Colossus of Rhodes dressed as Santa Claus and bought two – one pink, one purple – for her granddaughters.

'They'll look so cute in them,' she said, 'my daughter won't like them though. She's very particular. Which is another reason to buy them really isn't it? They've been in matching clothes since the day they were born, nothing less than John Lewis or M&S for them.'

'Troublemaker,' I said.

'Absolutely. Ooh look, a pencil sharpener in the shape of... well I'm not entirely sure what it is.'

'Well in that case you probably don't need it. Look what I've got for Stewart,' Kim said.

'You're buying him a present?' Anita asked, incredulous.

'It's an evil eye key ring. I hope it works,' Kim muttered.

'It's time for lunch,' Juliette said. 'In no time will be at the airport waiting to take off. I think we deserve a last treat; soon enough we will be chained to the kitchen sink again, that's when we're not doing the laundry.'

'Oh Lordy, I can't think about that now,' Kim groaned. 'Let's have some wine, let's buy something crazy for ourselves too. A mad hat with a donkey on the brim or a pottery savings bank which looks like a loo.'

'Huh?'

'I've seen both of those things,' she said almost wistfully, 'but I didn't buy them. Now I'm regretting it. They would have made the perfect present for Gemma. Simon too, come to think of it. Perhaps I'll go back and find them after lunch.'

We found a nice little taverna situated in a shady corner of a tree-lined square and sat down at a table outside.

'This time next week I will probably be making egg and chips for my kids' tea,' Kim said rather glumly.

'They might have cooked for you,' I suggested.

She gave a disbelieving laugh. 'Not a hope. I had a text from Gemma asking where the loo rolls were yesterday. I said they were either in the airing cupboard or in the shop. She texted me back to ask if I could pick up some on my way home.'

Juliette groaned. 'What? Look, repeat after me Kim, "I will not put up with this any longer". Repeat it three times every morning before you get up.'

Kim helped herself to one of the breadsticks on the table.

'I will not put up with this any longer. And I won't, I'm absolutely determined, there is going to be a new regime from now on. The first thing I'm going to do when I get home is find them a flat to share and I will pay their first three months' rent and then I'm going to get my locks changed. To make sure they can't sneak back in when I'm out at work.'

'Good idea,' Anita said. 'I've been thinking. Rick's only doing his best to deal with his spare time now he's retired. He might be bored too. But being a typical man, he won't say anything or do anything about it. I've decided I'm going to make Rick come to dance lessons or art classes or – I don't know – rock climbing with me. Something, anything that we can do together and if he won't I'll threaten to go without him.'

'He might let you,' I said.

'Not a chance, he'd think I was up to something.'

'What?'

'Mischief?' Kim said.

'And would you?'

Anita shook her head. 'No of course not! But when we were first married we used to have a lot of fun doing new things together. And we haven't exactly done anything earth-shattering for years. We've had fun here haven't we? Doing new things and none of it was that exceptional. We went out for meals, had a trip on the ferry, went in the hot tub, did some sightseeing—'

'Got arrested,' Juliette said. 'Let's not forget that bit.'

'Oh yes, well perhaps I won't tell him *that* particular detail, what I mean is we've had fun just chatting and hanging out. Rick and I could do that too. We always used to. I'm going to ask him if he fancies getting a hot tub as well. I've been thinking about it, there's a spot in the garden he hasn't manicured into submission. In between the shed and the patio. It could go there. In fact, I'm going to insist we have one, even if I have to order it myself. Who knows, it might spice things up a bit!'

'He'll think you've lost the plot,' I said.

'If all that fails, I think I *will* drape myself over his compost heap in my best underwear,' she added with a twinkle in her eye.

'You'll frighten him to death. Oh and by the way, we are coming back next year,' Juliette said, 'and we want you to come too. We are prepared to convert your honorary affiliation of the Old Ducks' Club into full, lifetime membership. All those in favour say aye!'

'Aye,' they shouted, raising their glasses.

I felt tears prickling my eyes, I was so touched. That after such an unpromising start, these women had welcomed me as one of them. I had new, genuine friends. It was a lovely feeling.

Juliette fiddled with her phone for a moment.

'Righty oh, I've just added Sophia to a new Old Ducks WhatsApp group so we can all keep in touch with each other. We can all send her our addresses too. Now then, Sophia. Speech!' Juliette shouted and the other two rapped on the table.

'Speech? Oh, I can't. I don't know what to say,' I said.

'Dry your tears and tell us how marvellous we are,' Anita said.

'You are, you've been such fun, I don't really know what I would have done without you three. I would have spent a miserable time moping and editing Lucian's book—'

They all booed at this point and Juliette made a thumbs down sign.

'—instead, I've eaten too much, drunk too much and enjoyed myself. And you've helped me think things through.'

'Ooh have we? That's exciting,' Anita said. 'Aren't we clever?'

'You have. I can see where I've been going wrong, but I rather think my flame got a bit damped down after Peter died. Peter was a lovely man; I'm not saying he wasn't. We had some happy years together. But he was so totally preoccupied with his work, that sometimes I didn't get much of a look in. Then, after he died, I suppose I was lost and a bit lonely and I started wasting my time with a man who didn't deserve it, didn't deserve me. I was so used to blaming myself for everything and leading a thoroughly uneventful life. Well I'm not doing that any more; I don't have to and it's all thanks to you. So thank you, Old Ducks and here's to the next time!'

We all toasted each other and then realised there was a waiter standing patiently next to us, his pen poised over his pad, ready to take our order.

* * *

'So, what about you Juliette?' I asked a while later. 'We've all been saying what we are going to do, how we are going to change our lives when we get home. What are you going to do?'

Juliette looked thoughtful and she even blushed a bit.

'Well I've been thinking about that. I'm going to get my piano obviously. But there's a rather nice man back in our village—'

'What? You haven't mentioned him before,' Kim said indignantly.

'I did, ages ago. Matthew. He and I have known each other for years. I kept him off the radar because I knew what you'd be like. He's the church warden.'

'I can see you being friends with a lot of people, but a church warden?' Anita said, incredulous.

'No, to be fair it's not as bad as it sounds,' Juliette said. 'He's just a really nice person. We sometimes meet up at the garden centre for coffee. We've been out on day trips a couple of times. Just to National Trust places, you know.'

'I think I'm going to faint.' Kim clutched her throat. 'Get my smelling salts. Garden centres? National Trust properties?'

Juliette laughed. 'Yes, I know it doesn't sound like me, but – well

– he's been a good friend over the last few months and being over here, I've realised I've missed him.'

'Well, I'm totally astonished,' Anita said, 'I had you down for a toy boy next or taking up with a DJ on the Costa del Sol. I absolutely didn't see this coming. Church warden? Meeting up for coffee?'

'Oh you can laugh all you like, I knew you would, but I'm looking forward to seeing him again. He sent me a text saying he'd put my recycling out and watered my pots when there was a bit of a dry spell. I just thought that was really nice of him.'

Kim leaned against me, pretending to swoon.

'Recycling? Pots? Where is Juliette and what have you done with her?'

'Dry spell, well I know what that feels like,' Kim grumbled. 'I wish someone would come and water my pots, so to speak.'

Juliette chuckled. 'Even I need to make a few changes. I didn't like that "getting arrested" thing one bit. Sitting in that place made me think. I'd quite like having some company for a change. I mean, you know, proper company.'

'You mean sex?' Anita asked. 'Good grief! And have you?'

'He's very fit and handsome,' Juliette blushed. 'Even if he is sixty-eight.'

'That's not a proper answer,' Kim said. 'I want to hear more about watering the pots. What does he look like?'

Juliette fiddled with her mobile for a few minutes and then held it out to us, showing us the picture of a rather distinguished-looking man in a tweed jacket with a muddy Border terrier on a lead.

'He has a dog?' Anita said, 'I thought you hated dogs?'

'No, I don't and that's *Maurice*. He's more like a person than a dog. He's grown on me actually,' Juliette said, looking at the picture rather fondly.

'Maurice,' Anita said faintly. She took another look. 'Actually, he's rather sweet, he and Matthew have matching eyebrows.'

'Matthew named him after Maurice Chevalier,' Juliette said.

'Well, you are full of surprises,' I said. 'Can I come to the wedding?'

'Very funny.'

* * *

After a very long lunch and a lot of laughter, we wandered back through the market towards home. Kim found the tasteless loo piggy banks and bought two. Juliette bought a straw hat decorated with the Colossus of Rhodes that she was going to hang on her wall, and a rather pretty little ceramic dish for Matthew.

'He sometimes invites me round for drinks after church. He likes nuts,' she explained.

'That's why he likes you I expect,' Kim said.

'Very droll.'

'So tell me some more about Matthew,' I said.

We were waiting for Kim to finish looking at some luminous sweets that she was planning to buy for her friends at work.

'He's ex-military, his wife died some years ago. We met at the village fete in the summer. It was really hot that day, he was buying an ice cream from the van and he bought me one because I was in the queue behind him and he said he thought I looked friendly. I was wearing my new red dress with the daisies all over it. And as Matthew was handing the ice cream to me it fell off the cone all down my dress. And I just laughed, and he laughed too and we just hit it off.'

'How lovely,' I said.

Juliette smiled. 'He rather is.'

'So why the secrecy about him?'

'Oh, I don't know, it wasn't that I was being secretive, it just sounded so unlike me. I wanted to keep him to myself for a bit. Being friendly with a retired lieutenant colonel. He has medals and everything, in a cabinet. I used to think the worst thing about getting old is that no one realises I'm still young in my head. But Matthew does realise that about me. And he's the same. He's so nice, very kind. But very sensible. That's one of the things I felt so bad about when I was arrested. What would Matthew think? For the first time in ages, I cared what someone else thought of me. I felt I was letting him down as much as myself. Is that silly?'

'Not at all. And I hope it all goes well with him.'

She squeezed my arm. 'Thanks.'

'But don't lose your sparkle, Juliette.'

She grinned and hunched her shoulders with excitement.

'I won't. It's one of the things he likes about me. Now tell me about this boat.'

* * *

I was going to make a risotto that evening, stirred through with white wine, herbs and pecorino cheese, with roasted tomatoes and olives.

'I shall miss your cooking,' Anita said, 'and we seem to have rather a lot of wine to finish up.'

'I won't be long,' I said, 'just let me get this risotto done. I can't leave it, it needs a lot of stirring and tweaking. As soon as it's ready I'll bring the pot over.'

'I can't wait,' Kim said, sniffing the air. 'It smells wonderful already. I'll get the table ready.'

Half an hour later I took the risotto over to their house. The air felt cool and damp. There was a smell in the garden as the first rain-drops hit the dry ground. Petrichor I think it's called.

'Oh wow, that looks just fantastic,' Kim said as I took the lid off the risotto pot. 'There are some bowls in the oven heating up, and look, I've made a salad and some dressing. That's about the limit of my holiday cooking.'

Kim fetched a basket of bread and we sat around the table. Juliette filled our wine glasses while Anita lit some candles on the table. It sort of gave the whole thing a festive feel.

Juliette raised her glass.

'Here's to us ladies, thank you for making the holiday so special, thank you all. Especially Sophia, who helped keep me out of prison, and for making us such wonderful food too. It's been marvellous.'

We clinked glasses over the table, and it seemed they felt as sad as I did to think that soon they would be leaving.

'It's been my pleasure,' I said. 'Now, please tuck in before I start blubbing!'

It was a very special evening, especially as far as I was concerned. We chatted and laughed and reminisced about the places we had been. The risotto was delicious, and I felt a little leap of pride when they complimented me on it.

'Right then, now we have finished, let's take a dip in the hot tub,' Anita said.

'But it's raining!' Kim said.

'So? How wet can you get?' Anita retorted. 'Everyone outside in five minutes!'

I went to get changed and went back outside into the garden. Although it was raining quite heavily, the three of them were already in the hot tub. Juliette was in a dolphin print tankini and had a plastic pixie hood over her hair.

'What? *What?*' she said with mock indignation as I laughed at the sight of her. 'I'm the sensible one here. Pour yourself a drink and get in. We still have loads of wine to finish up. There's no time to waste.'

I did as I was told and climbed in beside them.

'Here's to next year,' Anita said. 'Same time same place. Perhaps we ought to book it now? See if the delicious Theo will give us a discount?'

'I'll ask him when I see him,' I said.

'I'll be very jealous, thinking of you still here when I'm back home,' Kim pouted, 'so I hope it keeps raining. It will make it easier to bear.'

'Well I don't, I will send you pictures of the blue skies and sunshine just to annoy you,' I said. 'Funny, I was always intending to go and buy fresh fish from one of the boats in the harbour. I imagined myself sitting in my garden, eating some delicious meal I had made.'

'Well you certainly produced the delicious meals,' Juliette said. 'Especially the risotto you made tonight. It was heavenly. I'm going to miss you. If only for that.'

'Oh that means a lot, thank you. I even bought a special table-cloth to complete the picture and hardly used it.'

'There's still time,' Anita said. 'You can have quiet evenings out in your garden with a good book.'

'Hmm,' I said. 'Sounds a bit different after what I've got used to.'

'You've got to let us know what's going on,' Juliette said. 'Promise?'

'I promise.'

'Pinkie promise?'

We solemnly linked little fingers.

'That goes for you all too.'

'Now tomorrow, this boat trip. What are you going to wear?'

20

At nine-thirty the following morning I was up, showered and dressed in my comfortable but least favourite jeans (slightly baggy) and a T-shirt, waiting for Theo to arrive. I was very excited at the prospect of spending the whole day with him, just the two of us.

He arrived just before ten o'clock and rapped on my front door. He looked very smart in a white polo shirt, a cherry-red sweater tied around his neck and chinos with lots of pockets down the legs. Was this what Greek men wore when they went sailing?

His face lit up when he saw me.

'Good morning! What a lovely day for a sail!' he said. 'I told you the weather would be good. I ordered it especially for you. I went down to the harbour yesterday making sure everything was ready, filling up with fuel. And I have a picnic.' He held up the insulated bag as evidence.

I thought about it for a moment. He'd needed fuel, so that was a good sign. At least I wouldn't be doing any rowing.

'That sounds brilliant,' I said. 'Fantastic idea.'

'*Kalós!* Good! I'm so glad. You will need a sweater. Bring a warm coat in case you get cold. We can go now if you are ready?'

I looked doubtfully at my outfit. People wore smart, nifty outfits on boats, didn't they? I hadn't found anything particularly smart or nifty. And proper sailors had proper deck shoes, so they didn't slip over the side. I was wearing my newest trainers.

He sensed my reluctance.

'You look great, absolutely fine,' he said, 'just put a few things in a bag. Bring your swimming things and towel. In case you want a dip.'

A dip. I briefly imagined myself leaping off his boat into the sea. Oh well. If he thought I looked okay then I probably did. After all, he wasn't going to like me more just because I had some deck shoes was he? Or like me less because I didn't.

* * *

We walked together through the alleyways towards the harbour, coming out into the sunshine through the Gate of the Port. From there we walked along the *Akti Sachtouri* with the harbour to our right. The water was blue and sparkling, the breeze from the sea refreshing. There were lots of people strolling about, admiring the various craft that were moored there. Some were huge – masted yachts which looked rather terrifying – others were smaller speed-boats. I was very curious, of course, to find out which one was Theo's.

Some had people on them, doing whatever it was that people did on boats. One couple seemed to be clearing out a lot of empty wine bottles into a recycling bin. Another was messing about with a length of blue rope and having an argument in rapid Greek that made Theo bite back a smile.

Now and then there was a shout of recognition from someone, and then there would be handshakes and introductions of '*my English friend Sophia*' which was very gratifying.

'Ah, so this is Sophia, at last,' said one as he shook my hand with a huge, calloused paw. 'Adonis Papandreou. I must find you that fish you wanted, Theo.'

There was a lot of smiling and the woman I took to be Adonis' wife looked me up and down rather suspiciously, although she was pleasant enough.

They talked a bit about the water and the weather while Mrs Papandreou introduced herself as Electra and asked the usual polite questions about how I was enjoying my holiday. She had proper deck shoes, brown and weather-beaten, that spoke of many hours on their boat. I shuffled my trainers rather self-consciously.

Eventually we moved on only to be stopped by a shout from another boat and more introductions; this time it was two grizzled old sea dogs with a battered air and an equally battered fishing boat; they were introduced as Achilles and Pluto. How marvellous. Imagine the grief you'd get in school in England if your mother had called you either of those.

They shook my hand too and wished me a good trip. It was lovely how friendly everyone was, and how many people knew Theo, obviously liked him and wanted to talk to him. I was almost basking in reflected glory. The walk along the quayside which should have taken us a few minutes, took half an hour; it really did feel as though I was a local. And still I didn't know which boat was his. Would his be a small dinghy, a yacht with a lot of complicated ropes and rigging or one of the big white gin palaces at the far end of the quay? We passed one of those and it was filled with glossy, hair-flicking girls all vying for the attention of someone who looked old enough to be their father. Perhaps he was their father? Let's hope so.

'Theo! Theo!'

We were halted by a loud shout from behind us.

We turned to see an elderly man, silver-haired and probably in his nineties, being pushed along the quayside in a wheelchair by a fierce-looking woman in a waterproof coat and a woollen hat pulled low over her brows. She was evidently feeling the cold which was surprising as it was a glorious morning.

Theo gave a broad grin. 'Uncle Nico,' he said.

He bent to embrace the old man and they chatted for a minute before he turned to include me.

'Uncle Nico, this is my friend, Sophia,' he said.

Uncle Nico's beetle eyebrows raised and his dark eyes twinkled at me as he shook my hand.

'Ah, *this* is Sophia.'

So, he had heard of me too.

'And this lady is his carer, Irene.'

The formidable-looking woman gave me a brisk nod.

'Hera tells me you are staying here for a holiday,' Nico said, 'and now you are going out in Theo's boat.'

Did everyone know everything?

'I'm looking forward to it,' I said.

'A beautiful day,' Nico said, 'and then tomorrow you must come to my house for lunch.'

I looked at Theo.

'Lunch Uncle Nico?' he asked. '*Tomorrow*?'

'Lunch. Tomorrow,' Nico agreed firmly.

Theo gave me an apologetic smile.

'Uncle Nico is very bossy,' he said.

'I'm very old, which means I must not be upset,' Nico declared. 'I will see you tomorrow at one o'clock. I will tell Hanna. Have a pleasant day.'

Nico made a funny little spinning movement with one finger and Irene turned his chair around and wheeled him away.

'Who is Hanna?' I said as we watched them go.

'His sister, my aunt, she is a terror,' Theo said, which was not reassuring. He was looking slightly worried.

'What's wrong?'

He smiled. 'Nothing.'

* * *

'Here we are,' Theo said at last, '*Partheniki* – Sea Maiden. I hope you like her?'

I did like *Partheniki*, she was gorgeous. I hopped on board feeling very glamorous. No sails to worry about, no oars, just a medium-sized speedboat with gleaming white sides and comfortable-looking leather seats. There was even a little cabin with a tiny fridge.

'I haven't had her for very long, just a few months. *Partheniki* is my... epieíkeia... my indulgence.'

'Lovely,' I said, 'she's so lovely.'

Theo stowed the picnic below deck – a technical term I remembered – and handed me a life jacket. After a few minutes untying ropes and flicking switches, he fastened a cord around one wrist and reversed the boat out of its parking place, or whatever the right term for it was.

'This is the kill switch, in case I fall overboard,' he said, pointing to the cord, 'then the engine cuts out so it won't take off with you or come back and run me over.'

'You won't fall overboard will you?'

He laughed. 'I'll try not to.'

We left the harbour at a stately pace, making our way past the remains of the Naillac Tower which I was told had been destroyed by an earthquake many years ago, and then we turned right. Was that port or starboard? I wasn't sure. Once we were clear of the harbour buildings and out into open water, Theo pushed a lever forward and we were off. I'm not sure what speed we were going but it seemed very fast to me. Sitting in the comfortable leather armchair next to Theo, I was fairly well out of the wind, but I pulled my coat around me all the same.

'Are you all right?' he asked.

'Brilliant,' I said, glad that the sea was so calm. I hoped I wasn't prone to seasickness. Up until now I hadn't really had the chance to find out.

The land skimmed by on our right-hand side – starboard I found out. Or more accurately, *dexió méros*. On the coastline I could see deserted beaches and, occasionally, houses and hotels. I wondered if anyone was watching us whizzing past, leaving a white wake behind us as we cut through the glassy sea. Did they wonder about us in the way I had wondered about the girls on other boats? Perhaps I had it wrong. Maybe they hadn't been young, frisky girls, perhaps they had actually been women like me, older, greyer excited and just a bit surprised at themselves.

'Where are we going?' I said.

Theo turned to look at me and grinned. 'Somewhere I think you will like. You'll see. It won't take us too long, not for a first trip.'

So there might be a second trip?

I sat back in my seat, one arm along the side of the boat. I felt very glamorous. What had I done to deserve this? To be here, on a splendid craft with this lovely man. But thinking about it, did I *need* to deserve this or did people – people just like me – out of the blue, for no real reason, just occasionally get lucky?

* * *

After about an hour he slowed the boat and pointed to the shore.

'Recognise it?' he said.

There was a little rocky outcrop and between it and the land, a sheltered bay.

'Should I?'

'You should, I brought you here once, but that time was by road. And it was early evening.'

He concentrated on steering the *Partheniki* towards the bay, eventually stopping in deep water, not far from another boat where an older couple – well, another couple like us I suppose – were sitting drinking out of matching mugs. We gave each other a cheery wave as Theo threw the anchor overboard.

'You don't recognise it? Anthony Quinn Bay,' Theo said. 'It looks a bit different from the sea instead of the car park, doesn't it? You said you wanted to come back and see it.'

'Oh yes, I remember! It's lovely,' I sighed.

'One of the most beautiful beaches on the island. In high season there is snorkelling, and a glass-bottomed boat too. Anthony Quinn bought the bay when he was filming here many years ago. There were problems afterwards but well—' he rocked one hand from side to side, '—let's not talk of that now. Are you hungry? I have a picnic, remember?'

He went to fetch the insulated bag and opened it.

'I haven't brought too much, just a snack, but the sea air always makes me hungry,' he said.

I looked up at him and smiled. 'Me too.'

He hesitated for a moment and then he leaned down to kiss me. His face was cold next to mine, his mouth warm.

'I have wanted to do that all morning.'

'Oh, good,' I said.

I was smiling so hard, I must have looked slightly crazy.

My heart was skipping little beats with the excitement and the joy of the afternoon.

'I may want to kiss you again later,' he said warningly.

I laughed. 'Oh good.'

'In fact, I'm sure of it.'

He passed me a bottle of water and set out some bread and ham and a tub of plump green olives on the little table. I didn't think such simple food had ever tasted quite as delicious.

Sitting in the sunshine, eating and chatting, I felt relaxed and happy. Properly relaxed and really happy. At that moment it seemed to me that I was absolutely in the right place at the right time. Was all this just luck? Was it just the latest in a string of fortunate coincidences?

That dull, wet afternoon in Oxford, when I had felt so unhappy and wretched, I'd opened my laptop and looked for somewhere to go, somewhere small, warm and far away from where I had been. And Theo's little house had popped up. There had been great pictures and reviews left by previous guests; it had seemed too good to be true at the time. Now I knew it was every bit as marvellous as it had sounded.

Perhaps I would add my comments when I returned home. The charm and simple comfort of the house, the serenity and comfort I had found there. (Perhaps I wouldn't mention the neighbours.)

I'd had time to think, I'd made three new friends, had some fun, some excitement, laughed with them and confided in them. But this bit, this adventure, was an unexpected bonus. I couldn't have imagined this in my wildest, most optimistic moments. Things like this didn't happen to women like me, ordinary women with fears and failings, and yet it seemed they did. At least they did for me because I had taken a chance. I had struck out in a new direction and it was one I was enjoying.

Life was a funny thing; some of the worst bits were unexpected just as the best bits were too. That old saying about one door closing just as another one opens was true.

I sat looking at the view, feeling the slight rock of the boat in the clear water below us, the sun on my face. I took some slow, deep breaths, wanting to draw this emotion, this place deep inside me so that I would never lose it. Perhaps this feeling, this peace, this contentment, was mindfulness? Perhaps I knew what it was after all.

* * *

'You like this place?' Theo said after a while.

'It's one of – no, it's the *most* beautiful place I've ever been,' I agreed. 'Thank you for bringing me here.'

I could tell he was pleased.

'*Efcharistisi mou*. It's my pleasure. When I see a place like this, I know there is some good left in the world, despite everything. Despite the troubles, problems, disasters. There is something worth living for.'

'Did you ever think there wasn't?'

'Sometimes, when Olympia left for Australia, when Elena died, when I began to feel my age for the first time. When I was lonely. When sometimes the night was dark and the future uncertain. Then I sometimes wondered. But now? Well, here I am, I have my health and strength and things that I enjoy. Now I know there is life left in me and hope.'

'That's very good to hear,' I said.

He stretched his arms in the air, then linked his hands behind his head and sighed.

'And you? You have life and hope too?'

'I do,' I said, 'which surprises me because when I arrived in Rhodes I was in a very different frame of mind. I was confused and angry and tired. It seems like a lifetime ago, and yet it wasn't.'

'And you were sad, I think?' he said gently.

'I was sad, but more than that, I was angry with myself.'

He reached out and covered my hand with his. 'You don't have to do that, not any more.'

'I know, I have realised that. Thank you. *Efcharistó*.'

He smiled. '*Parakaló*.'

He reached into the bag and brought out a small box that I recognised as coming from the bakery.

'*Amygdalo*. Almond cookies. They are my favourite.'

He passed one over to me and I bit into it; sweet and delicious. Just like this day.

21

We sat in the sun and chatted for a while, we talked about our lives, our hopes and our thoughts and sometimes we were quiet, just enjoying each other's company. That was lovely too. The other boat finished its stay and pulled up its anchor, ready to go.

'Stegna,' the man called across, pointing out to sea to show us where he was going.

'*Apolamváno!*' Theo called back. 'Enjoy yourselves! Well, I suppose we should be going too.'

'Yes, it's getting colder now the sun is setting. Too cold to swim.'

'You'd be surprised. The water is still very warm at this time of year. Maybe next time.'

'Next time,' I agreed.

He grinned. 'I haven't enjoyed a trip so much in a long time.'

'Why?' I was fishing for compliments.

'You make me laugh, and you were just the right person to bring here.'

I sat and glowed with satisfaction for a moment.

You see, I'd always thought deep down that I was basically an okay person, and yet there had been times recently when I'd really doubted it. That I had made poor choices, that maybe I didn't deserve to be happy as a result.

'Do you remember, ages ago, you said something to me in Greek, and I asked what it meant? And you said you would tell me if I came out on your boat? Well?'

He smiled.

'I wondered if you would remember that. I said *échete ta pio ómorfa mátia*. You have the most beautiful eyes.'

'Oh.' I felt a bit shaky for a moment.

He turned to kiss me again and then he pulled up the anchor and I stowed away the remains of our picnic in the little cabin. Then I settled myself back into my seat.

'This has been lovely,' I said. 'Such a beautiful place and you are excellent company.'

He smiled at the compliment and squeezed my hand.

'You too. I've enjoyed today a great deal. Perhaps we could do this again? Soon?'

'Yes please,' I said. 'I'd like that a lot.'

'But I must start on the decorating as soon as your friends leave,' he added. 'Today you have been a bad influence, a distraction, I have been *tempélis* – lazy.'

'I'd be happy to help you,' I said, and it was true, even though decorating had never been my strong point. Actually, I hadn't done any for years. Decorating a room when several hundred books lined the walls was not an appealing prospect. I did suggest it once and Peter had looked at me as though I had suggested going to Glastonbury.

Perhaps I would have to think about it when I got back to Oxford? Somehow the prospect didn't hold nearly the same appeal as slapping some white paint on the rough, stone walls of a medieval house.

* * *

We reached home enveloped in the start of a wonderful sunset. The sky was glowing with a perfect apricot colour, the Palace of the Grand Master was illuminated and the lights from the harbour were endlessly reflected across the water.

One of the weather-beaten fishermen we had met earlier – it could have been Achilles or possibly Pluto, maybe it was Adonis – hailed Theo and thrust a package into his hands as we passed.

'So,' he said as we walked back home, 'are you hungry? You must be! A day out on the water with only bread and ham to eat is a poor feast.'

'I'd love a glass of wine too,' I said.

'Come home with me and I will see what I have to offer you,' he said.

Our eyes locked for just a brief second, and I had to look away. Was he talking about food? Or something else entirely?

Actually, the prospect of both things had definitely been on my mind. Today I'd had the opportunity to look at him; he had a strong, lean body, muscular arms and I'd liked watching his tanned hands on the controls of the boat. All of those things made me feel like *'something else entirely'* was a good idea.

'Okay,' I agreed, and had to look away to hide a smile.

* * *

We got back to Theo's house and he poured us a glass of dark red wine which was exactly what I had been hoping for. The warmth as it slipped down was perfect. Then, as I stood watching, he had a look in his fridge and cupboards, bringing out the ingredients for a salad and unwrapping the package he had been given. It was fish of course. Two, thankfully gutted, fish.

'Ah, Adonis has given me *lavráki* – sea bass. You'll like this I hope?' Theo said, turning on the oven.

'Only if you cook it. It's not my speciality.'

He grinned and came across to kiss me. 'I'm going to spoil you.'

'I don't think I've ever had a man who cooked for me,' I said. 'I shall watch with interest.'

He took a wickedly sharp knife and I watched as he expertly filleted the fish. That in itself would have been more than enough to impress me. Then he put some foil and paper on the worktop and placed the fish onto it, wrapping it up with whole garlic cloves, a glug of olive oil, some sprigs of rosemary and a glass of white wine. He sealed the whole thing up and put it into the oven.

'Ten minutes,' he said, 'now we can make a salad.'

'I can do that,' I said.

We worked together; I ripped up salad leaves and sliced tiny tomatoes, he toasted pine nuts and blanched some green beans. Then he scattered on some capers and olives. And chopped some parsley with impressive speed while I sat back with my glass of wine and watched him.

It was all very pleasurable and incredibly sexy if I was honest. Perhaps I could see why famous chefs got such glamorous women as companions. Having a man do this was really rather erotic. This definitely wasn't something I was used to. In the past I had been pathetically pleased if a man emptied the dishwasher or noticed that the kitchen bin was full and actually did something about it.

Having said that, *I've emptied the bin for you* is not a phrase designed to get a woman in the mood for love.

I'd read something recently on a problem page, a man asking what on earth helping with housework had to do with keeping his wife feeling frisky and affectionate. I think he was serious. He was also doomed to a life of increasing frustration and disappointment. In my opinion anyway.

Theo pulled out some plates and cutlery and set the table, even lighting some candles. They cast a soft glow over the room which was almost magical.

'That's lovely,' I said.

'My mother used to say *you don't need a gold fork to eat good food*,' Theo said, 'and she was right. You just need time and good friends to share it with. Now sit, enjoy your wine and I will bring everything to you.'

He put a crusty loaf on the table, some oil and the pottery bowl of salad in front of me. Then he got the fish out of the oven, opened up the parcel and slid the fillets onto plates. A delicious aroma filled the room.

'I'm looking forward to this,' I said.

He came to sit opposite me and raised his wine glass towards me.

'Me too. Please. Help yourself and I hope you enjoy it.'

I did.

It was one of the best meals I'd ever eaten, despite the simplicity of it all. I briefly wondered if the Old Ducks had noticed I hadn't come home.

'Did your mother teach you to cook?' I asked, dipping my bread into the olive oil.

'She did teach me; she was a good cook. And that's unusual. Not many Greek women expect their sons to cook. They expect them to marry.'

'So your wife – Elena? She was a good cook?'

'Elena was a great cook, she taught Olympia well too. She had a framed quote on her kitchen wall, *the people who give you their food give you their heart*. It's a nice thought.'

'What was she like?'

'Kind, bossy, determined. Funny.' He looked pensive for a moment and then re-filled my wine glass. 'And perhaps just a little like you.'

What was I supposed to say to that? I couldn't think of anything that didn't make me sound desperately unsophisticated. Luckily, he changed the subject.

'And your husband? Peter? What was he like?'

'An academic; intelligent, kind, absent-minded. He used to forget about food and appointments and—' I stopped.

'And you. Did he forget about you?' Theo asked, filling the silence.

'Sometimes,' I confessed. This was all getting a bit deep and personal for me. I finished my meal and put my cutlery down. 'That was delicious, thank you. *Efcharistó.*'

He smiled. '*Parakaló.* You're welcome.'

He stood up and held out his hand to me. I took it.

He led me to the garden where the stars were brilliant against the dark night sky.

There again, that scent of herbs and warm stone walls. The sound of a church bell somewhere in the distance.

He turned me towards him and tilted my chin up.

'Sophia,' he said. His voice was warm, affectionate and full of humour. 'Look at me. I told you I wanted to kiss you again, and I would like to do it now.'

And he did.

Wow, I mean double, treble wow.

It was without doubt the most romantic moment of my life. Just the two of us standing in the dark, our arms around each other. His back hard under my fingers, his stubble grazing my face, his hands in my hair.

'Sophia, Sophia,' he murmured.

As I followed him upstairs to his bedroom a thought struck me, and it pleased me with its oddness. Tomorrow was my sixtieth birthday. Unless I was very much mistaken, I was going to wake up with him, start a new decade of my life with this man. Not the second *half* of my life because I was unlikely to live to one hundred and twenty, but I was going to start my life again; I was ready to move on.

I had learned so much about myself and began to understand some of my many faults. But now, I was going to make my own choices; I was, after all, a free agent. I was going to find the things that made me happy and do them. Above all, I was going to value myself. I was going to forgive myself.

* * *

There's a very big difference between having sex and making love. Yes, I know that's an obvious statement but I'd only just realised it. No, I didn't know where I'd been for most of my life either, but it was never too late to learn. That was going to be my mantra from that day onwards. In the grand scheme of things, I knew a lot of stuff but also not a lot of *really important* stuff.

I hadn't known how it felt to hold a man in my arms and not know where I ended and he began; to become one. To forget my own name, to breathe him in, to taste his skin. To feel his eyelashes on my cheek, his gentle kisses on my neck. To have the feeling that the earth really might have moved. Just for me. Either that or there had been an earthquake. I mean I knew there were earth tremors in the region but even so...

22

I woke up the next morning in a tangle of bedsheets with nothing on. Not a stitch. Which in itself felt weird. No cotton nightie or pyjamas. Certainly no blue bed socks, which I had been known to wear on cold nights.

I stretched out in bed and luxuriated in the feeling.

Perhaps I would dump my collection of nightwear along with Peter's books and that shoebox full of deceit that I kept under my bed. Perhaps I would be like Monroe and just wear Chanel N°5 in bed from now on? Perhaps I would—

'Good morning,' Theo said.

I turned my head to look at him.

And I smiled.

This was wonderful, the feeling that I didn't need to feel guilty or worried or unsure. He wouldn't scramble into his clothes and rush out wittering on about getting back. I knew this felt right and good.

'Hello,' I said.

His hair was ruffled, his face half hidden in the pillow.

He reached out to stroke my cheek.

'Did you sleep well?'

'I did,' I said.

'So did I. Happy birthday.'

I blinked a bit. 'How did you know it was my birthday?'

'It was on your booking form, remember?'

'Oh yes. Well spotted. And well remembered.'

He reached into the bedside cabinet.

'I hope you don't mind; I have a present for you. It's just some-thing to remember me by, to remember your holiday.'

He handed over a little box wrapped in blue paper.

'I hope you like it.'

I could have said something like *oh you shouldn't have* or *you didn't need to get me anything* but I didn't. I never got many presents as a rule, and I would never turn one down.

I pulled the paper off and opened the box. Inside was a little gold bracelet with one charm attached, of the Rhodes Colossus.

'Oh Theo! I love it,' I said, absolutely delighted.

I held out my left hand so he could fix it on for me. When he had finished fiddling with the clip, he kissed the little bracelet.

'Now I'll go and fetch you some tea if you like? There is a dressing gown you can use in the airing cupboard.'

This was great news; I might be revelling in my lack of clothes at that particular moment, but it didn't mean I was going to wander around naked too.

He got of bed and pulled on a dressing gown, but not before I'd enjoyed the view of him. I felt like giggling, burying my head under the pillow. I felt happy, positively naughty.

Then as soon as he had gone out, I scrambled to the bathroom and found that dressing gown, freshly laundered and folded. I wondered for a moment whose it was. And who had worn it last? But then I realised it was probably his; it was far too big for me and almost trailed on the ground. Good. I didn't want to think I had been stepping into dead men's shoes, so to speak. I think I mean into other women's dressing gowns. No, it was fine.

I went back to the bedroom and looked out of the window; it was still early morning, the sky was a dark lavender colour, a promising splash of peach coloured clouds on the horizon where the sun was rising.

I wrapped my arms around myself; I wanted to have a little triumphant dance. I wondered again if the Old Ducks had noticed I hadn't gone back to my house last night. Of course they would have.

'Your tea, madame,' Theo said behind me. He put the two mugs down on the bedside tables and came to stand behind me, holding me gently against him. 'It looks like a good day.'

I was very content. No, I was more than that, I was excited, I was thoroughly happy.

Good heavens.

* * *

I went back to my house to shower and change into some clean clothes. About ninety seconds later, even before I had a chance to put one foot on the bottom stair, the three Old Ducks were hammering on my patio doors.

As I opened them, I could feel myself blushing.

Juliette had been to the bakery and dumped a bag of croissants on my dining table.

'So?' she said.

'Did you have fun?' Anita added.

'How much fun?' Kim said.

Juliette went to find plates and knives.

'We waited up for you, and you didn't come home, did you? I think that's very unfair, abandoning us like that to go off enjoying yourself, and just as we are about to go home too. *So...*'

'You are unbelievably inquisitive,' I said, holding my hands to my hot face.

'You'd be the same if it was one of us. I'm guessing you had a lot of fun. Well good for you,' Anita said. 'We went to the beach and hired some chairs. I got hit on the head with a football. I'm sure it was an accident, but these young Greek men are so gorgeous, I didn't really mind. There were some very attractive waiters there I must say. We kept seeing boats going past and wondering if it was you. You'll have to tell us where you went and what you did. I'll make coffee, shall I? And then you can tell us everything. Well not absolutely everything, I mean we're not that bad. Just the edited highlights.'

I held up my wrist to show them my new bracelet.

'Theo gave me this,' I said, 'it's my birthday.'

'When?' Juliette said accusingly.

'Today, I wasn't going to say anything—'

'Why on earth not? You mad thing!' Kim cried. 'This is actually your birthday today?'

'Yes, today,' I said.

'Happy birthday! We'll have to celebrate when you get back later. I'll get some champagne in the fridge,' Juliette said. 'We'll toast your sixty-first birthday!'

'Actually, I have an admission, it's my sixtieth birthday today. I've been an Old Duck under false pretences,' I admitted.

'You tricky thing,' Kim said. 'I think we'll have to have a special meeting and expel you.'

'Sorry. Anyway, it gets better, or possibly worse,' I said. 'We met Theo's uncle while we were out yesterday and he's invited me for lunch today.'

'OMG, now she's meeting the family!' Juliette said, fanning her face with half a croissant and dropping pastry flakes down the neck of her dress.

'No, just one aged uncle, and possibly his sister Hanna, who has been described to me as a terror,' I added.

'I bet she is too, I bet she will look at you with an evil glint in her eye and ask you awkward questions. That's what they do, old aunts,' Kim said. 'Stewart had three of them who were positively poisonous. Like the witches in Macbeth without the cauldron. Or the humanity. They came to our wedding because Stewart was too scared not to invite them and they sat together making snide comments. Asking if I was pregnant or just fat. Did I think it was appropriate to wear white? Hanna will be like that.'

'Oh thanks, that's very cheering,' I said, buttering a croissant.

'What are you going to wear? Shall I do your make-up?' Juliette said.

'Er, no but thank you,' I said, remembering the false eyelashes and the three shades of eyeshadow.

'You'll have to be on your best behaviour,' Kim warned, 'and not fall over anything.'

'I was planning both of those things,' I agreed.

Anita took up the thread. 'And ask after her health. Old ladies like that. My aunt can talk for hours about her blood pressure and cholesterol. That's if scary Aunt Hanna speaks English at all. She might not and then she will just watch you without saying anything until you faint with the stress, face down on the table. Probably do a face plant into the salad.'

'Stop it! I'm not listening!'

'And ask them both about themselves. Show some interest.'

'Well I am interested,' I said.

'Don't talk about Lucian or Oxford or having an affair with him,' Anita said.

I sighed. 'I'm not completely daft.'

'And she will probably have an evil old dog on her lap, so make a fuss of it,' Kim said, 'but don't try and stroke it because it will probably bite you. Stewart's Auntie Mim had a Pomeranian with teeth like needles and the same temperament as Mim. I sometimes think Mim would have bitten me too given half a chance.'

'My grandmother had a cat like that,' Juliette said. 'It would hide under the chairs and leap out to sink its fangs into passing ankles.'

'Hanna might have a cat,' Anita said. 'A really old one, curled up on a special chair, so don't sit on it by mistake.'

'Oh God, you lot are really freaking me out,' I said. 'Ask about cholesterol, don't talk about myself, admire the dog, don't sit on the cat...'

'And eat everything put in front of you,' Kim added, 'and say everything is delicious. Even if it isn't and you want to vomit.'

'Don't vomit,' Juliette added.

'Ask about her grandchildren,' Anita said brightly, 'they always like that. She'll have a photo album nearby so she can bore you with pictures of them. And whatever you do don't mention the fact that one of them is cross-eyed and needs a haircut because that one will be her favourite...'

'And you should take her a gift,' Juliette said, 'but that's difficult because old ladies hate everything. She won't want chocolates because she'll be diabetic. No flowers because she'll be allergic. No soap or perfume – ditto. No ornaments because the house will be stuffed with them already—'

'Jules is right. There will be bookcases filled with hideous things her grandchildren have made for her. I guarantee it,' Anita said.

'So what shall I take?' I said. 'Some wine?'

'Ooh no, she'll think you're an alcoholic. She'll only drink weak tea out of a feeder cup,' Kim said. 'Although Stewart's aunts could drink a dockside pub dry given half a chance.'

'This is impossible,' I wailed, putting my hands over my ears.

'Wear flat shoes, so you don't trip over the dog basket,' Anita said. 'If you wear heels, she'll think you're a strumpet and no better than you should be.'

'Ask about her feet,' Kim said. 'Old ladies always have trouble with their feet.'

'Feet?' I said, incredulous.

Kim nodded. 'It's a given. Trust me. Bunions, corns, that sort of thing.'

'But stand up for yourself as well,' Juliette said. 'You're an Old Duck now. We don't put up with any nonsense.'

'So be polite, eat what I'm given, ask after her grandchildren, don't stroke the dog, but don't take any nonsense. Right, I'm going to have a shower,' I said, 'and a quick nervous breakdown.'

23

Just after midday Theo called for me and we set off for Nico's house and lunch. I'd decided to wear my smartest trousers, some flat ballerina pumps and a rather lovely blazer I had bought just before I came away but never worn. The Old Ducks came to see me off, standing on their front doorstep calling out last minute advice.

'I should take a gift shouldn't I?' I asked Theo. 'But I couldn't think of anything.'

Theo held up a package wrapped in white paper.

'Don't worry, I have something for them. I always take them some Metaxa,' he said.

'*Really*?' That was beyond unexpected.

'Oh yes, they both love it. I think that's what keeps them going. That and arguing with each other,' Theo said.

'That's nice,' I said faintly.

After walking for about half an hour through the alleyways, past a beautiful little church, tree-lined squares and an elaborate three-tiered fountain, Theo stopped and knocked on a wooden door set back from the street behind an iron fence.

It was opened and to my amazement, there stood Hera. She was her usual elegant self in a striped silk dress, her eyes alight with mischief.

She came forward with a little exclamation and hugged me.

'I wasn't expecting to see you,' I said. 'How lovely.'

Hera arched her eyebrows and gave Theo a look. 'Really? Come on in.'

She took our coats and led us through the hallway towards the living room.

Theo, walking in front of me, stopped and I nearly cannoned into him.

The room was large and spacious, but it was full of people, I mean absolutely packed. There wasn't an empty chair left and people were standing around with wine glasses in their hands. It looked suspiciously like a party.

As we came in, everyone stopped talking and turned to look at us – or rather, at me. It was terrifying. And then people started to get up and came forward to be introduced.

Theo gave me an apologetic look.

'Sorry about this,' he whispered.

'You might have warned me there was a party,' I muttered.

'This isn't a party, it's just family,' Theo said.

'Good grief.'

Hera laughed. 'Didn't Uncle Nico tell you? We have a family lunch every month, just a chance to catch up. Theo, you should have told poor Sophia.'

'I didn't think she'd come,' he said.

'Of course I would,' I said unconvincingly.

'Well you are here now, there's no escape. Sophia, this is my husband Stephanos,' Hera said.

I shook hands with a good-looking man in a suit and he said something about being pleased to meet me.

'I won't monopolise you now,' Stephanos said, 'other people are very interested in meeting you. Perhaps we will talk later?'

'Come and talk to Uncle Nico,' Hera said.

Uncle Nico. He stood up with a bit of difficulty and came over, leaning heavily on a cane to bow over my hand with great politeness.

'Sophia. How pleased I am to see you again!'

There were aunts, cousins, nephews and nieces, all of whom wanted a good look at me, all of them smiling and welcoming and very curious. It took some time to get round all of them and I knew I would never remember all their names. But they were obviously interested to meet me. Some of them asked about Oxford, how long was I staying in Rhodes. I had the feeling they knew a great deal more about me than I realised.

'Sorry about this,' Hera said, 'but when they found out you were coming here for lunch, there was no going back. They all wanted to meet you. The problems of a big family, you get to meet most of them all at the same time!'

'I'll never remember who everyone is,' I murmured, panicking slightly.

'Of course not, just remember Uncle Nico and that lady over there with the black dress.'

This didn't narrow it down much as there were several ladies in black dresses.

'The one with the pearl earrings and the crucifix necklace, that's Aunt Hanna, she is in charge of all things. I will introduce you to her later, she's better when she's had something to eat. And trust me, she will let you know when she wants to speak to you. But you must remember this chap? I know you have met previously!'

Hera pulled a young man to her side; he was tall and very handsome, his hair slicked back with some grooming product. He wore a smart suit and tie. Of course, I knew him already.

'Alexis, of course I remember,' I said, 'so you are back from the beach and in the office again?'

Alexis pulled a face. 'Don't say it too loud, my mother thinks I am neglecting my work.'

'And so you are,' Hera agreed, 'now come and get something to eat, Sophia. The family have been cooking all day. And beware, they will be most offended if you miss anything, you will have to try everything! I mean it. They will be watching. And please, whatever you do, don't say you prefer one thing to another. Family feuds have been started over less than that believe me, just say *everything* is delicious.'

Oh yes, I'd had this sort of warning.

She led me out onto the patio, and everyone started to follow us as though I was declaring the feast formally open. Outside it was slightly chilly but very pleasant. There was a canvas canopy decorated with bunting and underneath it a huge table, loaded with dishes and platters and bowls. A startling amount and variety of food and dips. Dolmades and salads and cakes studded with cherries and crystallised fruit in jewelled piles. It was astonishing.

Theo was beside me, reassuring me.

I reached out and touched the table. The wood was cool and smooth with the patina that spoke of hundreds of meals and hands and polishing.

'This is the one your father made isn't it?' I said.

He nodded. 'You have a good memory.'

'It's beautiful, he must have been a wonderful craftsman.'

Everyone within earshot nodded approvingly.

I took a plate and helped myself, well aware that my choices were being closely watched.

'This is wonderful,' I said loudly at last, 'everything is so delicious.'

The atmosphere lightened a bit. Whatever the first test was I had passed.

* * *

The sheer numbers of them was intimidating but they seemed to be lovely people too, interested and welcoming. And I kept seeing people I thought I recognised. And when I caught their eye they nodded and smiled at me too.

In the end I grabbed Theo's arm.

'You have to tell me who they are,' I whispered, pointing them out. 'There are two men in particular... I'm sure I sort of recognise them.'

'Ah they have smartened themselves up for the occasion. No wonder you don't remember who they are. The one with the blue sweater is Achilles, he is my cousin and the man talking to him is Pluto, he is married to my cousin Daphne. They are both fishermen, we met them at the harbour. Over there is Hercules, he owns the taverna where we had dinner the other night, he is another cousin. Alexis you know already, Hera's son. And Cass, she isn't here today but do you remember her? The first night we met? The Australian waitress. She is my son-in-law Mark's sister.'

Oh, I thought she might have been your girlfriend.

'You really do have a lot of relations!' I said.

Theo laughed. 'Well, I did warn you.'

One of the children who had been wandering about plucked at my sleeve. I turned to look. She was about six or seven, with beautiful dark eyes and a head full of glossy curls.

'Hello,' I said, 'what's your name?'

'Iris.'

'That's a lovely name.'

'Say something,' Iris said.

Behind her there were several other children watching and listening.

'Say something English.'

'They want to hear your accent,' Theo prompted.

I thought about it.

'Candlewick bedspread.'

Iris giggled, covering her mouth with her hands.

'Say more things,' she said at last, 'funny things.'

'Bubble wrap, fish fingers, Buckingham Palace, sausages,' I said.

The children all burst out laughing and ran off back to the food.

* * *

Some of Theo's elderly aunts were lined up in armchairs along one wall in the sitting room, their eyes busy, seeing everything. It certainly seemed to prove the suggestion that the Mediterranean diet led to longevity.

At last, the terrifying Aunt Hanna stamped her cane on the floor and called me over with the crook of one finger. She indicated that I should sit next to her. I made absolutely sure there wasn't a cat already there first. She had been eating baklava and she gave me her empty plate to put on the table. While I settled myself she brushed flakes of pastry from the impressive bosom of her black dress.

I was a widow too, was I supposed to be in black? Juliette wouldn't approve of that at all, and I wasn't sure I did either.

'So,' she said, 'you are Theocritus' friend we have all heard so much about—'

Theocritus?

'And you are here on holiday. An English tourist. Who has made friends very quickly it seems.'

She made it sound rather sordid.

Oh God.

'And what do you think of Rhodes?' she added, with a piercing look.

Well, I had been trying to learn a few more words of Greek since I was last here, so I thought it was a good opportunity to show willing.

'*Eínai ómorfo edó*,' I said. 'It's very beautiful.'

I looked around for Theo, hoping he would come and rescue me, but he was still outside, surrounded by a gang of young lads I guessed were his nephews.

My gesture towards the Greek language did not go unnoticed.

Aunt Hanna gave a grim smile.

'Ah, you have been learning Greek, good. You like it here?'

'I love it here,' I nodded, hoping to deflect her.

Not a chance.

'Will you stay here or will you leave?'

Good grief, this was worse than I had expected.

'I must go home soon,' I said.

'But you will come back?'

'I'd love to,' I said, my brain incapable of coping with any more Greek.

'Yes, you must. Because Theocritus is a good man, and you are not young. There is no time to waste.'

Oh, cheers Aunt Hanna.

'I am old, I can say things like that,' she said, a tiny spark of humour showing in her eyes although her expression remained severe.

'Yes, you can,' I agreed.

'And you are a widow?' she looked pointedly at my red sweater.

'Yes, I am,' I said.

There was a long, horrible silence.

'How are your feet?' I blurted out at last, slightly manic.

Hanna fixed me with a cold stare.

'I have two.'

'How marvellous,' I gushed, wishing the ground would open up underneath me. I gave a nervous gulp. 'That's always good to hear.'

We stared at each other for another long moment.

'And do you have children?' she asked, her eyes like boot buttons.

I glanced briefly at the heavy gold cross that lay on her chest, covered with a few remaining flakes of baklava. I decide to take my cue from that.

'We did not have the blessing of children,' I said.

Aunt Hanna made a strange, barking noise that I realised was a chuckle.

'Blessings. You young people make me laugh.' She gestured at the old lady sitting next to her and then nudged her with a sharp elbow. 'Did you hear what she said, Eugenia?'

Eugenia, who looked about one hundred if she was a day but who was clutching a glass of wine all the same, turned stiffly in her chair, her face a furrowed map of confusion.

'What? What did she say?'

'She said children are a blessing. *Ta paidiá eínai mia evlogía.*'

'*Ti?*'

'*Ta paidiá eínai mia evlogía.* Children,' Aunt Hanna shouted.

'*O opoíos eípe óti*? Who said that?'

'She did, Sophia said that.' Hanna pointed at me with one bony finger.

'Ah,' Eugenia said, and then she rattled something off.

'I won't translate that,' Aunt Hanna said with a sniff. 'There's no need for that sort of language. But then she is deaf as a stone and twice as stupid. But you are still good to look at, I can't think of the right word. You have kind eyes. You can tell a lot about someone by their eyes. You will be kind.'

It wasn't a question, it was an order.

'I will,' I said, wondering how long this inquisition was going to continue.

'Because if you aren't—' she took hold of her stick which was tucked down the side of her chair and banged it on the floor a couple of times.

Everyone turned to look at us; one of the younger children giggled.

Oh God. Never mind about a bad-tempered dog in her lap, somehow I didn't doubt for a moment that Hanna would whack me if I annoyed her.

She smiled suddenly.

'If you are kind, we might be friends. I'm promising nothing.'

'I'd like that too,' I said.

'Aunt, are you trying to frighten poor Sophia?'

Thank heavens, it was Theo. Or should I say Theocritus?

'You are a wicked old woman,' Theo said, bending down to kiss Hanna's cheek with obvious fondness 'Take no notice of her, Sophia. She's all bark and no bite.'

'Ha! What would you know?' Hanna said, giving him an affectionate look.

Hanna put a cool hand over mine.

'I'm glad to meet you, you may be good for my nephew's heart,' she said.

I felt Theo's hand, gentle in the small of my back.

And I think he may be good for mine, I thought.

'Now before you go, I think you should take the labels off your jacket,' she gestured vaguely at my new blazer.

I looked down rather wildly and eventually saw a swing tag poking out shyly from under my lapel, attached by a gold safety pin. How had I not noticed that?

I removed it and stuffed it into my pocket, I felt a complete fool.

'And now go and eat more food,' Hanna said, waving her stick at the table, 'or everyone will be offended. And you don't want that do you?'

Actually, I was already pretty full. I'd had giant croissants earlier and I'd only just finished eating. Everyone was still milling around the table snarfing up platefuls of food and salads. Now some of the younger ladies were bringing out more platters of desserts and cakes.

Hanna knocked her cane on the floor to catch my attention.

'And bring me some *portokalopita*. The one Nina made, not the one Penelope brought, she uses too much vanilla and not enough syrup.'

Obediently I went back to the table.

Everyone paused to watch me.

'Aunt Hanna wants some *portokalopita*,' I said, hoping someone would point out what it actually was, 'Nina's not Penelope's.'

There was a moment's silence and then a stout, middle-aged woman threw her apron over her face and left the room crying. Two other older ladies followed her, shushing and clucking. I could hear her wailing and babbling in the distance as the other two tried to calm her down.

'I'm guessing that was Penelope,' I hissed to Theo.

24

I spent the next hour trying to make amends for my mistake by sampling everything on the table. The hapless Penelope returned, red-eyed and reproachful after a few minutes and I made a great fuss about her dessert, eating two pieces which would indeed have benefitted from more orange syrup. I made a lot of appreciative noises and then realised the other ladies were watching me, wanting me to try their offerings.

Gamely I ploughed through something called *loukoumades*, which were deep-fried and loaded with sugar so much so that I could almost feel myself spinning. Then a little cup of *rizogalo* which was like a very sweet rice pudding, *milopita,* a cinnamon-spiced apple pie. Then I moved on to some *kourabiedes,* which were little nutty biscuits plastered in icing sugar which splattered all over my face and sweater when I bit into them.

By that point I was definitely having a sugar rush of gigantic proportions and watching the older generation, who were ramming them down at speed, it seemed unlikely any of them were diabetic.

On the other hand, I was absolutely full, covered in powdered sugar and wondering how much more I was expected to eat.

'Have you tried my *galaktoboureko?*'

It was the woman I now knew to be Nina, she of *portokalopita* fame. She gave me a small, conspiratorial smile.

I sent a despairing look at Theo who was on the other side of the table and he bit back a grin.

'I'd love to,' I said, 'everything is so delicious.'

Nina went off to fetch me some and I gave a little whimper.

* * *

'So *Theocritus*, how do you think that went?'

We were hand in hand, walking home a few hours later through a dark evening though I was so full I could hardly walk. I had terrible heartburn and I was also trying very hard not to burp.

Theo laughed. 'I knew Aunt Hanna would tell you, it's quite a name isn't it. Even more Greek than you thought when we first met?'

I put my hand over my face. 'Don't remind me!'

'It's a very old family name,' he said.

'It was a surprise,' I admitted, 'but it's lovely, it suits you. Did I do okay with your family?'

He squeezed my hand. 'You were excellent, everyone thought so. You made a good impression I'm pleased to tell you. I knew you would.'

'Well that's a relief. I won't remember everyone's name though. Apart from Nico and Hanna.'

Theo laughed. 'I warned you. She's a terror. But she liked you too, so you can relax.'

'She did?'

He laughed. 'She did. She always bangs her stick on the floor when she's pleased, or when she wants something. She was sending out a coded message to the room; she liked you.'

'I wish you'd told me that at the time. I was afraid she was going in for the kill. Oh God, I even asked her how her feet were. She must have thought I was crazy.'

He laughed. 'She has recently moved in with Nico. They are both in their nineties, but you'll see, it will give them both a new lease of life, arguing with each other. They will live to a hundred, you wait. Neither of them will want to be the first to die.'

'But who will look after them?' I asked. 'Aren't they too old to live on their own?'

'Nico has a housekeeper who has been with him for years, you met her at the harbour the other day. Irene looks very fierce, but she is a good woman and she will have her work cut out to keep the peace between those two. They have been arguing for eighty years, they'll never stop. And of course, there is family, there are always people dropping in, close at hand.'

'That's nice, I mean being in the middle of all their family like that. Old people can become very lonely can't they?'

I took a deep breath of the cool sea air to try and clear my headache.

'Not here,' Theo said. 'I don't think that happens. The older generation live with the younger ones. They are respected.'

I had occasionally, in my most depressed moments, wondered what was going to happen with me when I was old and maybe infirm. Really, I had no one to call on, to care for me, to look after my affairs. Being in the middle of a big family sounded infinitely better than seeing out my days in a home where I knew no one.

'Hanna will be selling her house, you should look at it,' Theo said. 'You might like it if you wanted to buy somewhere on Rhodes. It's just a thought.'

'It's an interesting thought,' I said, surprised at how much the idea appealed to me, 'you'll have to tell me more about it.'

We stopped walking for a moment and watched as the lights from the town twinkled out across the dark water of the harbour.

'I'm so full. I have eaten far too much,' I said.

'I'm proud of you,' Theo said.

I laughed. 'What for? Eating my body weight in desserts?'

'For being you,' he said. And he kissed me.

* * *

At last we got back to the little house I was already thinking of as home, and I let myself in. I was looking forward to getting my shoes off and changing into my dressing gown. My trousers were not only splattered with powdered sugar but now also rather tight around the waist. What I really needed was a glass of water and a nice lie down. I wondered if I had any indigestion tablets.

'Surprise!'

'Hooray!'

'Happy Birthday!'

I blinked, startled as the lights came on. The room was full of balloons and bunting. Someone had set off a party popper. The Old Ducks were standing around my dining table which was loaded with platters and bowls of food arranged around a very large birthday cake. Juliette was just lighting the candles on top of it. Anita was popping the cork off a bottle of champagne with a shout of delight.

Behind me I could hear Theo laughing.

'We didn't want you to miss out on having a birthday party and your official re-election into the Old Ducks' Club!' Kim shouted. 'Here's to a great holiday, and here's to the next time. Cheers!'

She handed me a glass of champagne which I took with a feeling of some trepidation.

'Well this is definitely a birthday I will never forget,' I said raising my glass to them. 'Here's to the Old Ducks!'

'That was the idea,' Juliette said, giving me a hug. 'It's hours since lunch, you must be starving. Now grab a plate and tuck in!'

25

The Old Ducks left the following morning. The sky was cloudless and to Kim's obvious disappointment, it looked like it would be a sunny day.

We all did a last sweep of the house and then I walked down to the harbour with them as they trundled their suitcases behind them. The taxi was there waiting already in the agreed place, a rather stylish people carrier with plenty of room for them and their luggage. Not to mention the bags of souvenirs and bottles of olive oil they had collected during their stay.

We had a group hug and I think we all felt rather sad. I certainly did.

'Old Ducks forever, remember,' Juliette said as they got into their car and slid the door closed. 'See you soon!'

We all waved at each other as they drove away and into the traffic.

People said that didn't they? But I wouldn't see them again soon.

Rhodes suddenly seemed a lot quieter already.

I walked around for a while, looking at the fishing boats and watching as a beautiful white cruise ship left the harbour. There were people on the many balconies, some of them waving as they left. I waved back to them, wondering where they were cruising to next. Perhaps they were heading to Crete or further afield to Sicily.

Today, instead of just assuming they were a lot of old people crammed together on a boat as Peter had always described it, the prospect of a cruise seemed exciting; after all, they were on what was effectively a five-star hotel taking them to new places every day.

I rather fancied that all of a sudden although I had never been on one. I could even sail from Southampton, travel to the Mediterranean or across the Atlantic to New York. Now what a prospect that would be. Seeing places I had never expected to see except on Google Earth.

Would I feel awkward going on a cruise alone? The prospect of the awful phrase 'single supplement' loomed large. Maybe I would, maybe I wouldn't. I'd think about it. There was no reason why I couldn't go, why I couldn't see more of the world, and who knew, find out more about myself. What I liked, what I didn't like too. Thinking about it, all I needed was a passport, some money and my courage. After two weeks with three of the most determined women I'd ever met, it seemed entirely possible. There was no doubt I had learned a lot from them.

* * *

The house seemed very quiet too without the Old Ducks next door. I had become accustomed to seeing them in their garden perhaps or hearing them banging on my patio doors with a cake or perhaps an invitation to come round to their garden for a barbecue. We had tried that once or twice, and it was only a qualified success because we kept forgetting to turn the food over and burning things. Still, that too had been fun. There had been a lot of laughter over the last two weeks.

My mobile pinged with the arrival of a message from Juliette on the WhatsApp group.

We are at the airport. The driver was shouting at other cars all the way here. We want to come baaaacccckkkk!

I replied.

Missing you already, it's very quiet here 😞!

I imagined them in the airport, scurrying around the shops, buying last-minute gifts, some duty free. Getting on their plane, settling themselves.

I made a cup of tea and went out into the garden to drink it. I took a deep breath and closed my eyes against the sun. This really was such a wonderful place; I was becoming very fond of it. Too much so perhaps.

'Ah, you are back!'

I opened my eyes to see Theo in the next-door garden and I grinned at him.

Now that was one way of taking my mind off losing them.

'*Kaliméra!*' I called.

'I think you mean *kaló apógevma!*' he said. 'It's afternoon. Perhaps you have lost track of the time?'

'I have,' I said, 'I've been seeing my friends off to the airport, and then I watched a cruise ship leaving the harbour. It's such a lovely day.'

'Ah you will be missing them,' he said, 'you will miss their company.'

'Yes, I will,' I said.

'Things did not turn out as you expected?'

'Not at all, but in a good way,' I said.

'That's great to hear.'

Theo started clearing up the garden, wiping the table, putting the chairs upside down on top of it. Instead of leaping up to help him and letting my tea go cold, I watched him. I was enjoying sitting there in my chair, not doing anything.

'Is anyone else booked in? I hope they didn't leave too much for you to do?' I said.

'No, they were the last of the season this year. And it's not too bad at all,' he said, 'it is generally the family groups who leave the mess, but I understand that if they have children to get ready to leave. There is always something left behind. A toy or a wet swimming costume. Such ladies as these on their own are no trouble.'

Well that was generous, I thought, considering the facts.

He started sweeping the patio, clearing up the fallen leaves and probably a few of Kim's cigarette ends.

'Apart from when they first arrive, and they can be a little... *eínai ypervoliká enthousaisménoi*... excited,' he added.

'You're right,' I said with a smile.

'Or when they get into a little trouble,' he added with a comical look.

'Very true.'

'But I like meeting new people, and if they hadn't come here to stay, I might not have met them or you,' he said.

'That's true as well.'

He leaned on the end of his broom. 'And I would have had to do my painting and decorating on my own. Which would be very sad.'

Ah yes, the painting and decorating.

'When are you starting that?' I said.

'Maybe tomorrow morning. I have things to do today. Will you help? You don't have to, I just thought it might be pleasant to spend some time together.'

'Yes, of course,' I said. 'I'll be there.'

I wondered what I would wear, something I wouldn't mind getting paint on I supposed, which really didn't rule out a lot of my holiday wardrobe. I realised that in the last few years I had been buying clothes to just cover me rather than flatter my figure. And I still did have a figure.

But that made me think about going shopping and some things that had struck me over the years. Why was it that men's shirts were better made and cheaper than women's blouses? And why didn't designers make dresses with decent length sleeves and – the actual, genuine Holy Grail – *pockets*? They would make an absolute fortune. There wasn't a woman born who didn't need pockets, for a phone, some tissues, random stuff, and yet you'd think they were prohibited by law. One of life's mysteries.

When I had the chance, I was going to find a dress with sleeves and pockets and buy them in every colour that wasn't black or navy blue. Some more colourful things. Maybe not as bright as Juliette would choose, but something along those lines. And something flattering, something attractive, maybe even slightly fitted.

'It was nice to see Hera again. She seems lovely, and so kind too.'

'Oh yes, but she is home now. I wish we saw more of her but she is so busy.'

'It was kind of her to come and sort things out for Juliette. She rescued us from a very difficult situation.'

'She's very capable, very clever,' he said.

'Would you like a cup of tea?' I said at last.

'Thank you, no, I have things to do. I will leave you in peace to drink yours, and I will see you soon,' he said.

He finished his sweeping and tidying and kissed me before he went back indoors.

I felt almost a little disappointed, but then again not really. I knew he was nearby, but he wasn't crowding me, pressurising me. It was pleasant to have some time to myself here in this quiet garden with just my tea and the birds chirruping. For the first time, being on my own didn't seem like a negative thing.

A ginger cat slowly walked across the top of the wall at the end of the garden on some casual errand, and then jumped down out of sight. I leaned my head back against the chair and closed my eyes again. Now this was lovely.

* * *

I had a little snooze and thought about what I was going to do with the rest of my time in Rhodes. I really should get out and see more of this gorgeous island. Perhaps I had been wrong not to hire a car. There was a fabulous coastline, the ancient site of Kamiros which predated anything the Knights Templar did, Kallithea Springs, Tsambika Monastery if I could face the roughly 300 steps up to it to experience the wonderful views. And although I wasn't a fan of beaches as a rule, some of them looked gorgeous. I would look up other ferry tours and bus tours and timetables, I couldn't just rely on Theo to drive me about. Although he didn't seem to object. Perhaps I would hire a car next time I came here. Because there was going to be a next time.

And I still had to do the buying fresh fish from the boat thing. Although in a way, we had done that. Perhaps I would research some recipes first or watch some tutorials online. I knew Rick Stein made cooking fish look easy and just threw in handfuls of ingredients with a merry laugh to make a Michelin-starred meal, but I doubted I could. And I was bound not to have the one herb that made it special. I was terrible for overcooking fish anyway, I never trusted the *flash fry for thirty seconds* business; apart from anything else, to get the pan hot enough to achieve that meant the kitchen would fill up with smoke and set all the alarms off. I was used to producing fish that was like old shoe leather and no amount of

cunning little garnishes and dollops of tartare sauce could disguise
the fact.

In the meantime, I needed to do some washing and general
tidying up. All the going out and late nights had meant I'd been a
bit sloppy around the house. I'd opted out of the maid service
coming round each week and had found clean towels and sheets in
the airing cupboard. Perhaps it was time to do some laundry. Actually, I thought I'd quite enjoy that; a bit of domesticity and cleaning
could be quite therapeutic on occasion, and at least I only had
myself to think about.

I found all the cleaning things I needed and had a good go at it;
the house was so small it didn't take long anyway, and the washing
was soon hanging outside on the rotary drier. I looked around me
with pleasure. How wonderful not to have a house with several
bathrooms to clean, stairs to hoover – and possibly fall down –
shelves full of books and box files that collected dust, a lawn that
always seemed to need mowing. There was a great deal to be said
for a simpler life. This was an interesting thought. Would this frame
of mind work for me as a lifestyle choice? What would I miss I
wondered?

Would I be able to downsize my whole life? Stop keeping things
I had no need for, stop buying things at car boot sales in the hope
they would fill some void in my life which I could see now was
caused by basic dissatisfaction, not the actual need for yet another
cotton scarf or flower vase? It was a very interesting thought.

I put away the dusters and polish, made myself a sandwich and
another cup of tea and went outside to enjoy them both.

I thought about the possibilities. It was rather exciting. I could
almost imagine myself getting rid of my big house on the Wood-
stock Road and living in a sort of classy hermit's cave with a few
possessions on roughly hewn stone shelves.

I didn't think it would bother me to live alone now. I probably didn't need the sounds of my postgraduate lodgers arguing over the fridge contents in their shared kitchen, or the thumping of some Mahler symphony (Nigel) tussling through the walls with Miles Davis at full throttle (Leo). But I would need electricity of course. And running water. And a washing machine, a television and central heating and a fridge and freezer, quite big ones because of course I would not be going out shopping so much. Would I get rid of my car? Driving and parking in Oxford was an absolute nightmare anyway. Perhaps my idea of a *classy hermit's cave* was a bit unrealistic. If I stayed where I was I could turn my small garden over to vegetables when I got back and become almost self-sufficient.

The Good Life in Oxford starring Sophia Gregory.

But that would mean I'd need to buy a lot of tools and vegetable accessories that I didn't have. Dibbers and balls of twine and special tins for seed packets. I had occasionally watched *Gardener's World* on television, marvelling at their knowledge of Latin names and which plant should go where. How would I learn all that? I knew nothing about gardening. And would I need a greenhouse?

See, it wasn't quite that simple when I thought about it. And where would all my clothes and shoes and winter coats go? And I'd need Wi-Fi. The problems of twenty-first century life.

26

I decided to go to bed early that night after a quietly enjoyable evening on the sofa eating pita bread and taramasalata from the market. It was delicious. And nothing like the usual stuff I bought from the supermarket.

It was funny spending an evening on my own, and yet now I wasn't lonely; at last I felt comfortable with my own company. Theo was nearby, but not crowding me, there was none of the desperation I had felt with Lucian, a mad pleasure when he was with me, and a terrible restlessness when he wasn't.

I turned on the television and watched some more of the Greek soap operas.

The same women with the big eyebrows seemed to be locked in the same argumentative relationship with the man with the tattoos except now they were now standing in the dark somewhere under a motorway bridge and it was raining on them. At least it meant their clothes stayed on but how they managed to chase after him in stilettos I had no idea.

The chat show that followed had a man dressed as a clown having a heated discussion with a woman in a tight black trouser suit who had anger management issues. It was absolutely riveting. But perhaps I wouldn't need television in my superior hermit's cave after all. I had the feeling I would get fed up of it all pretty quickly.

Up in bed, enjoying the clean sheets, I smiled approvingly at the newly cleared bedside table. Then I logged on to the internet, did a little bit of browsing and sent a message to the Old Ducks group. Then I went to sleep, perfectly happy. In the morning I had a date with some paint rollers and Theo.

* * *

At eight-thirty the following morning I was up, showered and dressed in jeans and a T-shirt waiting for Theo to arrive. I was really quite excited at the prospect of spending the day with him and doing the decorating. What on earth was happening to me?

He arrived just before nine o'clock and rapped on my patio door.

'I haven't had breakfast yet, perhaps we should,' he said.

We went out together first to the bakery at the end of the lane and bought croissants, warm and flaky from the oven. We ate them in my kitchen with apricot jam and salted butter and a cafetière of fresh coffee. He took his coffee black with sugar. He ate with evident pleasure.

'I do love these, I don't indulge too often, but this feels a special occasion,' he said. He winked at me across the table.

'It does,' I said. 'I love that bakery. I'm going to miss it when I go back.'

I was aware I hadn't said *when I go home*.

'You may change your mind when we have been painting all day and you are bored and your muscles are aching.'

'When that happens, I will make my excuses and go!' I said.

'That seems fine,' he said, he reached across the table, took my hand and kissed it, 'but I will lure you back with wine and bread and honey.'

'I can be lured,' I said. I admired my bracelet again. 'And thank you for this, it's so lovely.'

'I'm happy you like it. Now, we should do more than just talk about painting. We should get on with our work. I brought all my things over yesterday. Are you okay wearing that or do you want to borrow something?'

The thought of wearing one of his old shirts was a bit too much like having a teenage crush so I declined.

'I'll be fine,' I said, standing up. 'I'll just clear up a bit here and then I'll be right over.'

He caught my hand. 'You will come back, won't you?'

I realised he wasn't talking about this morning, he meant something else entirely.

'I will, I promise,' I said, 'of course I will.'

He pulled me down towards him and kissed me.

'Now you've had the chance to get over meeting my family I'll take you out this evening for a special meal in honour of your birthday, and to reward you for the painting, would you like that?'

'I would like that very much indeed,' I said.

'I'll get everything ready,' he said, 'I'll see you next door.'

After clearing away our breakfast things, I dithered about for a bit. I changed my T-shirt for an older one and ran a brush through my hair. Should I put on some make-up? No, probably not. I wavered about this for a few minutes and was about to leave the house when I dashed back and put on some mascara. I should at least have some eyelashes. And then, remembering Juliette, I added some lipstick.

Theo had pulled the furniture into the middle of the room and covered it in dust sheets. He was wearing exactly the sort of generic blue workman's overalls I'd already imagined, and I briefly wondered if he was wearing anything underneath. I swallowed down a snort of laughter. I'd better not think about that or I'd never get anything done.

Paint was poured out into roller trays; he started one side of the room, I started on the other. I hadn't really noticed that the walls were at all grimy, but a sweep of new, white paint showed that they were. There was something very enjoyable about decorating when it didn't involve wallpaper. I had no idea how to do that and no particular desire to learn.

He put the radio on and there was music in the background. We didn't talk much, it was just companionable and restful. There was a lot to be said for that.

'Have you done much decorating?' he asked at one point.

'No, my house in Oxford has a lot of furniture, a great many books and far too much clutter. The prospect of clearing a room is too awful to contemplate. And anyway, Peter would never have tolerated the mess and muddle. He could be a bit resistant to change. I don't think he would have been able to choose a new paint colour. Or any colour to be honest.'

'It's good to do this,' Theo said. 'I always do it when the season ends, and the house is going to be closed up for the winter. A fresh start.'

Yes, a fresh start. We all needed that sometimes, didn't we?

'It's a lovely house,' I said. 'It has a nice feeling. My friends enjoyed their time here. They want to come back next year.'

'They would be very welcome,' Theo said.

He was working alongside me by now; he covered the walls faster than I did. He also had a stepladder so that he could reach to the top of the walls while I concentrated on the lower levels. I wasn't great up ladders.

We had almost finished when he came down to fill up his roller tray again.

'We are getting on so well, we are nearly finished, the workload is halved,' he said, standing back to appreciate what we had done.

'I'm enjoying doing it, really I am,' I said. I was standing admiring my work too while he went back up the stepladder.

I'm not sure how it happened. I think I knocked against him, or maybe he lost his balance for a second. The flag stone floors were uneven after all, so it wouldn't have been surprising.

'No! Look out!'

Foolishly, I turned towards him, just as his full tray of paint splattered against my head. Then there was the cold and very unpleasant sensation of a great deal of white paint soaking me from head to toe.

I stood for a moment, speechless and shocked. And then I let out a wail.

'Aaagh!'

'Oh Sophia! I'm so sorry!'

I stood stock-still, holding my arms out from my sides, not daring to move in case I made even more mess than there was already.

I heard the stepladder rattle as Theo clambered down.

'Oh dear. How could I be so clumsy?'

I blinked hard and looked down at myself. I could have been iced.

'What shall I do?' I said.

Paint dripped into my mouth and I spat it out rather inelegantly.

'I think we need to get you outside, so you can – well take your clothes off I suppose,' he said. 'I'll put another dustsheet down for you to walk on.'

His voice was a bit funny. I realised it was because he was trying very hard not to laugh.

I walked, stiff-legged, robot-like out of the house onto the patio while he arranged the dustsheet and some pieces of cardboard for me to walk on and suddenly I started laughing too. How I was ever going to get all this paint off I had no idea. Perhaps he would have to hose me down?

He had some kitchen roll in his hand and he gently wiped the paint off my face, still chuckling.

'I'm so sorry,' he said.

'It's fine,' I said, trying to stop laughing and catch my breath, 'it's absolutely fine. Honestly.'

He dabbed at my lips and then kissed me, coming away with paint all over his face, which made me laugh even more.

'I've got to get out of these clothes and into a shower,' I said. 'How am I going to manage that?'

'I don't know. Look, I'll get another dust sheet, you can get undressed under that while I hold it up.'

'Perhaps you could find a couple of plastic bags for my feet?' I said, 'so I don't tread paint all over the floor.'

'Okay, good idea, stay there,' he said.

Well obviously I would, there was nowhere else to go really.

He came back with a fairly clean dustsheet which he wrapped around me after I took my clothes off. It was not as easy as it sounds. It's very hard to peel off paint-soaked jeans however baggy they are. Then he held out two supermarket carrier bags for me to step into while the paint dripped down my legs. I rested one hand on the top of his head while he did so, leaving a fairly recognisable handprint in his silver hair.

'Are you going to be okay?' he said, 'getting upstairs and into the shower?'

'I'll be fine,' I said.

'Please be careful.'

I took a deep breath and started my ungainly progress towards the patio doors.

'I think you need to tie something around these carrier bags,' I said after a few steps, 'otherwise they are going to slip off.'

Theo went back into his house and came back with some big elastic bands which he slipped over my feet and up to my knees to keep the carrier bags in place.

This, now this, was a moment of true glamour.

I bet Joan Collins would have liked to give this a try when it came to being alluring.

'I look ridiculous,' I said, and started laughing again.

'You do,' he agreed, 'but very sweet too. I'll come round with some fresh towels. Now go and clean up, I'll see you very soon, my little painted lady.'

I plodded through the house towards the stairs, trying hard not to drip paint everywhere, longing to get into the shower. Paint is, after all, very cold. And wet.

As I passed my front door, someone knocked.

I don't know why I opened it. I supposed I thought it was Theo with the new towels. Perhaps I just wasn't thinking straight. I vaguely hoped he didn't have a camera in order to record my appearance for posterity.

'Shall I strike a pose?' I said as I opened the door.

I adopted the classic one; hand behind my head, hip stuck out under the paint sodden dustsheet. I was aware paint was dribbling down my face again.

'Sophia! What in God's name are you doing?'

My eyes flashed open.

I blinked hard a couple of times. Partly through shock, partly because of the dribbles of white paint tracking down my forehead.

Yes, there was no doubt about it.

'Lucian!'

'What the hell are you up to?' Lucian said.

'Aaagh!'

I clutched the dustsheet a bit more tightly around myself, which felt even more horrible than it sounds.

I took a step back away from him in my rustling, carrier bag wellingtons, I supposed under some concern that otherwise I would get paint all over him too, and he stepped forwards into the house, pulling a large, wheeled case behind him.

27

He dumped his case in the middle of the room and pulled out his mobile phone. He stood, oblivious of me, checking his emails.

'What's the Wi-Fi code?' he said.

'You don't need to know because you're not staying,' I said, hitching up my dustsheet with as much dignity as I could. 'Go away.'

He sighed. 'Look Sophia, I'll explain everything in a minute. For now, I need the Wi-Fi code, it's important. I am waiting for a lot of emails. From my publisher for one.'

I handed over the laminated postcard with the Wi-Fi code on it.

'Can't you read it out to me, I can't find my reading glasses.'

'Capital G. Lower case o. Capital A. Lower case w, a, y,' I said.

He typed it in obediently.

'It says password incorrect – oh I see what you're doing. Very amusing.'

He grabbed the card out of my hand and fumbled in his jacket pocket for his spectacles. Then he typed in the correct password.

'Right, password accepted. Now explain to me why you are

wandering around half naked covered in paint,' he said. 'And I need a drink. Where do you keep the whisky?'

'I haven't got any whisky. What are you doing here?'

'Wine then,' he said.

He started opening cupboards and eventually found a glass and an opened bottle of red wine. He pulled the cork out with his teeth and spat it on the floor. The cork was only pushed a short way into the bottle by the way, Lucian didn't have the sort of dentition to do that without a corkscrew. That would have been very odd.

He took a deep slug of the wine and sighed.

'Ah! That's better, now for God's sake, what *are* you doing?'

'What are you doing more's the point?' I said, feeling my anger rapidly rising. 'I didn't invite you here. I don't want you here.'

'Well that's as may be, but I'm here now,' he said, finishing off his wine and refilling the glass. 'Perhaps you should—' he gestured with his glass at my unusual garb.

'I'm going upstairs to have a shower,' I said furiously. 'Stay here, don't touch anything and don't do anything.'

He gave me a mock salute and sat down on the sofa with a groan.

I went up as fast as I could without losing my plastic bag boots or falling down the stairs, and then got into the shower. I stood and scrubbed myself and shampooed my hair four times and it still didn't feel right. Paint washed out didn't it?

I remembered my father rinsing out his brushes in white spirit; I hoped it didn't come to that. I hoped I wouldn't need to just shave my head.

I waited at the top of the stairs, listening to see if Lucian was still where I had left him. He was on the phone, so I eavesdropped for a few minutes.

'Yes... yes... no... I'm doing what I think is right... no, well that's just what I would have expected... I'm doing what I think is right...

yes you would say that wouldn't you... she is delusional... I told you... she's not... she said what? That's libellous. I'm going to... no listen will you...'

I went into my bedroom and closed the door, wedging a chair under the handle for good measure. Then I tried to decide what to wear; I wanted to feel business-like and in control of the situation, which I obviously wasn't. I chose some smart-ish trousers and a dark sweatshirt. And then I brushed my wet hair out of the way and put on some make-up, like a sort of armour. What lipstick would Juliette have chosen for this occasion, I wondered? I chose a dark red one that I seldom used. I looked pale, I wasn't sure about being interesting as well.

As I went downstairs there was silence. Lucian was sitting where I had left him, with his hands on his knees. He looked somehow older than I remembered, with deep lines running down from his nose towards his mouth. His hair looked greyer. He'd opened another bottle of wine and had a full glass in front of him.

He looked up when he heard me.

'There you are at last,' he said. He didn't stand up; it was as though he didn't have the energy.

'Lucian, what are you doing here?' I said.

I noticed a few drips of white paint on the stairs and I went to get a cloth to wipe them up.

'I needed to get away,' he said. 'It's not just you that needs a break from work.'

'Break from work? This isn't a break from work, Lucian, I've resigned.'

'Yes. You resigned, so you took up decorating instead I suppose,' he said sarcastically.

'I was helping a friend.' I scrubbed at one particularly big splash on the kitchen floor. 'Not that it's any of your business how I spend my time when I'm on a holiday I have paid for.'

He dropped his face into his hands.

'Why are you here? And how did you know where to find me?'

'You left an address with the main office in case there were any emergencies. Well, this is an emergency,' he said.

'What is?'

He looked evasive. I knew what that meant.

'And don't bother lying to me Lucian,' I said.

He took a deep breath. 'I'm in a spot of bother. I thought I knew Gina My Wife pretty well, but when she found out about Poppy, she went a bit crazy.'

'Could you please stop calling her *Gina My Wife* like that? It's like she doesn't exist as an independent human being. Only an adjunct to you and your greatness.'

He looked up suspiciously.

'She said something similar actually. Have you been talking to her?'

'Don't be ridiculous.'

'Gina My – Gina got in touch with the vice chancellor. She told him what had happened. She told the children, she told her parents, she told her sister – who sent me a very offensive message by the way. I've never seen such language. She told our neighbours, and Malcolm Wilson has never been able to keep a confidence. The whole university will know by now. She even went to seek out Poppy and when she found her, they had a nasty row in the Oxford University Press bookshop. Which was, of course, full at the time, full of students, a lot of them *mine*. And someone took a video with one of their blasted phones. I'm guessing it will be all over social media by now. The upshot of that was that Poppy put in an official complaint. About Gina. And me too. I mean okay, I might have overstepped the mark, but she wasn't exactly innocent. It takes two. And I don't remember her complaining at the time.'

'She's an absolute child compared to you,' I said, wiping some paint off the worktop.

'Child? Hardly. She led me on, there's no doubt about it,' Lucian blustered pompously.

'And of course, you were so weak-willed you couldn't say to her, hey Poppy, put your clothes back on, I'm old enough to be your grandfather. I might have a heart attack or a stroke or something. You don't want that on your CV, do you?'

'Oh God, I don't know,' he grumbled, knocking back some more wine and topping up his glass. 'Stop being so literal.'

'So, then what happened?'

'I've been temporarily suspended, pending enquiries,' he muttered.

'I'm not surprised,' I said.

'Look can you stop wandering around wiping things and listen to me?' he said. 'I've been travelling for hours, I need to rest. I need something to eat. I had a sandwich at the airport and that was a long time ago.'

'Don't tell me what to do. Go and find something to eat. And stop drinking my wine.'

His mouth tightened in annoyance and he topped up his glass yet again until it almost overflowed.

'I came to you because I thought you understood me.'

'I do understand you, Lucian. That's the problem.'

'So please, can you be the old Sophia again? The one who was always so supportive and kind? The one who made me such lovely meals.'

He looked at me with hangdog eyes, appealing for sympathy.

'Please, I'm desperate. I'm at the end of my tether. The university is going to question me, question her and probably anyone else who wants to slander me. Unless I can get her to withdraw her complaint. And get Gina back on my side. I know what it's like these days. One person says something and everyone else wants to jump on the bandwagon.'

'Lucian, I really don't care. It was an abuse of your position, can't you see that? I was old enough to make my decisions, however wrong they were, but a twenty-year-old girl away from home?'

'She was twenty-one.'

'Don't split hairs.'

'You and I had something special, Sophia. We were going to – you know?'

'We were going to what? Get married? I don't think so.'

'I was going to say we were going to have a future together. When the children were off my hands.'

'You keep calling them children, but they are all in their thirties, Lucian. When exactly *were* they going to be off your hands? And no, we weren't going to have a future together, and in a way I'm grateful that I found out about Poppy. It opened my eyes.'

'Oh God, Sophia,' he said, 'be kind, I've got no one at the moment.'

'That's very sad for you.'

He stood up and came towards me.

'Please Sophia.' He fixed me with his grey eyes, which were still beautiful of course. 'I need you. Please help me through this.'

Before I could stop him, he'd thrown his arms around me and was practically sobbing on my shoulder. Unfortunately, I was still holding the damp cloth in front of me and some of the paint transferred itself to his leather jacket.

Behind me I heard the patio door open.

'Sophia? You've been a long time. Are you alright?'

Oh God, it was Theo.

He stood watching me, watching us, his hand still on the door handle. A couple of towels under his arm.

'I'm sorry. I came to see if there was anything wrong,' Theo said, 'and to give you these.'

He dropped the towels on the coffee table.

I pushed Lucian away, depositing more paint on his shirt.

'Theo, yes I'm fine.'

Theo looked at Lucian, who was scrubbing at his jacket with a handkerchief.

'I'm sorry I didn't know you had visitors,' he said.

'I don't,' I said. 'At least, I wasn't expecting anyone.'

'Shall I leave you to it?' Theo said.

'No! Please don't go. This is someone who has called in very unexpectedly. He's just leaving.'

'No I'm not,' Lucian said.

'Yes, you are, Lucian.'

Theo turned and gave an incredulous laugh. '*This*? This is Lucian?'

'He's just turned up,' I said, awkwardly, 'I didn't invite him.'

'I'll just go and finish clearing up,' Theo said and left.

I turned and punched Lucian's arm as hard as I could.

'You bloody idiot!'

'Ow! There's no call for that. I never thought you capable of physical violence. Who was that? I demand to know who that man is!' Lucian said, rubbing the spot on his arm where I had hit him. 'I demand you tell me. What have you been up to?'

'You *demand*? Who do you think you are? I don't have to explain myself to you!' I said and stamped out of the house.

'But I'm starving,' he called after me rather pathetically.

28

Theo was in the living room of the Old Ducks' house, sorting out the paint pots and collecting up the dust sheets. It looked as though he'd managed to clear up most of the mess we had created, though there were still some splatters of white on the stones outside where I had shed my clothes.

Theo turned as I came in. 'I hope you are okay?'

'Well yes, but no, I'm not at all okay with this.'

'Then what will you do?'

'I'm sorry.'

Theo turned back to his paint pots, cleaning some excess paint off the roller onto the wall.

'Sophia, you don't need to apologise to me. You don't need to explain yourself to me. You are an adult; you can do whatever you think is right.'

'I'm trying to get him to leave,' I said.

'Of course.'

He turned away; I had the feeling he didn't quite believe me. This made me feel doubly uncomfortable.

I made my way back to my house. My mobile rattled in my pocket and I stopped. It was a WhatsApp message from Juliette.

So how's it going? Everything okay? I've been out with Matthew!!! He's so nice. 😊

I sank down onto one of the patio chairs and composed a reply.

How lovely, I hope things go well for you both. Everything here was going great. Then Lucian arrived today. Just turned up at the front door. I don't know what to do.

I waited for her to respond, casting a nervous look at my back door, wondering what Lucian was doing in there.

No!!! That's terrible. Tell him to sling his hook. 🙁

I've tried. He's having problems.

Oh poor old him – said no one ever. 🙁

And then one from Anita.

Just about to go out flat hunting for A & G. Tell Lucian to leave pronto!

I will.

I went back inside at that point while my phone pinged and rattled with messages.

'Where have you been?' Lucian said.

He had moved from the sofa and was looking in the kitchen cupboards.

'What are you looking for?' I said crossly. 'Stop poking about.'

'I'm hungry,' he said, 'you'd be hungry too if you hadn't had anything to eat since first thing this morning. And then had to travel for hours on a budget plane where everything is overpriced and there is a stag party behind you with cans of beer and huge bags of Doritos stinking the place out. Nothing said to them. And I had hardly any room, so my knees were practically under my chin. *And* there was a child wailing somewhere. It was all my nightmares at once.'

I walked in front of him and slammed the cupboard door shut, almost trapping his fingers.

'*Ow!* Watch out!'

'Go away.'

'Oh come on, Sophia. I thought at least we could be civil to each other.'

'Well, I thought I was being fairly civil actually, Lucian. I haven't hit you with a blunt instrument, tasered you or phoned the police to tell them I have an unwanted intruder. And trust me, the Greek police would probably do both of those things.'

'You punched my arm,' he said reproachfully, 'and you got paint on my new jacket. I needed to see you, I needed somewhere to go, time to regroup. That's all. I'd also quite like a shower before I go,' he said.

My spirits rose.

'So you're saying you'll have a shower and then you'll go?'

'Absolutely. I'm not one to outstay my welcome,' he said pompously.

'Then go and have a shower. Take these towels with you.'

'Are they his towels?' Lucian said suspiciously.

'Yes, they are. It's these or you can dry yourself off on your hand-kerchief.'

He stamped off up the stairs with his case, turning halfway to speak to me.

'Something to eat would be nice too, if it's not too much trouble?'

'It is,' I said.

'Thanks,' he blew me a kiss, 'perhaps some of your lovely pasta alla puttanesca? I've really missed that.'

'Not a chance in hell.'

I heard the bathroom door close and a bit of thumping about and then it went quiet.

I cleared away the wine bottle and washed up the glasses and cleaned away the last traces of him from my sitting area.

Was I still going out with Theo this evening as he had suggested? I hoped so, but I wouldn't blame him if he had gone off the whole idea. I mean what would I have done if an old girlfriend of his had turned up out of the blue? If I had found him with his arms around another woman?

By then it was late afternoon.

It was funny, I'd always found that an irritating time; that space between the day and the evening when nothing really happens if you aren't in the middle of cooking something for the evening meal. Which I definitely wasn't.

Lucian was still upstairs, I could hear his footsteps clomping about, stopping, moving around again. I hoped he wasn't poking through my stuff.

'Lucian,' I called up the stairs, 'It's time you left.'

No reply.

After a few minutes I went up. He was out of the bathroom, leaving two wet towels on the floor behind him and he hadn't bothered to use the shower screen wiper thing. I followed the trail of wet footprints and tentatively opened my bedroom door.

'Lucian? Are you okay?'

I couldn't believe my eyes. Another damp towel lay in a heap on the floor in front of me and Lucian was actually, astonishingly, in bed. In my bed, with his laptop open on his knee.

'Oh hello,' he said, 'I thought I'd just have a little rest. I hope you don't mind?'

'Yes, I do flaming well mind,' I shouted, 'get out!'

'I don't feel very well,' he said, 'so I thought I'd have a little lie down.'

I grabbed the end of the bedclothes and tried to tug them off the bed. He seized hold of his end of them and for a few minutes we had an undignified tussle which he won, clutching the sheets around his neck and head like an outraged nun.

'Get out of my bed!' I shouted, 'or I'll call the police!'

He fell back against my lovely plump pillows and groaned.

'I think I might have food poisoning,' he said.

'I swear to God, if you throw up on my bed, I really will kill you!' I said, clenching my fists and advancing towards him.

'Leave me alone. I'm ill,' he wailed feebly.

I stamped back downstairs in a furious temper and went outside to where the afternoon light was fading and sat down in one of the patio chairs. I felt like crying. Everything had been going so well, the future had seemed to hold such possibilities and now this.

'Are you all right, Sophia?'

It was Theo, lovely Theo, standing uncertainly in the next-door garden.

'No, I'm not all right,' I said, and infuriatingly my lower lip started to tremble.

'Perhaps I understand. You are sad because your friend has gone?' he said.

'No! Absolutely not! I'm frustrated because he *won't* go. He's had a shower and got into bed and he's saying he's ill and I can't seem to get rid of him and... and...'

I paused to draw breath and try to calm down.

'...and I was so happy!'

I heard Theo laugh, but it was in a sympathetic and kind way.

He knelt down in front of me and gave me a hug.

'Poor Sophia. The man is foolish.'

'That's putting it mildly,' I said, 'he's a selfish—'

I didn't finish the sentence. I didn't want to start with the expletives just yet.

I mopped myself up and blew my nose.

'Sorry,' I said.

I wasn't a child, but this had been such a threshold point in my life, a new and exciting time that had been waiting to start. Lucian had barged back in, into my lovely little house, into my shower and now into my bed.

'You need something to cheer you up, we will sort this out tomorrow,' Theo said. He hugged me again. 'Come on, forget about him, let's go out.'

'You still want to go out?' I said, looking up at him hopefully, 'I thought you would change your mind.'

He laughed. 'Why would I change my mind? We still need to celebrate your birthday properly. We still need to eat.'

'I've left my lovely bracelet in the house; I took it off when we started the painting.'

'Then let's go and find it, and then dry your tears, we will go out, we will drink wine, we will toast your birthday, we will enjoy ourselves. Come on!'

So that's what we did. I found my gold bracelet on the kitchen worktop where I had left it, and a good job I had or it would have been covered in paint. Theo bent over my wrist, carefully fastening the catch, making sure it was secure. Then, despite the fact that I was hardly dressed for a glamorous evening out, we set off together and as we reached the end of the lane, Theo took my hand.

Young people didn't seem to do that any more, did they? Hold hands. I wondered why not. Perhaps it wasn't the cool thing to do any more. Sometimes you saw an elderly couple arm in arm, but perhaps that was more for mutual support? But holding hands with someone was different. Was it possessive or affectionate or a bit of both? It was a sign though, wasn't it? This person is with me. I liked that.

'Let's have cocktails first,' Theo said as we passed a tremendously chic wine bar. It was all mirrors and glass-topped tables and steel chairs. We were still early so it wasn't too crowded either. Just a couple of sharp-suited chaps with the sort of very pointy shoes that young men seemed to like these days. There was a languid redhead draped over one of them, her calculating cat's eyes looking at Theo over the rim of her Martini.

'What would you like, birthday girl?' he said. He smiled at me and I think I was blushing. It was a good job the lights were low.

Anyway, I was beginning to feel better.

I looked at the very long menu which was chalked up on a board behind the bar, while the barman, immaculate in his white shirt and black trousers, polished a glass and then jiggled a bottle of champagne in an ice bath at the end of the bar.

'I was going to have a margarita because I know I like them, but I'll have a Beam Me Up Biscotti,' I said at last. 'I don't know what it is but I've never heard of it and it sounds fun.'

'Make that two,' Theo said. 'We can be beamed up together.'

It was indeed fun; it was strong and tasted of coffee and orange and made me feel a lot better. Perhaps that was the courage of a strong drink on an empty stomach? Well I would take that for the time being. The afternoon had rattled me more than I'd perhaps realised. The past seeking to wriggle back into the present, where it had no place to be. I wasn't going to allow it.

When we had finished, we wandered off down the street towards the harbour. It was getting colder now, and dark. I shivered, wishing I had brought a warmer jacket. Theo put his arm around me.

'Not too cold?'

'A bit,' I said.

I didn't want him to take his arm away. I liked the touch of it there. I could feel the heat from him warming me. Perhaps that was sort of symbolic. He had warmed me in so many ways. Other couples were passing us, some of them arm in arm, similarly unhurried, enjoying the evening. I felt a part of it, I was like them. At last I was in a relationship where I felt comfortable and valued and content.

We reached the taverna at last, looking out over the harbour where the lights were glowing in the dusk. The boats, the buildings, the strings of lights looped between lamp posts and awnings. It looked almost magical.

We were greeted with many smiles and handshakes by the owner who I think was another of Theo's cousins and then we were shown to a wonderful table upstairs where we could look out over the dark sea. The wine-dark sea; that was Homer wasn't it? I didn't think there could have been a better spot anywhere.

I could feel my mood rising again, my confidence in myself returning little by little. I could get through this. Nothing was lost after all; we were still friends. I was still me.

Lucian might be sleeping, drooling over my bedlinen, snoring fit to rattle the windows; at that moment I didn't care. I could deal with him and I would.

* * *

We had meze, a dark green ceramic platter filled with little dishes of tasty treats. Garlicky hummus, fava dip, olives, crisp hot pita breads, tiny dolmades and keftedes, feta cubes, breadsticks, roasted red peppers and crudités. Plump shrimps, salted almonds, artichoke hearts in olive oil that tasted of the sun. Ripe cheese and little bruschetta. Everything was delicious and perfect. One flavour melding beautifully into another.

'This is such a treat,' I said. 'Do you know, when I first came here, I had to learn to eat all over again. I mean I know how to *eat* obviously, but to eat slowly. To savour everything.'

He approved of this. 'We are all in too much of a hurry these days. The Greeks are not a race for fast foods as a rule. We like to take our time over our meals. We like to talk.'

'Yes, that too,' I said.

'So, will you talk to me, Sophia?'

I looked into his dark eyes. I knew what he meant.

'Of course,' I said at last.

'Then please tell me. What is this Lucian to you? Why is he here? Why does he look at you with need in his eyes? And why do you look at him with distaste in yours?'

I paused, touched my napkin to my lips, drank some wine.

'We were in a relationship,' I said slowly at last. 'A relationship which has ended.'

'And yet he is here, today, in your house?'

'I didn't invite him, I told you that.' I took another sip of my wine. 'He is having trouble at home. His job is at risk, his family are angry with him. His wife—'

'His *wife?*'

Oh God. Of course, Theo hadn't known this, hadn't realised my part as the other woman. Although the story was more complicated than that because actually, I was the *other*, other woman.

I took a deep breath. I wanted to tell him, I was going to be honest, but I was afraid of how he would react when he learned of my unacceptable behaviour. And only recently I'd had the nerve to be annoyed with him when I thought he was messing me around. Talk about double standards.

I sat up a little straighter in my chair.

'Yes, he is married. I'm not proud of what I did. I could make excuses; I could say I was lost and lonely when Peter died, and it would be true. I could say I was at a low point in my life and that would be true too. I could say I was flattered and excited and astonished that another man – any man – would want me or need me and that would be true. But I could also be honest and say I behaved badly, that there are no excuses, that I am ashamed and sorry for everything. And that would be the absolute truth.'

'I see,' he said.

He sipped his wine and snapped a breadstick in half.

'And now?'

'Now? I want to start my life again. I want to be a better person. Stronger. To believe in myself.'

'And how will you do that? When this man still lives near you, is still expecting your support?'

I thought about it. Theo was right. I needed to think long-term, to plan my life from this day on. Not just drift from one week, one month, one year to another, making and regretting bad decisions. Making the best of things. Hoping I was doing the right thing for the right reasons. Getting older and perhaps regretting the path not chosen. Or the path I had.

The solution came unexpectedly to my lips, and as I said it, I knew it was the right thing to do.

'I have a house, in Oxford,' I said at last, 'and I'm going to sell it.'

His eyebrows lifted in surprise.

'And do what?'

I topped up my water, the ice cubes slipping out, splashing into the glass.

'I need to think about it, but it's what I want to do. I'm going to travel, that's the first thing. See some of those things we talked about. The Northern Lights and the Rockies and... oh, I don't know yet. The wonders the world has to show me.'

He smiled at last and put his palm over the back of my hand for a moment.

'I'll have to find you that cockleshell for your hat. It's good to have a plan, Sophia. And that sounds like a very good plan.'

We looked at each other for a few seconds and then I turned my hand over and grasped his. We sat in silence just being with each other.

And palm to palm is holy palmers' kiss.

Some long-buried Shakespearean quote had surfaced from my memory. How very odd. Any love of Shakespeare I might ever have nurtured had been ground out of me years ago at school.

Around us, the tables were busy, waiting staff bustling about with trays and glasses and platters. People were talking and laughing. There was the clink of cutlery on plates, the rattle of ice in the pitchers of water. There were the scents of lemon and garlic and herbs, roasting tomatoes and warm bread.

I had the shocking, gut-constricting, worrying feeling that something was happening. Something unexpected and disturbing.

I knew quite clearly what I needed to do with my life. And I was even starting to plan how I was going to accomplish that. I had embryonic ideas and thoughts about what I could do, what I should do.

It didn't matter that I'd had my sixtieth birthday. It didn't matter that I had a slightly dodgy knee. That I needed reading glasses and my hygienist occasionally tutted about my gum health.

Despite all my determination to be independent and sensible, all the things I had thought and said over the last weeks, despite everything. I had been trying to understand what I was feeling, and failed, but now I knew.

I was falling in love.

29

We finished our food, and then had coffee and little glasses of Metaxa. The taste was really growing on me. Perhaps I would get some when I was back in Oxford. Perhaps then I would sit drinking it, looking at the label with its owl-toting warrior. I'd remember this holiday and undoubtedly it would depress me. Maybe it wasn't such a good idea after all.

Theo looked at me across the table and raised his glass to me.

'Happy birthday, Sophia.'

There was a sudden stir behind me, and then a burst of singing.

I sat open mouthed as the owner, who reintroduced himself as Hercules – put a little silver plate in front of me containing a ring of mixed berries around a perfect panna cotta. It had *charoúmena genéthlia* written in chocolate sauce around the edge and one candle stuck in the middle.

It looked as though most of the waiting staff had congregated upstairs to sing to me too. It wasn't 'Happy Birthday' as we know it, but something else which ended with a round of applause. Some of the other diners were taking pictures on their phones, they all seemed to be smiling. I was in floods.

Theo came to give me a hug.

'Don't cry, you silly thing,' he said. 'Happy birthday.'

'Thank you,' I said, gulping a bit and drying my tears on my napkin, 'that was so lovely.'

'Well I know you like panna cotta,' he said with a smile. 'Remember that first day we went out together?'

'I'll never forget it,' I said. And it was true, I never would.

'You see, already we have memories together.'

We left the taverna with much ceremony, Hercules bowing over my hand and wishing me a happy birthday and even the bar staff smiling and waving as we went. I thought it must be like this when celebrities went anywhere.

Theo tucked my hand under his arm and we walked slowly despite the chill of the evening. I felt enveloped in the warmth of a lovely friendship, a splendid meal and his company. But the closer we got to home, the more immediate the problem of Lucian became. Where was he, what had he been doing?

'It's no good, I'll have to go inside and see if he's okay,' I said. 'Will you come in with me?'

'Of course, if you want me to. You're not afraid of him?'

'No, nothing like that, I would just feel better if you were there.'

I opened the front door. The lights were all on but there was no sign of him. But there were certainly signs of where he had been and what he had been doing.

The worktops in the kitchen were covered with debris. Bowls, plates, dirty cutlery and glasses.

On the coffee table was yet another empty wine bottle and an almost empty bottle of whisky. So he had ventured out. Beside that was a tumbler covered in greasy finger marks and a mug of cold coffee that hadn't been touched by the looks of it.

'What the *hell* has he been doing?' I said.

There were opened packets of cashew nuts, crisps and some green olives in a plastic dish. Food and crumbs were scattered over a wide area. Half a loaf of bread was on the chair, with signs that he had just ripped chunks out of it. There was a triangle of Brie with a perfect bite mark across it.

'Oh my god, what a mess!' I cried.

'I think he was hungry,' Theo said.

'How could he do this? What was he thinking?'

'I'm guessing he was upset, he probably wasn't thinking.'

'I could kill him,' I said.

I moved towards the stairs, but Theo caught my arm.

'Leave him. He will probably be asleep and most likely drunk. We can sort this out in the morning.'

'But—'

'Come on, you can stay with me tonight,' Theo reassured me, 'everything will be fine. I'll turn the lights out down here. Tomorrow, we will do this tomorrow.'

I gave a huge sigh. 'Yes, you're right.'

I followed Theo out and up the alley to his front door.

He turned just before we went in.

'And don't apologise for him, Sophia. There's no need to apologise to me for his behaviour.'

'I feel terrible about this.'

He laid one finger across my lips.

'Be calm. Push it away.'

I followed him into the house where, of course, everything was tidy and peaceful.

I shrugged off my jacket and hung it up on a hook behind the door.

'He's going to feel awful in the morning.'

'Lucian? Well yes, probably,' Theo said, 'but that's his problem too. Now come on. It's bedtime. You can go into the spare room if you prefer?'

I looked at him and smiled.

'No, I wouldn't prefer,' I said. 'I'd love a cuddle.'

He found me a spare toothbrush and a dressing gown, and we went to bed. It was lovely. We just lay there while the moon rose and glowed through the window, sending a pale light onto the floor.

Theo put his arm around me and I snuggled into his warm body and gradually my cold feet warmed up.

'Tomorrow is another day,' Theo murmured, his voice reassuring. 'Don't worry any more about it now.'

'I won't.'

'We might need to leave him until the afternoon,' Theo added.

'Ha!' I said, 'I don't think so.'

He chuckled. 'You're very fierce, birthday girl. Should I be frightened?'

'Not really,' I said. And I gave a little growl which made him laugh even more.

He kissed my hair. 'Sleep well.'

It felt so absolutely right. To be there snuggled up in bed with him.

I went back over my evening, how lovely it had been, how thoughtful Theo had been towards me. How kind.

I wasn't going to let Lucian spoil those memories for me. He wasn't going to spoil or waste any more of my time.

* * *

When I woke up, I could hear Theo moving about downstairs. The clink of mugs, the sound of a kettle being filled. A few minutes later he came upstairs with two mugs of tea.

'Ah you are awake, here is your tea,' he said, putting a mug on the bedside table beside me.

He sat down on the bed next to me.

'How are you feeling this morning?'

I thought about it. I felt fine actually. The old me would have lain awake all night fretting or being angry at what had happened; the new me was busy being happy. I was gaining in confidence; I knew that I could deal with this without losing the plot.

'I'm fine, I slept really well.'

He bent to kiss me. 'Good. I'm glad to hear it. Now, what would you like to do today?'

I sighed. 'Well, clear up the shambles next door I suppose.'

He put on a mock stern expression and held up one finger.

'Not a chance. Let's just go for a walk this morning. We can go out along the harbour wall and find breakfast on the way. We could take a look at the boat too, make sure it's okay. Is that a good idea?'

'An excellent idea, but I do need some clean clothes. I'll go in really quietly and find some.'

'You promise not to start cleaning?'

'I promise I won't start cleaning.'

* * *

Next door, the sound of Lucian's snores echoed down the stairwell. I went up the stairs, the smell of alcohol increasing as I opened the bedroom door. Lucian was asleep, sprawled across the bed, one leg dangling over the edge, mouth gaping, a white track of dried saliva trailing down his chin. That sight alone would have quelled any sympathy I might have had for him. He didn't look like a suave, sophisticated professor any more, he just looked like a rather unattractive lump in need of a shower and a shave.

I quickly found some clean clothes and closed the bedroom door quietly behind me. I had a quick wash in the bathroom and got dressed. Some jeans, a shirt and warm sweater and on top of that, a raincoat. I still didn't have the deck shoes, but my best trainers would do.

I checked my appearance in the hall mirror and gave my reflection a jaunty thumbs up. I could do this; I could do anything.

Theo was waiting for me.

'Ah good, you are not coming out with a full rubbish bag,' he said.

'I promised I wouldn't clear up and I haven't.'

This was very unlike me. I usually got very anxious when I saw a filthy mess like that one, normally I would have been reaching for a mop and bucket and some disinfectant. Today I just closed the door and walked away from it.

We went through the streets at a leisurely pace, trying to decide where to have breakfast. After all the food of last night, I supposed I shouldn't really have been hungry, but I was.

'There's a café along here that makes wonderful *ladenia*,' Theo said. 'You must try it.'

We sat inside because the wind was so cold and drank big bowls of creamy coffee and ordered the *ladenia*, which were square flatbreads covered in baked tomatoes, herbs, capers and feta cheese, like a Greek pizza. They were delicious. I could have stayed there for the rest of the morning just chatting and people watching, but in the end, we went back outside and continued on towards the quay.

It was cold and grey that morning, a brisk wind coming in off the sea. Beyond the sea wall we could see the water whipped up into waves, a fishing boat coming towards the safety of the harbour.

'No sailing for us today,' Theo said. 'It looks very choppy out there.'

'I wouldn't want to test my boast that I've never been seasick,' I laughed.

We sat on a bench in the shelter of a wall and watched the sea.

'Tell me about your family,' he said.

'There are a couple of cousins in Scotland. I see them occasionally. Both are married and have children. So I'm a sort of aunt. Apart from that there aren't many of my family left that I know about. What about you?'

'You've met my sister. You know about my daughter in Australia. You know now we are not a small family. My mother was the youngest of eight, my father was one of five. You have met some of my family but not all. I have seventeen cousins and between them they have about thirty children. But we are scattered now. Some in Rhodes, relations on the mainland, some in France, one in America. The Greeks were a great seafaring power, they've never lost their sense of adventure.'

'How marvellous to have such a big family. They seemed so nice, so welcoming.'

He took my hand and tucked it into his pocket with his.

'My family was around me when I was growing up and my mother ruled the kitchen. Always noise and arguments and family dinners around that big table.'

'It must have been wonderful.'

'Oh it was. There are still many of my relatives on Rhodes you haven't met yet. If it was the spring or the summer, I could invite them all, they would come, I know it.'

The thought of being faced with even more people, watching me, greeting me, smiling, curious, was both terrifying and fascinating. How would that feel, I wondered, to be part of a family that size? And yet I wasn't actually a part of his family.

The vision of myself in an attractive summer dress, under a vine, sitting at a table of twenty people, everyone chattering and laughing, everyone accepting me faded. I was going back to Oxford soon, in a week's time. No – I counted on my fingers – the time was slipping away from me, in five days. And something inside me began to feel sad.

30

We got back to the house just after two o'clock. We had stopped for a glass of wine and a salad along the way, and our pace had been slow. I certainly wasn't looking forward to the confrontation that lay ahead.

I opened the front door, hoping against hope that Lucian would be up, showered, dressed and apologetic. That he would have cleaned up, perhaps replaced the wine he had drunk, maybe even bought a gift which he would present with his apologies.

No such luck.

The room was just as he had left it, the snores were as stentorian as ever from upstairs. The air was hot and unpleasant with the stink of whisky and the Brie which was now running off the paper and onto the plate in an oily slick.

'Oh, for heaven's sake,' I said furiously. 'I did hope he had done something about this but obviously not.'

Theo stood thinking for a moment and then turned the television on and ramped the volume up to high.

'We'll wait outside, shall we?'

There was a loud shout and a thump from upstairs; it sounded very much as though Lucian had been woken by the noise and fallen out of bed. I muffled a snort of laughter.

Theo steered me outside into the garden. The sun had come out now and it felt more private. Under the pergola the chairs were dry enough to sit on.

'I don't think he will be long,' Theo said.

Above us, a window opened, which was then followed by the sound of Lucian complaining, a loo flushing, and water pouring down a drain, presumably as Lucian showered. I hoped he didn't mind drying off on damp towels from the previous evening. I bet he did.

There was a great deal of coughing and nose blowing from within, and the noise from the television stopped. Eventually Lucian ventured outside, blinking against the light, still wearing the dressing gown, each step punctuated with a groan that spoke of a hangover. Neither of us moved.

He looked terrible. He probably felt worse.

He had rather a grey tinge to his skin and dark shadows under his eyes. I wondered how he would deal with this assault on his dignity. I took a deep calming breath and Theo caught my gaze; his eyes were sparkling with humour. I bit back a smile.

'Oh, there you are,' Lucian said, scratching his head. 'There's a bit of a mess in there isn't there? What *have* you been doing?'

'*Me*? What have *I* been doing?' I said outraged, my composure vaporising.

Lucian winced. 'My head,' he said. 'Don't shout, for the love of God.'

Theo stood up, unfurling his tall frame from the chair in a way that was almost catlike.

'Good afternoon,' he said.

Lucian blinked at him. 'Who's this? What time is it?' He looked at his watch. 'Two-thirty? Good grief. Hang on, I met him, didn't I?'

'I am the owner of this house,' Theo said.

'Oh.' Lucian had the decency to look embarrassed.

'You have made my house into a pigsty,' Theo said quite pleasantly. 'I expect you to clear up the mess you made.'

'I didn't do that!' Lucian said, outraged, and then he faltered. 'Did I?'

'You did,' I said.

'Ah yes, but I was ill. I thought I had food poisoning.'

'I think it more likely you have alcohol poisoning,' I said.

It was really amazing how good this felt. Being calm and matter of fact.

My old reaction would have been to lose my temper with him, maybe even cry with frustration. But then I would have gone inside grumbling to sort out the devastation. I wasn't going to do that.

Lucian scratched his head and stood looking puzzled.

'Oh,' he said, 'well we'd better get it cleared up then. You couldn't make me some tea first could you? Milk one sugar?'

I stood up. 'I suppose so.'

'And have you got any paracetamol?' he said as I passed him. 'Two?'

He rubbed his temples with his fingers.

I thought about it. 'No, sorry, I did have some, but the Ducks took them all.'

His face creased into irritated incredulity and his eyes, which were bloodshot and no longer in the slightest bit attractive, bulged slightly.

'*What?*'

* * *

Theo's phone rang and he stood up and walked away to answer it.

There was a brief and rapid conversation, in Greek of course, so I couldn't tell what it was about, and he kept looking at his watch.

'Okay,' he said and ended the call.

'What's up?' I asked.

He pulled a regretful face. 'I'm sorry, I have to go out. To Lindos. I have a house there, one of my renovation projects. I need to go and sort out a problem with the plumbing, the tenants have reported something. You could come with me but—'

Theo looked meaningfully at Lucian.

'No, of course not,' I said.

'Oh, don't mind me,' Lucian said waspishly, 'I think I'm able to be left on my own. I'm not a child.'

'Not a chance,' I muttered under my breath.

Theo looked at his watch again. 'If I leave now, I can be back before dinner. I thought we might go somewhere new this evening. What do you think?'

'Lovely,' I said, sensing light at the end of the tunnel.

'Don't make it too late,' Lucian said behind me, 'I'm going to need an early night.'

'You're not invited,' I said.

'Well what am I supposed to do?' he grumbled.

'Something else,' I said. 'You could start by finding a hotel.'

I went with Theo to see him off. He put an arm around me and gave me a hug.

'Don't let him bully you, I can see he's going to be difficult.'

'I'll be fine,' I said, 'don't worry.'

Theo kissed me and gave me another hug, and then left. I was sad to see him go and doubly disappointed that I was going to be left to deal with Lucian on my own. I'd have to be pretty determined with him.

* * *

Lucian was still sitting outside drinking his tea which must have been tepid by now. Rather kindly, under the circumstances, I went in to find him the necessary rubbish bags and cleaning things he was going to need.

When I came back outside, he was still sitting there, slightly bent over to one side with his eyes closed.

'I've got everything ready for you,' I said brightly.

'I feel terrible,' he replied in a weak voice.

'Well the exercise will do you good, take your mind off things.'

'You're not the same any more, Sophia, you're not as kind.'

'I'm not as stupid,' I said, 'I think that's more accurate.'

He made a big fuss about getting up. 'I need to get dressed; you don't expect me to do your housework in my dressing gown do you?'

'Of course not, but it's your housework and that is Theo's dressing gown.'

Lucian looked at the garment with sudden horror and went upstairs.

Meanwhile I went to sit in the house and took a look at all the messages I'd received from the Ducks.

Juliette:

So what happened? Did you get him to leave?

Anita:

Rick and I have had a row. I'm calling him Richard now, which is a very bad sign. He says I've lost my mind just because I started talking about hot tubs.

. . .

Kim:

Have you got all his pants out of the dishwasher yet? 😞 I've put an ad in the local paper and the Post Office, offering maths tuition. I've had three responses from parents who want their kids to get through GCSE and one from a man asking if I did extra tuition after hours and did I have a cane? Bloody pervert. #yuk

Juliette:

Matthew has been asking about Rhodes, he's never been. He's suggested we should have a minibreak. A minibreak! What happened with ghastly Lucian? You've gone quiet. What did Theo have to say?!

Kim:

I've said yes to the flat. It's very nice two bed near the middle of town so they won't need to keep borrowing my car or asking me for lifts. I swear both of them are reverting to teen age. I don't think either of them is pleased, Simon says sharing a flat with Gemma will be weird and people will think they are some sort of incestuous cult hahahahaha!

Anita:

Good for you Kim, I hope it works out, flipping kids! Rick went to M&S and bought new pants. #stripes I'm sure you'd all want to know that.

Me:

Everything is okay, too much to tell you at the moment but I promise I will when I get a moment. Thanks for the messages, well done everyone; Old Ducks rule!

* * *

'I want to apologise,' Lucian sighed.

That was unexpected.

'What are you apologising *for*? Just so we are on the same page about this.'

'For the mess I made. I was thinking about it while I was in the shower and it must have been me, because you went out with Aristotle Onassis didn't you. And who is he to tell me what to do?'

'His name is Theo,' I said, 'and he owns this house and the two next door as well, so he has a perfect right to expect you to clean up. I was very embarrassed.'

'Sorry,' he muttered. 'Where did you go?'

'We went to a taverna at the harbour and had a lovely meal,' I said. 'To celebrate my birthday.'

He looked shocked. 'Why didn't you tell me?'

'It's been on the same day every year. It's not like I've changed it.'

'Oh God!' He buried his face in his hands. 'I've made a right dog's breakfast of things, haven't I?'

'Sounds like it. Lucian—'

'Yes?' he said expectantly.

'I'm going to sell my house in Oxford and I'm having a gap year.'

He frowned. 'A gap year? You're a bit old for that aren't you?'

'Ever the charmer, aren't you? No, I'm not too old for anything. I'm going travelling.'

His mouth hung open with amazement for a few seconds and then he looked hopeful.

'Can I come with you?'

'No of course you can't come with me, you moron,' I spluttered.

'Worth an ask I suppose,' he said, very glum. 'I suppose you'll be going off with Aristotle Onassis, will you? He looks the sort.'

'No, and what *sort* do you mean?' I said.

'Slimy. All charm.'

'Well I could do with a bit of charm after five years with you,' I said.

He frowned. 'Was it five years? It wasn't five years. Really?'

'You're hopeless. Now get on with the clean-up.'

'Oh dear. You are going to help me, aren't you?'

'No, I'm going to watch.'

* * *

In the end, of course, I did help him, because otherwise we would probably still have been there. Lucian was not the sort of man who had the first idea how to use a vacuum cleaner or damp cloth effectively.

We started off dumping all the scattered food remnants into a bag and then set about collecting up the crockery and glasses. He did at least have the decency to look at the nearly empty whisky bottle with distaste before he tipped the remaining few inches down the sink, muttering *never again*.

After an hour we had just about finished, and everything was neat and tidy once more. Lucian had some colour returning to his face and was almost back on form.

'Can we at least go out for a walk?' he said as the last glass was dried and put back into the cupboard.

'You need to find a hotel.'

'Yes okay, no need to get nasty again. I need some fresh air; this place is giving me such a headache. Just half an hour. I could get some paracetamol at the same time. I still don't feel quite the ticket.'

* * *

We left the house soon after that and walked through the alleys towards the harbour. These streets were familiar to me now; I knew my way around without having to look at a map, something that impressed Lucian who was well known for having no sense of direction. And of course, at that moment, no sense either.

'It's really quite nice here, isn't it?' he said after a few minutes. 'For somewhere Greek. I haven't been here for years; it hasn't changed that much.'

'It's lovely here,' I said. 'You xenophobe.'

He waved his hands about vaguely. 'Well, you know. Greece. All that financial stuff a few years ago.'

'It seems pretty good to me now,' I said.

'This place, or *him*?' Lucian said accusingly.

'Ha! Not really any of your business is it?'

By then we had walked along the quay past the fishing boats and out towards the place where Theo's boat was moored. I looked at it, remembering the lovely day we had spent on it.

We sat together on a stone bench. I huddled my scarf around my neck more closely; it was nice to be out in the fresh air, but it was chilly.

'So what's happening back in Oxford?' I asked.

'No idea. I've turned my phone off,' he said. 'Whatever it is, it won't be good. Complaints, enquiries, investigations.'

'Gina will be worried about you.'

He pulled a face. 'Will she? I doubt it. I don't think I'm used to all this walking. My legs are still aching.'

'You should get out more.'

He thought about this for a few minutes, staring gloomily out to sea.

'People keep asking me to play golf. I'd rather shoot myself,' he grumbled.

I put my hand on his arm. 'You won't do anything silly will you?'

He made a non-committal noise and shrugged. 'No one would care if I did.'

'Don't be ridiculous and stop it with the self-pity.'

'Well, someone's got to feel sorry for me,' he said.

A couple of rustic looking men were walking towards us one of them carrying a coiled rope over his shoulder. One of them spat on the ground as they passed.

'Charming,' Lucian said, looking after them. 'Disgusting habit.'

'You're a one to talk,' I said. 'You have disgusting habits of your own.'

He held up one protesting hand.

'If you mean the furry handcuffs that was her idea, not mine.'

'I really don't want to know, Lucian. You should be ashamed of yourself.'

'Don't start on me,' he grumbled. 'I'm hungry again. Can we pick up something to eat on the way back? And some aspirin or something?'

'Oh come on then,' I said. I wondered when Theo would be back. It was nearly five o'clock.

We went back through the town, stopping briefly for some take-away food at the taverna where Theo and I had met that first evening, and then at the small supermarket near my house where Lucian picked up some paracetamol and some snacks.

'Hardly decent food,' he grumbled. 'I can't be doing with all this foreign stuff. I'd give a lot for a proper English steak and chips now.'

'Perhaps your hotel will serve them,' I said.

'About that—' he said.

* * *

Theo still wasn't back at six-thirty, by which time Lucian had tried and failed to find a hotel. He seemed to be trying as best he could but either the places were closed for the season, full, or they didn't like the sound of his tone. Which was embarrassingly Englishman-on-holiday, thinking that shouting made up for his inability to speak Greek.

'It's no good, I'll have to stay here for another night,' he said.

'That's a terrible idea,' I said.

'Ask Aristotle Onassis for me when he gets back from grovelling around, unblocking the drains,' he said in what passed for a humorous tone.

'Lucian, you are going to have to work on your people skills; his name is Theo and he's got more class in his little finger than you have in your entire body. Being patronising is not going to help your cause.'

'Oh, someone's on edge,' he said. 'Don't tell me you are falling for that Greek nonsense?'

'What Greek nonsense would that be?' I said.

'Oh you know exactly what I mean. I can see the way you look at him. You used to look at me like that.'

'Not any more,' I said briskly.

'You *were* special,' he said. 'You were always there for me. You were kind and thoughtful. I loved how you looked after me, your wonderful cooking, how you were interested in my work and organised my workload so well.'

I threw up my hands in despair. 'See? You've just made my point for me. Everything was all about *you* wasn't it? I thought you were wonderful,' I said, 'and now I can't remember why. In fact, I'm blowed if I can recall what it was about you that I liked.'

'Ah, well that might just be your age,' he said thoughtfully, running one hand through his hair. It was thinning at the crown; he was very conscious of it. 'I mean it happens. Look at me, I could reel off the Rhodes Grand Masters going back to the year dot, but I forgot your birthday. I used to forget Gina's birthday and our anniversary as well. Every year until you started working for me and reminded me. Gina used to get really cross with me too, sulking and door slamming and I never caught on. Until you came along and pointed it out to me.'

'Here's a thought. You might make more headway with people if you think before you speak,' I said through gritted teeth.

Lucian gave a heartfelt sigh.

'Well, I'm tired, I'm going to bed. And I'm going to lock the door too, so don't think you can just throw me out into the street. I'll sort something out tomorrow. If he doesn't like it he can – to use a well-known phrase or saying – get stuffed.'

31

The snores from upstairs started at full volume five minutes later. For heaven's sake. I'd got used to living without that.

I went to see if Theo was back; there were lights on so I knocked on the door.

After a while he opened it.

'Hello,' I said, 'I was wondering where you were.'

'Hello. How is he?'

'Asleep, he is snoring like a warthog.'

'I thought he was going to find a hotel?'

'He tried, but no luck. Everywhere was full or closed, so he's staying for another night,' I said.

'As you wish.'

I wasn't going to accept that. Not now. I was going to speak my mind, not wrestle in the middle of the night with what I could have said and should have said.

'It's not what I wish. I want him to leave as much as you do, more in fact, but I can't just sling him out onto the street, can I?'

'A man like that would always find somewhere.'

He stood back politely and let me in before he closed the door.

I went through to where there was music softly playing, the wall lights illuminating the room. It looked like he had been reading, a glass of wine on the coffee table. Compared to the scene I had just left, which still reeked of whisky fumes, it was very appealing.

'I'm sorry, I can see you are annoyed, and you have a perfect right to be,' I said, 'but things have not turned out how I wanted. That's all. It's just one night. He will be gone tomorrow.'

'And what then? Will he keep coming back and pestering you before you give in to him? I see him for what he is, Sophia. And because many people have told me how you have been out and about with him. Walking along the harbour—'

Ah yes that would have been Pluto, of course. Or the other one.

'—in the square. Shopping together.'

Ah, the place where Cass worked. It was a small town, and everyone knew Theo, of course.

'Yes, I did go out for a walk with him. He was unwell and needed fresh air and something to eat. And some paracetamol. But that was all. I would have thought you'd at least trust me.'

He waved me towards the chair, and I sat down. Then he came to sit opposite me. He leaned forwards, his elbows on his knees.

'Sophia, I don't mind if you want to spend time with him or with anyone else for that matter. I'm not like that. Some might say I was a successful, happy man with a good life. But like everyone I am capable of self-doubt. Of being unsure.'

'Well it's the same for me,' I said, 'you don't have the monopoly on self-doubt.'

He went and got me a glass of red wine and put it on the table in front of me.

'There, you look cold,' he said.

'Theo, you can see him for what he is and so can I.'

'Okay, so what now?'

He didn't look at me, he seemed more interested in his hands. There was a large sticking plaster across the back of one. He lifted the edge of the plaster and stuck it back down again.

'Have you hurt yourself?' I said.

He pushed aside the question with a shrug.

'Oh, it's nothing. Just a scrape.'

'Have I hurt you?'

He looked up then, his eyes filled with doubt. 'I am too old to be hurt, aren't I?'

'Well I'm not,' I said.

I went to sit next to him and put my hand over his – the one without the plaster.

'I think we are good for each other Theo. I would never do anything to affect that. I don't want our friendship to be the latest in a long line of things Lucian has spoiled.'

'Then?'

I kissed him. His skin smelled of soap, clean and pleasant. His mouth tasted of red wine. I put my arms around him and felt him relax against me.

'Can I stay here tonight?'

* * *

The following morning, we were both still asleep when we were woken by Lucian hammering on the front door and shouting through the letter box.

'Sophia, Sophia! Open up! I have to go! *Sophia!*'

I stumbled down the stairs to open the door. Lucian was there, fully dressed, looking back to his normal, stylish self. His hair was brushed, his shoes polished. He even had a shirt and tie on. What had happened?

'Look, I haven't got time to hang about chatting,' he said, looking at his watch. 'I'm off.'

'You've found somewhere to stay?' I said.

He looked irritated. 'I think you might be losing the plot Soph, no, I mean I'm off. I'm going home.'

'Don't call me Soph,' I said, 'what are you talking about?'

He took a deep breath. 'I opened my emails. There were seven from Gina.' He sounded very pleased with himself.

'I bet there were,' I said.

'At first, she was angry and extremely rude. And then when she couldn't get hold of me she started being the old Gina, you know. Worried. And then this morning she actually rang me. I was a bit nervous when I saw her name, I can tell you. But she was crying, absolutely sobbing. Where had I been, what was I doing. That sort of thing. She wants to talk.'

'You're a lucky man, Lucian.'

'I think she's going to be reasonable. You know, about everything.'

'By the sounds of it she is going to be very foolish,' I said.

'Oh don't be taken in by her, Gina has a tongue of tempered steel when she has a mind to use it and I think she will.'

'So?'

He took a deep breath and gave me a sad look.

'Well, you're going to have to accept that we are over, Sophia. I know it's going to hurt, that you've been playing around, coming to Rhodes when you knew I would probably follow you to make sure you were okay. Then taking up with this man to try and make me jealous—'

'How *dare* you—'

'—but I have responsibilities back home. With Gina. And the children. I see that now. I was distracted and I was weak, but I'm not any more.'

'Well thank heavens the message has got through,' I said angrily.

'So now it's goodbye. I hope we can still be friends and remember the good times,' he said, giving me another rather saccharine look. Did he really believe all this nonsense?

'Please feel free to sod off, Lucian. You go with my blessing.'

He smiled, pleased.

'There, I knew you'd be reasonable in the end. I've a got a flight booked later on today. I'm all packed and I need to get to the airport. I've booked a taxi. One more thing and this is very important. Delete your file of My Book from your laptop, I don't want it falling into the wrong hands, so to speak.'

'*What*? What the hell do you think I'm going to do? Sell it on eBay?'

He rummaged around in his pockets, checking he had his passport and his wallet. 'Still, I can't hang about here yakking. Anyway, good luck with everything.'

With that, he was gone. I watched from the doorway as he walked down the alleyway towards the harbour where he would pick up his taxi. He looked quite a jaunty figure actually, with a spring in his step that said, *crisis averted*. I looked around, wishing I could find a rock to chuck at him, and hopefully hit him on the top of his pompous head. How could I have been taken in by him? I must have been out of my mind.

He didn't look back once.

I could hear Theo coming down the stairs; he was tightening the belt of his dressing gown.

'Well,' he said when I came back indoors, 'how does that make you feel?'

I thought about it, trying to breathe deeply and bring my heart rate down to its normal rate.

'Relieved,' I said at last, 'just relieved. I'm furious at him for causing so much trouble, but he's gone. I hope that is the end of it.'

I'd clenched my hands into fists. Theo took hold of them and gently shook them so that I relaxed.

'Push it away, remember,' Theo said with a smile.

32

So, what were we going to do with the rest of my time in Rhodes?

That day, I finished tidying up the house, making sure Lucian hadn't left anything behind, which amazingly he hadn't.

Soon I would be going to the airport for my own flight back to England. So, in effect, I had only three days left and there was still so much I wanted to do, places I wanted to see, time I wanted to be enjoying and spending with Theo.

Life beyond that was an uncertain place. I would need to get home, sort out clearing the house up ready to sell. How long did it take to sell a house these days? Weeks? Months? Maybe even years. How long did it take to get tenants out of the house? And what would they do? Where would they go?

I supposed that wasn't my problem. Houses got sold all the time, postgrads knew that. But to be fair, in the time I had known them none of them had been any trouble; Monosyllabic Nigel with his fruit flies, Leo with his vinyl jazz record collection and books on Tolstoy. Japanese Yuki studying some obscure aspect of computer sciences, his room filled with boxes of cables and piles of books.

How should I tell them? Would I need a solicitor to make it all formal? What if they refused to go and clung on through house viewings or put up posters in the windows complaining about me and putting people off?

I couldn't think about that. I had to allow myself to enjoy what little time I had left of my stay because I didn't know when I would return.

* * *

It was my last day. I wanted to go somewhere memorable, somewhere I could tuck away in my memory and take out on a grey day when the washing machine broke down perhaps or I was standing outside my house watching a lifetime of hoarding going into a van destined for the tip or perhaps a charity shop.

'Let's go to Kallithea Springs,' Theo said. 'I wanted to take you there days ago. It's years since I went, it's no distance and I think we could both do with a change of scenery. And a swim. And a walk.'

So that's what we did.

* * *

Kallithea Springs was amazing. Some might say it was a bit kitsch, but I loved it.

We parked close to the entrance where the flags fluttered in the sea breeze and walked in through the pillars.

Despite the fact that it was late October, the day was warm, the sea was blue and beautiful, and there were temples and walkways, fountains and wonderful mosaic floors to admire. Occasionally a stunning view through an archway to the Mediterranean.

'This place has been well restored,' Theo said as we walked through an arcade of arches, the sunshine dappling through the roof. 'It was very neglected for many years.'

There were people in the sea, splashing around in crystal clear water. There were two yachts moored a little further out and as we watched, a girl leapt from the deck of one, shrieking, into the water.

'Shall we swim first?' he said.

I changed into my tankini and followed him down onto the beach. I supposed, being used to the seaside in England, I was expecting to show some sort of stoicism, but the water was incredibly warm. We swam around for a bit, and then I floated on my back, looking up at the clear blue sky above us. It was bliss.

And then I saw a plane and a vapour trail crossing my line of sight. That would be me tomorrow, back above Rhodes, on my way home. Would the skies there be as clean and bright, or would I see the grey familiarity of England as we came down through the sullen clouds and onto a wet runway. I could almost imagine the scrum at the baggage reclaim, the arrivals gate, people in raincoats struggling with suitcases and bags of duty free. And me, on my own, looking for a National Express coach to take me to Oxford.

I swear my eyes stung with the prospect, but perhaps it was the salt from the sea?

I would come back, I would. And I would go to other places that would make me this emotional when I left them. I would be adventurous and brave. I would understand at last why people like Michael Palin were always going off for months at a time with camera crews and huge amounts of luggage, finding out things about different cultures and countries. I wasn't sure I was quite as daring or confident as he was, not yet. My imagined explorations involved hotels and shops and information centres. They did not include sandstorms, tents or wildlife invading my suitcase. I'd have to work up to that.

After our swim we went to the taverna for a drink and one of their delicious pizzas. We sat under a huge parasol at a table close to the water. I had relaxed; I was, in fact, quite chilled. I did have a plan for my future. Most importantly, I knew what I didn't want.

'You're very quiet,' Theo said after a while.

'I'm just thinking about the future,' I said.

'And how is it looking?'

'In one way it's clear, in another it's a bit fuzzy,' I said.

'Go on? Tell me how you feel.'

That was one of the things I really valued, that he actually wanted to know how I felt and was prepared to actually listen to what I had to say, instead of just interrupting and trying to offer a solution to my problems.

'I'm going back, I am planning some changes. I'm sixty, you know that now.' I lifted up my wrist to show him I was still wearing the birthday bracelet. 'And I'm going to be brave; I'm going to expand my expectations of myself.'

'That sounds exciting,' he said, toasting me with his glass of wine.

'But I'm a bit scared at the same time.'

'That's understandable. You need to take small steps to start off with. You don't need to climb Everest on your first day.'

'Actually, Everest wasn't on my list,' I laughed. 'It doesn't appeal.'

'Take small steps, start with something simple that is on your list and be brave.'

'I will,' I said.

'I'll miss you,' he said suddenly.

I looked up at him, committing his face to my memory wasn't quite enough. I found my phone and took a picture of him. Behind him, the sea, the rocks, the yachts and the same yelping girl inadvertently photobombing him as she jumped off into the water again.

'Will you? Will you really?'

He touched my cheek with one finger and smiled.

'I will.'

'You won't forget about me?'

He laughed gently. 'Never.'

I was comforted by this. I supposed he might move on to the next lone woman who came to Rhodes looking for peace and quiet, but somehow, I didn't think he would.

* * *

He took me to the airport the next day, my luggage fuller now with new clothes and mementoes of my holiday. I'd probably have to pay hundreds in excess baggage charges, but I was too miserable to care very much.

He hugged me and held me for a long time while people dodged around us and shouted at their children and looked for their planes.

I'd noticed that in every airport I'd ever been to there was always at least one youngish man, carrying some sort of canvas satchel, sweating and running with a desperate expression and a sort of bent knees style, as though by doing that he could conceal the fact that he was about to miss his plane. And there he was that day too, barging his way through the other people, into us, towards security. *Sorry, sorry, sorry.*

'He's in a rush,' Theo said as we watched him go.

'Perhaps next time he will get up ten minutes earlier?' I said.

'Perhaps he got stuck in traffic. Or perhaps he couldn't bear to say goodbye to his lady friend. Like me.'

He looked at me as though this time he was memorising my face.

This was getting really difficult.

I hitched my laptop bag up onto my shoulder and checked yet

again that I had my passport in the right place. Ready to show it to the many people who would want to see it.

'I must go,' I said.

'I know.' He paused and then hugged me very close. 'Please come back soon.'

He held my hand until the last possible moment and then he was gone, back to his lovely house, back to the sunshine and his boat. The Sea Maiden. *Partheniki.*

I went through to the departures lounge and found a seat out of the way, where no one could see me or ask questions. And I sat looking at the wall, while behind me the announcements continued, the people hurried past.

I took out my phone and flicked through to the picture I had taken of Theo. Was it only yesterday? The sunshine, the blue sea, the girl leaping off the boat behind him, his smile, the look in his eyes. I cried.

I didn't think anything in my life had ever felt that way. Nothing had prepared me for that moment. For that sorrow.

I wasn't even sure what it was. Why I was crying as though my heart was breaking. It wasn't mourning or sentiment or frustration; the moment just felt utterly and absolutely wrong. What a rotten and unexpected end to my adventure.

'Are you alright, madame?' said a soft voice behind me.

I looked up to see a young woman dressed in a navy blue suit with a perky cap on her blonde curls. So, cabin crew then.

I sniffed and mopped myself up a bit. I felt a bit foolish now, crying like a love-sick teenager at my age. But what had Hera said? A sixty-year-old heart can break as easily as a sixteen-year-old one. I looked at the picture again and then shut my phone down.

'Thank you,' I said, 'I'm fine.'

33

Oxford was just as unsatisfactory as I had remembered. I knew it was a wonderful city filled with history, and millions of people travelled from all over the world to see it, but it wasn't what I wanted, not any more.

I went home from Rhodes determined that I was going to put my plans into action. Instead of regretting the past and the choices I had not made, I was going to work towards the future. The minute my plane landed and I turned my phone back on there was a message from Theo; he missed me and hoped I would come back soon.

A couple of days later we had a WhatsApp call. It was both lovely and unsatisfactory. He was sitting in the garden, sunlight filtering through the pergola onto his face. I could imagine so clearly the house, the garden, the alleyways and the squares that we had explored together.

'I miss you,' I said.

He gave a rather sad smile. 'I miss you too Sophia. I wish you would come back, it's not the same without you. I have no one to throw paint over.'

'I hope you won't ever throw paint over anyone but me,' I said, trying to smile.

'I've been thinking. Come for Christmas,' he said, 'come here for Christmas.'

I thought about it. There was nothing here that would make me half as happy.

'I was going to ask you to come here,' I said, 'but my house might be sold by then, we would have nowhere to stay.'

'Then come here,' Theo said, 'Christmas here is wonderful. I know you were thinking of coming back in the spring, but I don't think I can possibly wait that long to hold you in my arms again. I've been looking at your picture on my phone and it's not nearly enough. What do you say?'

I smiled. 'I've been doing that too. Aren't we a silly pair? Will you come and pick me up from the airport?'

'Of course I will, I will be waiting there,' he said.

I felt my heart lift and we grinned at each other over the miles.

I told Nigel, Leo and Yuki that I was going to sell my house and regretfully I would have to give them notice. They went off to talk about it for two weeks, when they must have actually communicated properly with each other for the first time. I even heard laughter from their rooms and there were suddenly countless beer bottles in the recycling too which, for a while, made me slightly alarmed that the council would think I'd opened a bar without planning permission.

To everyone's astonishment, the upshot of that was that Nigel was revealed as a man of means. He had devoted so many years to his fruit flies research that he hadn't actually thought to spend some of his considerable trust fund. So, he offered to buy my house.

Nigel's father was a conveyancing solicitor who would handle the sale; Nigel went happily back to his fruit flies and I looked for places where I could store my furniture until I found somewhere to live. I was going to be out of there by the end of the year.

In the meantime I did a fairly good job of decluttering the place. I got rid of the things I didn't want and no longer needed, and a lot of my dull clothes. I didn't miss any of it, in fact, driving back from the council tip or the charity shop with a newly emptied car gave me a feeling of something positive achieved.

The weather was grim, dark mornings, dark evenings and cold rain that slashed at my face when I went out. The memory of Rhodes with its sunshine, blue skies and the thought of returning to see Theo at Christmas was all that bolstered me up.

I got back in touch with some of my old friends and shared several evenings out with them where they happily told me how much they had detested Lucian and his influence over me that had turned me into such a recluse.

I flew to Edinburgh to visit my cousins, who were really pleased to see me and the soul of hospitality. I'd forgotten how much I'd liked them. They even encouraged me to move nearer to them, but I wasn't tempted. Okay, it was November, but I didn't think I had ever been so cold in my life. I didn't think I was tough enough to live there, however gorgeous the city was. Still, it was lovely to reconnect with them and feel that I wasn't quite so isolated in the world.

On my way back from Scotland I went to stay with Juliette too and met Matthew over a very enjoyable lunch in his local pub. They were obviously very firmly an item.

Matthew seemed a regimented and sensible man; well he would be after a career in the army shouting at lesser ranks. He was handsome, tall, sinewy and absolutely devoted to Juliette. You could tell that every time he looked at her with a funny little smile that made his moustache bristle. I think they are what's known as an odd couple. He was so disciplined and no-nonsense, and she was still crackers. He was tweed and Tattersall shirts, she was sequins and stilettos; what the rest of the churchgoers thought of her heaven only knew. But it seemed to work, which was all that mattered.

'I'm a gnat's whisker away from moving into his house,' Juliette said confidentially over several glasses of wine that evening.

'How marvellous. I hope you do. Does he have room for you and all your clothes?'

'It's an old rectory, so yes he does,' Juliette said. 'Are you missing lovely Theo? It's okay, you can admit it, I won't laugh.'

'I am,' I said. 'I'm going out to see him at Christmas.'

'How marvellous! How romantic! I'm so pleased for you. I wonder what they do there. I mean, there can't be any possibility of a white Christmas. Do they have Santa?'

'I'll let you know,' I said.

She filled me in with the news of Kim who had recently signed up for internet dating sites. And moved her kids into their own flat.

'She's not getting anywhere with the dating and swiping yet but who knows, she might at least have some fun. The other day she went out with someone who had a picture of a young Cliff Richard as his profile picture, which obviously should have rung alarm bells. She said he looked more like Keith Richards.'

* * *

Then, at last, we were into December. Contracts on my house in Oxford were exchanged and Nigel's father expected us to complete on the sale at the beginning of the new year. So for a while nothing much changed. Nigel stayed in his room upstairs while Yuki and Leo carried on doing whatever it was they did.

The day before I left for Rhodes, I met a glorious-looking girl in the hall; she was coming down the stairs in some pyjamas decorated with cats. She could have been in a perfume advertisement too, with her blonde hair and sparkling blue eyes.

'Oh hello,' she said giving me a wide smile, 'you must be Sophia. I'm Hottie—'

Yes I bet you are, I thought.

'—I'm just getting the milk. Nigel's desperate. He's such a beast before he gets his first coffee.'

She went to pick up the milk bottles from the front step.

'Nice to meet you,' she said, her accent cut-glass Belgravia. 'Have a good trip to Spain.'

'Rhodes,' I said.

'That too. I'd better go, Nigel is in that funny, growly mood. You know, when he behaves like a very naughty boy.'

Nigel? Was this the same Nigel? Well I never. The times they were indeed a-changing.

* * *

I flew out to Rhodes, leaving Oxford behind in the fog. I had to fly to Athens and then get a connecting flight to Rhodes because in the winter I couldn't find a direct one. Still, I didn't mind, this one was exciting for so many reasons. Sitting looking out of the window at the terminal at Heathrow I thought back to all the things that had brought me to that place.

When I was younger, sixty was seen as old. But it wasn't, people my age did all sorts of things. Wing walking, abseiling off cliffs, marathons, and people said *well good for her*. No one said *isn't she good for her age* any more. I reckoned you had to be over eighty for anyone to take any notice when you did things like that. Actually, I wouldn't do any of those things at any age and if I did people might *say what the hell is Sophia doing?*

Perhaps my perspective had changed over the last few months; maybe when I was seventy I'd think differently but you still wouldn't find me abseiling off anything, however worthy the charity was.

* * *

The cabin crew were going along the aisles of the plane again, shutting overhead lockers and making sure we were all strapped in before take-off.

I knew you weren't allowed to call them stewardesses any more in case they got offended, although when I was little I would have loved to have been an air stewardess. It sounded such a glamorous life. Not now obviously, because I didn't think my knee would appreciate the miles they had to walk during a flight, but every time I saw airline crew strutting across an airport concourse, I did feel a twinge of regret that I never tried.

Still, I read something not long ago about how badly behaved and rude some people were to the crew on planes. Why would they behave like that? After all, did you want them to ignore your buzzer or did you want them to upgrade you simply because you said good morning and smiled?

I'd just been given a really nice seat with a lot of leg room exactly because of that. I complimented one of them on her beautiful hair, which was a complicated arrangement of plaits wound around her head like a sculpture. How she did it, heaven only knows.

'Would you like to take this seat, I think you will be more comfortable here,' she'd said, sweet as you like. She'd even called me *madame*. It could have been because I was using the folding walking stick I didn't actually need. Juliette put me on to that one; she said it was a good prop for playing little old lady on many different occasions and it worked.

Anyway, there I was unexpectedly in an exit row seat with a gin and tonic and some rather nice pretzels.

Out of the window I had a lovely clear view of the Channel, the land was far behind us. The plane had taken off on time and flown over London and the motorways filled with people going to work and school – something I loved seeing because I wasn't doing either of those things. I drank some champagne over France and the plane headed out towards the Mediterranean and my next adventure. Down below, a long way down, I could imagine French roads, villages and French traffic. Everything was different up there at thirty thousand feet or whatever it was.

The world was so huge and so beautiful, there was so much to see, so many people, new places. Okay, there were bad things out there too, I didn't think everything was great, but if everyone focussed on the bad stuff all the time no one would ever go anywhere or do anything. And that wasn't going to be me. Not any more. I was too busy being excited.

* * *

Attractive girl with the complicated hairdo walked past me and we smiled at each other; she was going to someone behind me who was complaining about something. What, for heaven's sake? The plane wasn't going fast enough? The champagne wasn't quite chilled enough? The pretzels weren't exciting enough?

I felt like turning around and saying *just get a grip, you're in millions of dollars' worth of airplane with unprecedented fuel efficiency*. I didn't know that before, but I'd been reading about it in the in-flight magazine in the pocket in front of me. Of course, I didn't actually say anything. After all, people were entitled to disagree with me, I was allowed to have my own opinions. That was something else I no longer worried about.

* * *

It was late at night when my plane landed in Rhodes because the stopover in Athens took so long. I supposed I could have flown at a different time and stayed overnight somewhere, but I was eager to just get there, so I didn't really mind. It was, of course, dark, the lights on Rhodes twinkling below me as the plane came in to land. When I got to the arrivals gate, Theo was there, muffled up in a padded coat, a scarf around his neck. His face lit up when he saw me. I flew into his arms and we stood hugging each other, both of us lost for words for a moment.

'I can't believe you are here at last!' he said.

'Nor can I!' I could hardly speak I was so excited.

He held me at arm's length for a moment, looking at me.

'You are very welcome,' he said, 'so very welcome.'

He drove us away from the airport and out towards the old town.

It was so different from the last time I had been here when the taxi driver had been talking non-stop, complaining. This time, although I was tired from all the travelling, I was more than content.

We caught up with each other's news; he had been busy doing some more decorating, had taken *Partheniki* out a couple of times for short trips but now she had been taken out of the water for the winter for some maintenance. I told him about my house sale progress, what I had been doing to clear away my things. I was taking a leap of faith, away from the past and definitely towards a new future.

'So soon you will be homeless,' he said, 'what will you do?'

'I'm not really sure,' I said. 'I have enough money to buy somewhere, house prices in Oxford are very high at the moment. I haven't decided.'

'That's a nice problem to have.' He reached over and took my hand. 'I'm so happy to see you again. It's been too long since you were here. I've missed you.'

'I've missed you,' I said.

He turned briefly to smile at me, his face illuminated by the glow from the dashboard.

'I'm glad you've missed me,' he said. 'I wouldn't have it any other way.'

The streets of Old Rhodes were bright with Christmas lights and decorations, it was glorious. There were illuminated images of the Virgin on the walls of the old town, and brightly lit shapes of ships and boats. There was a merry-go-round and a funfair on the harbour side. I gasped and craned my neck to see them all, it was wonderful.

'Sadly, you have missed the *kalanda* singers. Children singing Christmas songs. They always do that in the town at this time of year, perhaps they will be out tomorrow for you to hear,' he said. 'The illuminated boats – the *karavaki* – are very important to all Greeks at Christmas.'

'Oh, you have Santa Claus!' I said, seeing an illuminated figure on the harbourside.

'Of course, he is *Áyios Vassileios h*ere.'

It was wonderful to walk back down that little alleyway to reach his house and go inside into the warmth of the living room.

'It's so good to be back,' I said.

He dumped my case down and put his arms around me.

'Are you hungry?'

I rested my cheek against his chest. 'No, not at all, just tired.'

He kissed the top of my head and then went to pour us both a small glass of Metaxa and we clinked glasses together.

'Welcome,' he said.

'*Yia mas,*' I said. 'See, I haven't forgotten.'

'I haven't forgotten how lovely you are,' he said, 'let's go to bed.'

I knocked back my Metaxa in one and choked a little bit. Classy, that was me.

'Yes. Let's,' I said.

* * *

The following day was Christmas Eve and I woke up late; I supposed it was all the travelling that had tired me out. For a moment I wondered where I was. I looked around at the white walls, the pale morning light coming through the windows, and then I remembered.

I gave a deep sigh of contentment. Last night had been every bit as wonderful as I had remembered and hoped it would be. And we had the days ahead together, time to learn more about each other, and Christmas to share. It was going to be very different from others I had known recently. I was very happy. But, I noticed, I was on my own. Where had Theo gone?

I pulled on my dressing gown and went downstairs. Theo was sitting at the dining table and he was on the phone. He looked up as I came in and he waved. *I'll be a moment*, he mouthed at me.

I went to make myself a cup of tea, hoping he wasn't going to be called away with some errand to run or maintenance problem.

'That was Uncle Nico. He wants us to join him for lunch tomorrow. But meanwhile, I have a present for you,' Theo said.

'But it's not Christmas Day yet,' I said, 'that's naughty.'

'I'd like you to have this one now,' he said. 'I don't think Santa would mind.'

He pulled a little package out of his pocket and handed it to me.

Excited as a child, I opened it.

It was a filigree gold heart charm for the bracelet he had bought me for my birthday.

'Oh Theo,' I whispered, 'thank you!'

I held it carefully in the palm of my hand, it was exquisite.

'Well – now you know. You have my heart,' he said. 'But first...'
Theo stopped and turned to kiss me, 'Merry Christmas.'

'*Kalá Christoúgenna,*' I said.

34

FOUR MONTHS LATER

Well, I did it; a lot has happened for me and for the Old Ducks since that holiday last year. I don't think life has been the same for any of us since then. I'm looking forward to seeing them again when the Old Ducks' Club has its planned reunion in October. They've already booked their stay.

Kim is enjoying life on her own. Occasionally we get a hilarious tale of her latest internet date; none of them seem remotely suitable for her. Her children Gemma and Simon lived together for two months in the flat she found for them and then – fed up of the continual clash between himself and his sister who had morphed into a house-proud nit-picker – Simon moved out. He went back to his girlfriend a changed man, having realised exactly how much work is needed to run a house, so it wasn't all in vain. Gemma moved a friend in to help with the rent. Kim assumes Gemma is still saving for her deposit but very wisely doesn't ask too closely.

Anita retired in January and as far as I can tell she and Rick are hardly ever at home. Having dragged her protesting husband out to their local community centre for taster classes in pottery, art and bread making, they discovered an unexpected talent for square dancing and in the last few weeks they have even taken part in competitions with a whole new circle of friends. Last time I spoke to her she said they were going to think about getting a gardener because now the spring is here, Rick's borders are going to rack and ruin.

Juliette, as expected, moved in with Matthew, I suspect much to the disappointment and outrage of some of the other local ladies in the village who might have harboured hopes in his direction. I have a sneaky feeling she is enjoying it all and when I see them on Zoom calls, Matthew seems pretty pleased with himself too.

And me?

Well I went back to Oxford after Christmas to sort out the sale of my house to Nigel, who then moved into my old rooms on the ground floor, along with his luscious girlfriend who was actually called Hattie.

And then I went back to Rhodes and bought Aunt Hanna's house.

It turned out to be a large stone villa just outside the walls of the old city, with the added benefit of actual car parking space and room in the garden to build a pool, which I fully intend to do some-time soon. I'm not in any rush.

I suppose I could have moved in with Theo and he did offer, but I thought I would take things slowly, although thinking about it, some might say it is already a bit late for that.

Anyway, Theo and I went to see the Northern Lights in February, and they were just as magical as I had hoped. In September we are going to New York. I am going to see everything. The Statue of Liberty, Ellis Island, the Empire State building, Macy's, absolutely *everything*. I can't wait.

We even have tickets booked – at huge expense – for a Broadway show, something I never thought I would do, as I've never been a great theatregoer. It's not much fun to go alone. Theo and I have already agreed if we don't like it, we will walk out, get our interval drinks and we won't go back. I won't feel guilty or awkward at all, after all, I have no time to waste doing things or being with people I don't much like.

And that's one of the really great things about being older that I hadn't realised, you can get away with a lot. Being late, speaking your mind, wearing unusual hats, not wanting to eat tofu. You can go home early from things, get up late. Eat toast and Marmite in bed.

People just assume that when your hair goes grey your brain does too, but mine hasn't, not for a moment. I'm even learning all the names of Theo's relatives, which is taking some time because just when I think I have them all sorted out another one pops up. It makes a change from just having two cousins in Edinburgh. And they are supposed to be coming out to visit sometime this summer, which will be marvellous.

But now I have my new house sorted out. Sort of. I had what was left of my furniture shipped over from Oxford and some of it works and some of it doesn't, but it will do for now. There's a small amount of clutter, but nothing too excessive.

I'm having a house-warming party tomorrow. It won't be a small event of course, because you can't do that with a family as large as Theo's. And there is also the added benefit of them being unable to turn up without a plate or bowl of food and a bottle of wine. In a strange way the parties seem to organise themselves. I'm looking forward to it. It will be my first ever house-warming party. Fancy having to wait until I'm sixty to do that.

And I have two cats too, as I always wanted. Castor and Pollux are tabby kittens that Theo rescued from a building site and brought back for me. They are growing fast, sleek and spoiled and enormous fun.

* * *

Theo appears the following morning, ready to help me put up the strings of bunting and fairy lights which every party on Rhodes seems to need. It's a beautiful April day; the air bright and fresh with a wind from the sea.

Theo had been right too, the flowers and the lush greenery of the island are at their best in the spring. We had spent the last few weeks driving all over the island, finding new places to explore, appreciating the beauty of the place I was beginning to call home.

'Aunt Hanna asked if there would be baklava,' Theo says as he loops some lights over the branches of a tree, 'I'm just giving you a heads up.'

'Of course there will,' I reply, 'in fact, I ordered some from the bakery at the end of your alley. Remember how we used to love buying things there?'

Theo comes down the stepladder and starts decorating the next tree – I have a few in my garden including a wonderful almond tree which Aunt Hanna claims she grew from a nut when she was a child. It's nearly twenty feet high now and is covered in the most delicate pink blossom.

'See, I told you we could make new memories together,' he says.

'It's all been very surprising,' I tell him, 'meeting you, buying this house, having my first ever house-warming party tomorrow—'

He dips down to kiss my cheek as he passes me.

'It's nearly lunchtime. Do you want to go out somewhere?' I ask.

'Soon,' he says vaguely, 'I'll just finish this.'

I go into the house to make sure all the glasses and cutlery are ready for the following day; some of mine and several boxes borrowed from Uncle Nico. I take them out and put them on one of the tables in the garden.

'Could you go and get the other box?' I say, 'it's a bit heavy and I don't want to risk breaking Nico's things.'

'Sure thing,' he says.

I unfold my tablecloth – the same one I bought that first day in Rhodes all those months ago – and smooth it out. Then I start to organise the glasses into straight rows on top of it. This party is going to be lovely; I've got to know so many people since I moved here, not just Theo's family. And the one thing it is possible to rely on here is the weather, not like in England when it can be so unpredictable. People leave their garden chair cushions out for weeks at a time here. It takes some getting used to.

Theo comes back out into the garden holding the other box of glassware. He has a big grin on his face.

'Some visitors have arrived to see you,' he says.

'What? Who? They do realise the party is tomorrow?' I say and then I stop.

Coming out into the garden behind him are three familiar figures. And then that very memorable hyena laugh rings out.

'*Oh my God!*'

'Well you didn't think we'd miss this did you?' Juliette says, a vision in turquoise frills.

'Wild horses wouldn't keep us away!' Anita adds.

'Hurrah! It's us! We've called an extraordinary meeting of the Old Ducks!' Kim shouts.

And then they all run over the grass to hug me and, I'll be honest, I don't know who is crying the most, although I think it might well be me.

ACKNOWLEDGMENTS

So many people are involved in the production of this book, but special thanks are due to my agent, the wonderful Broo Doherty of D H H Literary Agency. She worked so hard on my behalf and has always been there, on the other end of a phone or email when I've needed her.

Thank you to Boldwood Books, especially Emily Ruston, my editor, who has been thoughtful, approachable and reassuring at a time when I most needed it.

Heartfelt thanks too to my copy-editor Cari Rosen who had such a keen eye and made many good suggestions.

Thanks are also due to Candida Bradford for her excellent proof-editing.

Thanks to the Literary Lovelies group who are always there with a cheer when things go right and a virtual hug when they don't.

Finally, thanks are due to my family for all their support and encouragement, and of course my marvellous husband Brian.

MORE FROM MADDIE PLEASE

We hope you enjoyed reading *The Old Ducks' Club*. If you did, please leave a review.

If you'd like to gift a copy, this book is also available as an ebook, digital audio download and audiobook CD.

Sign up to Maddie Please's mailing list for news, competitions and updates on future books.

http://bit.ly/MaddiePleaseNewsletter

Sisters Behaving Badly, another feel-good read from Maddie Please, is available to order now.

ABOUT THE AUTHOR

Maddie Please is the author of bestselling joyous tales of older women. She had a career as a dentist and now lives in Herefordshire where she enjoys box sets, red wine and Christmas.

Follow Maddie on social media:

f facebook.com/maddieplease

𝕏 twitter.com/maddieplease1

⌾ instagram.com/maddieplease1

BB bookbub.com/authors/maddie-please

ABOUT BOLDWOOD BOOKS

Boldwood Books is a fiction publishing company seeking out the best stories from around the world.

Find out more at www.boldwoodbooks.com

Sign up to the Book and Tonic newsletter for news, offers and competitions from Boldwood Books!

http://www.bit.ly/bookandtonic

We'd love to hear from you, follow us on social media:

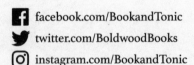

facebook.com/BookandTonic
twitter.com/BoldwoodBooks
instagram.com/BookandTonic